INTERNATIONAL PRAISE FOR *DEATH ANGELS*
BY ÅKE EDWARDSON

"A crime novel with snappy dialogue, depth and—most important of all—suspense from beginning to end."
—*Morala & Vadstena Tidning* (Sweden)

"Edwardson will not be hampered by the constraints of the crime
genre . . . with his sharp dialogue . . . and a backdrop of darkness
that recalls the early works of James Ellroy, one must proclaim
Åke Edwardson a master of the Scandinavian detective novel."
—*Le Monde des Livres* (France)

"A read which even on a really warm July day sends cold shiv-
ers down my spine . . . Edwardson's language is vivid and full of
nuance."
—*Hufvudstadsbladet* (Finland)

"A fast, sleek, hard ballad."
—*Die Welt* (Germany)

"Clever, exciting, atmospheric!"
—*Der Spiegel* (Germany)

ABOUT THE AUTHOR

Åke Edwardson has won three Swedish Academy of Crime Writers awards. His ten Erik Winter novels have been translated into more than twenty languages. He lives in Gothenburg, Sweden.

DEATH ANGELS

AN INSPECTOR ERIK WINTER NOVEL

Åke Edwardson

TRANSLATED FROM THE SWEDISH BY KEN SCHUBERT

PENGUIN BOOKS

PENGUIN BOOKS
Published by the Penguin Group
Penguin Group (USA) Inc., 375 Hudson Street, New York, New York 10014, U.S.A. • Penguin Group
(Canada), 90 Eglinton Avenue East, Suite 700, Toronto, Ontario, Canada M4P 2Y3 (a division of Pearson Penguin Canada Inc.) • Penguin Books Ltd, 80 Strand, London WC2R 0RL, England • Penguin
Ireland, 25 St Stephen's Green, Dublin 2, Ireland (a division of Penguin Books Ltd) • Penguin Group
(Australia), 250 Camberwell Road, Camberwell, Victoria 3124, Australia (a division of Pearson Australia Group Pty Ltd) • Penguin Books India Pvt Ltd, 11 Community Centre, Panchsheel Park, New
Delhi – 110 017, India • Penguin Group (NZ), 67 Apollo Drive, Rosedale, North Shore 0632, New Zealand (a division of Pearson New Zealand Ltd) • Penguin Books (South Africa) (Pty) Ltd, 24 Sturdee
Avenue, Rosebank, Johannesburg 2196, South Africa

Penguin Books Ltd, Registered Offices:
80 Strand, London WC2R 0RL, England

First published in Penguin Books 2009

10   9   8   7   6   5   4

Originally published in Swedish as *Dans med en angel* by Norstedts Forlag, Stockholm.

Publisher's Note
This is a work of fiction. Names, characters, places, and incidents either are the product of the author's imagination or are used fictitiously, and any resemblance to actual persons, living or dead, business establishments, events, or locales is entirely coincidental.

LIBRARY OF CONGRESS CATALOGING IN PUBLICATION DATA
Edwardson, Åke, ———.
[Dans med en angel. English]
Death angels : an Inspector Erik Winter novel / Åke Edwardson ; translated from the Swedish by
Ken Schubert.
        p.   cm.
ISBN 978-0-14-311609-7
1. Detectives—Sweden—Fiction. 2. Sweden—Fiction. I. Title.
PT9876.15.D93D3613 2009
839.73'74—dc22   2009027529

Printed in the United States of America
Set in Dante MT with Eras
Designed by Daniel Lagin

DEATH ANGELS

HE WAS NO LONGER ABLE TO MOVE. HE COULDN'T REMEMBER how long it had been this way. Movement was like a shadow play now.

He knew what was happening to him. He tried to make his way toward the south wall of the room, but the gesture was mostly in his mind, and when he raised his head to see where the sound was coming from . . .

Once more he felt the coldness between his shoulders and down his back, followed by the heat. He slipped and struck his hip as he fell, then slid along the floor.

He heard a voice.

There's a voice inside me, he thought, and it's calling to me, and the voice is me. I know what's happening to me. Now I'll go over to the wall, and if I stay calm it's going to be all right.

Mom! Mom!

He heard a whir like when time freezes and the world stops before your eyes. He couldn't escape it, and he knew what it was.

Get away from me.

Go away.

I know what's happening to me. I feel the coldness again. I'm looking down at my leg but I can't tell which one it is. I see it in the bright light. That's not the way it was at first. But when the coldness began, the light went on and everything turned to night outside the window.

I hear a car, but it's going the other direction. Nothing stops out there.

Get away from me.

He could still take care of himself, and if he were just left alone, he would be able to move around the room and over to the door. The man had come in, gone back out and gotten his things, then returned, closed the door and made it night outside.

He still heard the music, but it might be coming from somewhere deep inside. They had played Morrissey, and he knew that the name of the album came from an area on this side of the river—not very far away. He knew a lot about that kind of thing. That was one of the reasons he had come here.

He heard the music again, louder now, but not the whir.

The light was as bright as ever. It ought to hurt, penetrate him.

I don't feel like it's hurting me, he thought. I'm not tired. I could leave if I were just able to stand up. I'm trying to say something. Time is slipping away. It's like when you're falling asleep, and suddenly you give a start, as if you're climbing out of a deep pit, and that's all that matters. When it's over, you're frightened and you lie there, incapable of moving.

He didn't think so much after that. The wires and cables in his head had been clipped in two and his thoughts spilled out and careened around his brain and merged with the blood that was running down his back.

I know it's blood and it's mine. I know what's happening to me. I don't feel the coldness anymore. Maybe it's over. What's next?

I'm up on one knee now. I'm staring into the light, and that's how I'll drag myself toward the wall and into the shadows.

Something is coming at me from the side, and I'm turning away from it. Maybe I'm going to make it.

He tried to move toward the refuge that awaited him somewhere, and the music grew louder. There was activity all around him, coming from different angles. He fell and was caught, and he felt himself being lifted up and to the side. He made out the contours of the walls and ceiling as they closed in on him, and he couldn't tell where one ended and the other began. Then there was no more music.

The last wires holding his thoughts together snapped, leaving him alone with dreams and fragments of memories that he took with him when it was over and silence had descended.

The sound of footsteps faded into the distance, and his thin body slumped against the chair.

JANUARY 1997

1

IT HAD BEEN THE KIND OF YEAR THAT REFUSES TO LET GO. IT spun every which way and bit its own tail like a rabid dog. Weeks and months seemed to go on forever.

From where Erik Winter sat, the coffin appeared to hover in the air. Daylight poured through a window to his left and lifted it from the bier on the stone floor. Everything merged into a rectangle of sunshine.

He listened to the psalms of death, his lips unmoving. He was surrounded by a circle of silence. It wasn't the unfamiliar atmosphere that made him feel isolated. Nor was it his grief, but another kind of feeling, akin to loneliness or the void that you stare into when you're losing your grip.

The warmth of my blood is gone, he thought. It's as if the path behind me is overgrown with weeds.

Rising with the others, Winter walked out into the light and followed the pallbearers to the grave. Once the farewell handfuls of soil had been thrown, there was nothing more to do. Only after he had stood quietly for a few minutes did he feel the January sun caress his face like a hand dipped in lukewarm water.

He walked slowly westward along the street to the ferry dock. The civil war within a man is over, he thought. An armistice has been signed. Now only the past remains, and my grief is just beginning. If only I could simply do nothing for a long time and then start weeding the paths to the future. He smiled wistfully at the low sky.

He climbed aboard and went up to the car deck. The vehicles on the ferry to Gothenburg were covered with dirty snow. They clattered like hell and he put his left hand over his ear. The sun was still out, lucid and impotent over the water. He had removed his leather gloves as the casket was being lowered into the grave, and now he put them on again. He couldn't remember a time when it was ever this cold.

He stood alone on deck. The ferry chugged away from the island. As it passed a breakwater, he thought about death and the way life goes on long after it loses all meaning. The gestures still come from force of habit but leave nothing in their wake.

The ferry restaurant was full. The people seated to his right drifted over toward the big windows.

At first he sat hunched over his table without ordering anything to drink. He waited for the psalms to die down inside his head and then asked for a cup of coffee. A man took the seat next to him.

Winter sat up and unfurled his long frame. "Bertil Ringmar, of all people. Would you like some coffee?"

"Thanks."

Winter motioned to a waitress.

"I think it's self-serve."

"No, here she comes."

The waitress took Winter's order in silence, her face oddly transparent in the sunlight. Winter couldn't tell whether she was looking at him or at the church tower of the receding village. He wondered if you could hear the bells chime when you were on the opposite shore, or on the ferry when it was heading toward the island.

His posture is awkward, Ringmar thought. These tables aren't made for tall people. He looks like he's in pain, and it isn't because of the sunlight in his eyes.

"So here we are again," Winter said.

"It never ends."

"No." Winter watched the waitress put the coffee down in front of Ringmar. The rising steam thinned out at Ringmar's brow and traced a circle around his head. He looks like an angel, Winter thought. "And what are you doing here?" he asked.

"I'm sitting on the ferry drinking coffee."

"Why do we always have to split hairs with each other?"

Ringmar took a swig of coffee. "Maybe because we're both so sensitive to shades of meaning." He lowered his cup.

Winter saw Ringmar's face reflected in the tabletop, upside down. The lighting suits him, he thought.

"Were you out here to see Mats?" Ringmar asked.

"You might put it that way . . . he's dead."

Ringmar grasped his cup. It burned like ice, but he didn't let go.

"The funeral was quite an event," Winter said. "I didn't know he had so many friends. Only one relative, but the church was packed."

"Hmm."

"I was thinking it would be mostly men, but there were plenty of women too. More women than men, come to think of it."

Ringmar was looking out the window behind Winter, who assumed the church tower had caught his attention. "It's a hell of a disease," he said, turning back to Winter. "You could have called me."

"In the middle of your Grand Canary vacation? Mats was a close friend, but I can handle the grief. Or maybe it's just starting now."

Their silence gave way to the roar of the engines.

"It's a bunch of diseases rolled up in one," Winter said after a while. "What finally got him was a bout of pneumonia."

"You know what I meant."

"Of course."

"He had the damn thing for a long time, didn't he?" Ringmar asked.

"Yes."

"Shit."

"For a while there he thought he was going to beat it," Winter said.

"Did he tell you that?"

"No, but I could sense what he was thinking. Sometimes the strength of will can save you when everything else is gone. He even had me convinced."

"I see."

"Then some kind of misplaced guilt got hold of him," Winter said, "and it was all downhill after that."

"Didn't you mention once that he talked about becoming a policeman when he was younger?"

"Did I say that?"

"That's how I remember it," Ringmar said.

Winter reached up and brushed the hair back from his forehead, then left his hand on the thick strands that covered his neck. "Maybe when I started at the police academy. Or was thinking about applying."

"Could be."

"It's been a while."

"Yes."

The ferry trembled as if it had fallen asleep in the calm waters and been jolted awake. Passengers wrapped their coats more tightly around themselves.

"He would have been welcome," Ringmar said.

Winter let go of his hair and placed his palms on the table.

"I read they're looking for homosexual police in England," Ringmar said.

"Do they want to take homosexual police and assign them new duties, or train homosexuals to be police?"

"Does it make any difference?"

"Sorry."

"At least in England they realize that the police force needs to reflect the general population," Ringmar said.

"That makes sense."

"Who knows, maybe we'll have some gay officers here one of these days."

"Don't you think we already do?"

"Ones who are willing to admit it, I mean."

"After what I saw today," Winter said, "I'm beginning to think that I would admit it if I were gay."

"Hmm."

"Maybe even before today. Yeah, I'm pretty sure I would have."

"You're probably right." Ringmar's face relaxed.

"You shouldn't have to pretend to be somebody you're not and carry all that guilt on your own shoulders."

"I'm up to my ears in guilt."

The people by the big windows looked like they didn't know whether they should burst into song or drown their sorrows in drink.

Winter glanced outside as the ferry passed a lighthouse. "What do you say we go out on deck and greet the big city?" he asked.

"It's cold out there," Ringmar said.

"I need some fresh air."

"I understand."

"Are you sure about that?"

"Don't try my patience, Erik."

The day was gray and about to lose its freshness. The car deck had the muted glint of coal, and the cliffs surrounding them now were the same color as the sky. It's not so easy to tell where one ends and the other begins, Winter thought. Before you know it you're in the kingdom of heaven. One false step off the cliff and there you are.

By the time the ferry made its way underneath the bridge, the sun had already set. The lights of the city beckoned to them. Christmas was long past, and snowless patches dotted the landscape. The cold wave had frozen the ugliness in place like a photograph.

"I always think that late January is the nastiest time of year," Ringmar said, "but when it rolls around it's no worse than anything else."

"I know what you mean."

"That must mean that I feel just as shitty all year round or else that I'm always happy as a king."

"Uh-huh."

"I wish I was a king."

"Things aren't that bad, are they?"

"A long time ago, I thought that I was a crown prince. I was wrong. It turned out to be you. How old are you? Chief inspector at thirty-seven, or thirty-five when you were promoted? It's unheard of."

The sounds of the city had grown louder.

"Don't get me wrong, I'm happy for you," Ringmar continued. "But if I still had any hope left for myself, the workshop I was just at crushed it."

"What workshop?"

"You know, the one about taking the next step in your life and that sort of thing."

"Oh yeah, I'd forgotten all about it."

"You were lucky to get out of it."

"Right." Winter watched the traffic out on the highway. The line of cars reminded him of an agitated glowworm.

"I'm not a career climber, when all is said and done."

"Why do you keep talking about it, then?"

"Let's say I'm processing my disappointment. That's a natural thing to do every once in a while, even if you can't complain about the scraps that life has thrown your way."

"You're a detective inspector, for God's sake. A respected public official." Winter inhaled the night air. "Not exactly a king, maybe, but certainly a role model."

The wind was like coarse salt in Winter's face. The ferry bumped against the dock.

2

AS STEVE MACDONALD WALKED EAST ON ST. JOHN'S HILL, THE
sounds from the Clapham Junction station were everywhere but he
hardly heard them. The bigger and faster the trains get, he thought, the
more they lull you with their silence.

He entered K&M's café, ordered a pot of tea and sat down by the
window. The construction workers in the corner were having a bois-
terous breakfast, but he didn't listen to their conversation. Most of the
passersby were heading east toward Lavender Hill and the Arding and
Hobbs department store. It's always Christmas there, he thought, a Harrods for the plain and ordinary people who live south of the river.

Cheeks were flushed with cold. You could feel the winter inside the
café too, the fresh smell of clothing and the draft when the door opened
and closed. The winds from the north swept across south London and
everyone was unprepared like always.

We once ruled the world, he mused, but we're helpless when it comes
to wind and rain. We still think that we can wear whatever we like
and the elements will do our bidding, and we're never going to change.
We'd rather freeze to death.

He sipped his tea, but it was already too strong. We drink more tea
than anyone else but we don't know how to make it. It's too weak when
we boil it and too strong when we drink it and too hot in between.

". . . and so I told him, That will cost you a beer, you S.O.B.," one of
the construction workers said, concluding a story he had been telling.

The café reeked of fat and grease. People left impressions of
themselves that lingered in the air as they crossed the room. It's like

Siberia, Macdonald thought. Not quite as cold but the same resistance to movement.

He stepped outside and took his phone out of the breast pocket of his leather jacket. He dialed the number and waited. Looking up, he saw passengers walk out of the station's stone archway as he put the phone to his ear.

"Hello."

"I'm down here now," Macdonald said.

"Okay."

"I'll probably hang around all day."

"How about all winter?"

"Is that a threat or a promise?"

Silence at the other end.

"I'll start up at Muncaster Road."

"Have you checked out the pond?"

"Yes."

"And?"

"Anything's possible. That's all I can say right now."

"Okay."

"I want to see the hotel room again."

"Assuming there's enough time."

"I need to breathe in that air once more."

"Keep me posted."

Macdonald heard a click, and the line went dead.

Putting his phone away, he turned south on St. John's Road, waited for a break in traffic on Battersea Rise and continued along Northcote.

He turned left onto Chatto and gazed longingly at the Eagles pub. That was for later, he thought, maybe a lot later.

After another couple of blocks, he turned onto Muncaster. The row houses shone warily in the January sun. Their brick and plaster merged with the color of the pavement. A mailman appeared out of nowhere, wheeling a letter bag so red it made his eyes hurt. Macdonald watched him ring a doorbell. Postmen always ring twice, he thought as he opened a low wrought-iron gate. He lifted the knocker and banged loudly. Such a brutal way to announce your presence, he thought.

The door opened all the way to the end of a heavy iron chain, and he saw the outlines of a woman's face in the dim hallway.

"Who's there?"

"Is this the residence of John Anderton?" Macdonald rummaged around for his badge.

"Who wants to know?"

"The police." He held up the badge. "I'm the one who called earlier today."

"He's eating breakfast," the voice announced, as though interrupting it was out of the question.

She wants me to leave so she can finish making her kippers, he thought. The pungent odor of fried herring wafted through the crack in the door. "It won't take long," he said.

"But . . ."

"Just a few minutes of your time." He put his badge back and waited. The chain rattled as it was removed. They must have spent a fortune on security, he thought. Nothing left over for a sturdy door. One of these days it's going to collapse under the weight of its own apparatus.

She was younger than he had guessed. Not very pretty but in the bloom of youth, although that would soon be gone as well. She's probably worrying about it already, he thought.

"Come in." She pointed toward the living room. "I'll tell John you're here."

"Show him in, dammit." The man's voice echoed through the hallway, his words both aggressive and jumbled.

He's got a mouthful of eggs, Macdonald thought. Or bacon.

The kitchen reminded him of the café. The fumes from the frying pan burned his eyes.

Anderton was ruddy and stockily built.

He likes his cholesterol, Macdonald thought. I hope he doesn't croak while I'm here.

"Perhaps the constable would like a little something." Anderton waved at his wife and the stove at the same time. Apparently Macdonald could take his pick.

"No, thanks," Macdonald said. "I already ate."

"It's fried with curry," Anderton said.

"Very tempting, but I'll pass."

"Then what do you want?" he asked, as though Macdonald could use some fattening up. "Not even a hamburger?" His smile revealed a set of yellow teeth. "A Big Mac, maybe?"

"Tea would be great."

"We're out of milk," the woman said.

"That's fine."

"No sugar either." Her eyes were on Anderton.

I wonder if they're married, Macdonald thought.

Anderton inspected him in silence.

I could always ask for a little herring just to be polite, Macdonald thought.

"Here you go." The woman put Macdonald's cup down in front of him.

He picked it up and took a few sips. It was just strong enough and not too hot.

"I found some sugar after all," she said.

"What an honor to have a policeman in my very own home," Anderton said. "I didn't know they made house calls. I thought they took you down to the Yard in the middle of the night, even if it was just a case of a missing hamster."

Macdonald observed him. The poor guy is just as uptight as everyone else, he thought. Chatter is the daughter of nervousness. Maybe he eats these grotesque servings just to unwind. "We appreciate your getting in touch with us, Mr. Anderton," he said, taking a pen and notepad out of the right pocket of his jacket. He had hung his coat in the hallway.

"I was just doing my civic duty." Anderton stretched out his arms as if auditioning to be a statue on the Common.

"Not everyone is so conscientious."

"Not that I have a lot of information to give you."

"You saw a man. Is that correct, Mr. Anderton?"

"Call me John."

"Okay, John, you told us that you had seen a man talking to a younger guy."

"The sun was setting and I had been down at the Windmill Pub, and after we had a couple of beers, somebody said that the night—"

"I'm most interested in what happened at Mount Pond."

"Like I was saying, it was getting dark. I left the pub by myself and turned off Windmill Drive toward the pond."

"What for?"

"Huh?"

"Why didn't you walk straight ahead across the avenue?"

"What difference does it make?"

The woman was finished straightening up and stood by the stove with a towel in her hand. She looked out at the street with her back turned to them.

"If it's so damn important, I had to take a piss," Anderton said. "There's some thick bushes between the pond and bandstand that come in handy if you have to answer the call of nature on your way home from the pub."

"So you were by the pond."

"I was pretty close to the pond, and when I was through, I saw this character come by with his arm around a young guy."

"Were they touching?"

"The character had his arm around him, that's right."

"Why do you call him a character?"

"Because he looked like one."

"What do characters look like?"

"To be honest, more or less like you." Anderton grinned.

"Like me?"

"Ruffled hair, leather jacket, tall and athletic with dark wrinkles in his face that could scare the shit out of anyone."

"Just like me, in other words."

"Right."

What a find, Macdonald thought. He's about to drown in grease, but he's got a sharp pair of eyes in his head. "So you were standing there looking at them?" he asked.

"Right."

"Tell me in your own words what you saw."

"Who else's words would I use?"

"Just go ahead."

Anderton tilted his cup, looked in it, reached for the teapot and poured. The tea had gotten much darker while they were sitting there, and he grimaced as it passed his lips. He ran his fingers over his balding scalp, the skin red where it had been stretched. "To tell you the truth, I wasn't especially curious. It's just that there was nothing else to look at. But I said to myself, this character is twice as big and twice as old as the kid, and they sure as hell aren't father and son."

"But he had his arm around him?"

"Like I said. But it was mostly him who was doing it."

"What do you mean?"

"He was obviously more interested than the kid."

Macdonald looked down at his blank notepad. The less I write now, the less irrelevant stuff I'll have to sort through later, he thought. "Was he using force?" he asked.

"Where do you draw the line between force and affection?" Anderton asked, as though he were giving a philosophy lecture at the University of London.

"Where do *you* draw it?"

"He wasn't dragging the kid along, if that's what you want to know."

"Were they talking?"

"I heard voices, but they were too far away for me to catch any words." Anderton rose from the table.

"Are you going somewhere?"

"I was going to boil more water. Permission granted?"

"Of course."

"Do you know what language they were speaking?" Macdonald asked.

Anderton sat back down. "Wasn't it English?"

"We don't know yet."

"Why would they be speaking another language?"

"Did they seem to understand each other?"

"The character was doing most of the talking, but it looked like the kid understood him. Of course, they weren't there very long."

"I see."

The kettle began to whistle. Anderton went over to the stove and fixed more tea, his back to Macdonald. "I was just about to come out of the bushes when they left." He sat down again.

"Did they see you?"

"I have no idea. The kid turned around once and he might have noticed me. But what difference does it make now? He's dead, right?"

"How long did you watch them walk away?"

"I didn't stare at them until they disappeared over the horizon, if that's what you mean. I was in a hurry to get home and watch *East-Enders*. And it was already getting dark."

"Which way did they go?"

"Straight south across Windmill Drive."

"We're going to need your help to put together a composite sketch of this man."

"But I barely saw his face. I can't just make things up, can I?"

Macdonald sighed.

"Okay, okay, I wasn't trying to be a wise guy or anything."

Macdonald jotted down a note to himself.

"I'll do whatever I can. It's not like I don't realize what you're up against, and I do feel sorry for the kid. Not to mention his parents. I mean, I called you guys, right? First thing I did when I saw it in the *South London Press*."

"Yes, a lot of people would have been afraid to come forward at that point."

"I hope you get your hands on the motherfucker. We're behind you all the way."

Macdonald had the impression Anderton was including everyone in the former British Empire.

Macdonald made his way through the traffic to Clapham Common South Side and entered the Dudley Hotel at the corner of Cautley Avenue— twenty-five pounds a night, up front. He broke the seal on the door and walked to the middle of the room. The stench of blood was everywhere. You're used to blood, he told himself, but nothing like this. He'd grown up on a farm and seen a thousand pigs slaughtered, but it didn't turn his stomach the same way. Human blood has a cloying sweetness that throws you off balance, he thought.

So this is where they were going. It might have been right after Anderton saw them. Assuming it was them. The kid had been here for two days. Why had he chosen this hotel, of all places? What would make a Swedish kid stay down here in Clapham? Nothing wrong with Clapham, but you'd think someone his age would have found a cheap joint up in Bayswater. Or Paddington. He would have had plenty of other young foreigners there to hang out with.

The wallpaper, off-white originally, was now a sickening orange.

Macdonald closed his eyes and concentrated on the echoes from the walls. Before long he heard a muffled scream and the sound of a body writhing on the floor.

His right eye ached, forcing him back to the present.

How had the man convinced the kid to bring him here? Was it only sex? Or had he promised something else? Drugs?

Why here? Did he know people in Clapham or up in Battersea? Or over in Brixton?

He'd been robbed, but that wasn't the motive. All that had happened afterward.

We can't even confirm his identity with his teeth, Macdonald thought. They're not in the British records.

The victim had scrawled his name and hometown in the guest book when he'd checked into this shabby bed-and-breakfast on the south side of the former capital of the world. His name was Per Malmström. He was from Gothenburg. That's all they had to go on.

That's somewhere on the west coast of Sweden, Macdonald thought. Per was blond, like so many of his compatriots. What have they got that makes them all towheads? We're also exposed to the same merciless winds and sky.

The Gothenburg police must know about it by now, assuming INTERPOL is on the case.

He closed his eyes again, listened to the walls roar, the floors shriek.

3

A BOY IN HIS LATE TEENS HAD BEEN SPOTTED WITH A MAN IN downtown Gothenburg. Nobody could recall exactly where—maybe the Brunnsparken area. They hadn't been seen together before that.

Three people might have caught sight of them after they left Brunnsparken, and that was a hell of a lot to go on. Who knows, maybe there were more than three.

They were obviously together, but they didn't look like father and son.

According to a couple of witnesses, the kid had dark, badly cut hair, and since Winter knew how unreliable such testimony could be, he made a quick mental note and let it go at that.

There's always a trail to follow, he thought as he walked by a sports complex. It might feel like you're not getting anywhere, but it's just a question of patience.

The icy soccer fields below him were in hibernation, dreaming of last year's glory. In three months, players would be kicking the shit out of each other, the gravel soft and redolent of sweat and menthol.

Soccer isn't a sport, Winter thought. It's a million little injuries, the feeling of loose bone chips rattling around your knees. I could have been something, but I wasn't injured often enough.

Nobody remembered what the man looked like. But they showed no reluctance to describe him anyway. He had been tall, average height or a bit short. Compared to the kid? No, compared to the streetcar, somebody said, and Winter closed his eyes as if he were exorcising the world's ingratitude.

The man's hair had been blond, black and brown. He had been wearing a suit, leather jacket and tweeds. He had horn-rimmed glasses, dark sunglasses and no glasses at all. He was stooped over, his posture was perfect, he was bowlegged and he had long, muscular legs.

What kind of world would we live in, Winter mused, if everybody looked at it the same way?

Winter had seen for himself that the kid's hair was dark. Whether it had been "badly cut" was impossible to tell. The coroner and forensic specialists were done, leaving Winter alone in the dorm room at the Chalmers University of Technology. The body had already been carried out.

The walls reeked of blood. It's not a real smell, he thought. It assaults the mind more than the senses. The color is what does it, the pale remnants of life splattered on ugly yellow.

The sun crept in from the right and cast its harsh light on the opposite wall. When he squinted, the colors disappeared and the wall became a luminous rectangle. He closed his eyes and felt the blood dissolve in the sun's heat, heard the wall murmur about what it had witnessed less than twelve hours earlier.

As the murmurs turned to shrieks, Winter put his hands over his ears, crossed the room and opened the door to the hallway. He closed it again and heard the roar inside the room, and it struck him that the same ear-splitting silence had reigned while the crime was being committed.

Winter walked past the bar, turned around and retraced his steps. The decor was subtle and understated, but in sharp contrast to the pale sky outside, with colors that offered coolness in the summer and warmth in the winter. Johan knows how to pick his interior decorators, Winter thought, sitting down at one of the two tables by the window. A young waitress came up and he ordered a malt whisky.

"With ice?" she asked.

"Excuse me?"

"Do you want ice in your whisky?"

"But I ordered a Lagavulin."

She gave him a blank look. She's brand new, he thought. It's not her fault. Johan hasn't trained her yet.

"No ice," he said, and she walked back to the bar. Five minutes later she returned with a round, sturdy glass. Winter looked out at the street. People walked in slow motion as if on a conveyor belt. Soon spring will be here, he thought, and you can stroll barefoot along the beach.

"I haven't seen *you* for a while." Johan Bolger sat down across from him.

"I know."

"Did she ask whether you wanted ice?"

"No."

"Are you sure?"

"She seems to know what she's doing."

"You've always been bad at telling white lies, but I forgive you. Actually, plenty of our customers take ice in their malt whisky. Not everyone is a snob like you."

An old woman slipped and fell on the icy cobblestones outside. She slid along with one leg sticking out and screamed when something snapped. Her hat lay on the street and her coat was half unbuttoned. Her purse bounced along the pavement, flew open and spewed out its contents in a little semicircle.

Winter could hear her shrieks. A couple crouched down next to her, and he saw the man talking on his cell phone. If I were in uniform, he thought, I could go out and chase the idlers away, but there's nothing to do now.

Bolger and Winter watched in silence. After a few minutes, an ambulance backed in from Västra Hamngatan Street. The crew lifted the woman onto a stretcher and drove off without turning on the siren.

"The days are getting longer," Winter said. "Just when you get used to the darkness, the light starts coming back."

"Does that depress you?"

"It gives me hope."

"The eternal optimist."

"Something terrible is about to happen, and I'm going to be right in the middle of it."

"That doesn't sound so hopeful."

"It makes me sad," Winter said. "I've always believed in goodness, but that seems to be slipping away from me."

"That faith was your own self-therapy."

"Do I sound confused?"

"To be honest, yes."

"Then I must be on the right track."

"So, playing the Good Samaritan isn't your thing anymore?"

"That's not what I meant. I'm just not so much into making the world fit into my own belief system."

"Does that make any difference?"

"A policeman doesn't have to spend all his time racking his brain about why people betray and kill each other."

"Then who would do that dirty but necessary work?" Bolger waved in the direction of the bar.

The waitress approached and Bolger asked for a Knockando without ice in one of their thin new glasses.

"She looked like an old pro when she took your order," Winter said.

"There's hope for everyone. Except for those who have to clean up after you, or alongside you."

"Clean up?"

"You know what I mean." Bolger took his glass from the waitress.

"Mats's death hit me pretty hard."

"One day grief ends and turns into something else," Bolger said after a strained silence. "You could have asked me to go to the funeral with you. He was my friend too."

"True enough."

"I could have been offended."

"It wasn't really my call, Johan. I thought you might turn up anyway."

"It's so goddam . . ."

"What were you going to say?"

"Nothing."

"What are you mumbling about?"

Bolger hunched over his glass.

They listened to the voices of the other customers.

Winter was wearying of the conversation and all the unanswered questions. What was weighing on him? Probably that he didn't want to watch people disappear from his life anymore, regardless of how it

happened. He quickly dismissed the thought, deciding it was the atmosphere of the bar that was conjuring up all those phantoms. He hadn't
touched his whisky, and now was no time to start. He let go of his glass
and stood up to leave. "See you, Johan."

"Where are you going?"

"To work."

"On a Saturday night?"

"Who knows?" Winter said. "Somebody else might have just disappeared."

A memo from INTERPOL lay on Winter's desk. My God, he thought,
will this never end? What a naïve question.

The memo left out the gory details. Nor had he expected any. The
facts spoke for themselves.

What the hell was Per Malmström doing in London anyway?

He heard his own heavy breathing as he picked up the receiver.
Someone had to notify Per's parents, and he knew that someone was
him. The dreaded task generally went to an experienced officer—not
necessarily the chief investigator—but Winter shouldered the burden
like somebody who puts on a heavy raincoat before braving a storm.
You bow to the inevitable without looking for an escape hatch.

A policeman's job doesn't get any worse than this, he thought. "I
have some information for you," he told Karin Malmström.

He wrote down her address. He hadn't needed to ask, but he did it
reflexively as if it might save a little time.

He would give Hanne Östergaard a call later. She was a good listener, and the pressure was starting to get the better of him.

The big adrenaline kick didn't come from the actual burglary. His pulse
raced every time the lock sprang open, but that wasn't it either.

It was the waiting, making yourself invisible and still remaining
fully alert, your eyes and ears everywhere.

She's leaving now.

There he goes.

You had to study their daily habits. Who was going to work, and who
was just out for a short walk. Who was suddenly afraid that she had left

the stove on. Who was sure that he had forgotten to turn off the lights and went back day after day to check.

A pro had to keep track of everything. He wasn't a true pro yet, but he was getting there. He had ransacked three apartments, and he already knew that working by yourself was a definite advantage. The guys who stripped cars always had a partner, but he didn't want to depend on anyone else.

He left his hiding place under the stairway, walked up half a flight and had the door open in three seconds flat. He was already an expert at not scratching the frame.

He felt a warm pressure in his body and stood still in the hallway until his heart slowed down.

Silence was both his friend and his enemy. He never made a lot of noise. If the tenant in the apartment below was in bed with the flu, he wasn't going to be so impolite as to disturb her.

He started with the living room because that's the way it had happened the first time. After four months, he knew everything there was to know about living rooms. It's a good thing you're not a book thief, he always laughed to himself. People don't usually own many books. You're a burglar but you own books. A petty criminal, but also a husband and a father.

He had held down another job once or twice, but he never thought about that anymore. Some people can handle the rat race and some can't, and he had made his choice.

This tenant owned books. He had seen in the man's face that he was a reader but couldn't tell the kinds of books he was into.

It would be fun to check out the titles, he thought. But he didn't take unnecessary risks.

He rummaged through the drawers and glanced at the walls but saw nothing worth taking. He crossed the hallway to the bedroom.

Next to the unmade bed, a few feet from the door, was a garbage bag. There was something in it. It felt soft from the outside. He took hold of the bottom of the bag and carefully emptied it. A shirt and pair of pants fell out. Both of them looked like they had been dipped in something sticky that had now completely dried. I'm starting to see things, he thought. I've had enough for one day.

Back home, the burglar had difficulty concentrating. Snowflakes danced outside his window, and he could feel a draft through the sill. Some children were picking up the snow as soon as it hit the ground, while his son stood there with a carrot in his hand. A nose for a snowman, he thought. Why does that remind me of Michael Jackson?

"A penny for your thoughts," his wife said.

"What?"

"You looked like you'd just discovered the theory of relativity."

"I was thinking about Michael Jackson."

"The singer?"

He kept his eyes on the children. The lower part of the snowman's body was done. No legs, of course. A snowman with legs—that was a new concept.

"You meant the singer, right?" she repeated.

"What did you say?"

"Hello, anybody home?"

He turned and looked at her. "Yes, Michael Jackson. Kalle's got a carrot in his hand, and he's waiting for them to put a head on the snowman so he can give it a nose." He glanced back at the children. "Michael Jackson had a nose operation or something a year or two ago."

"That's news to me."

"It's true. Is there any more coffee?"

She got up and took the coffeepot from the counter.

"So what did you do all day?" she asked after he had poured some milk in his cup, followed by the coffee, and taken a few sips.

"What do you mean?"

"You looked a little upset when you came home."

"I did?"

"You weren't your usual self."

The snowman had a head now, and Kalle had stuck the carrot into a blank surface that would soon turn into a face with pebbles for eyes and gravel for a mouth.

"Did you have a bad day?" she persisted.

"No."

"I thought you were in a better mood the last few days."

"The caseworker at the employment office always looks right past me," he said finally.

"Past you?"

"She sits there, and we talk and talk, but her eyes are on the window behind me. Like some job was about to climb in. Or she feels like jumping out."

"A job *will* climb in soon. Take my word for it."

She knows me through and through, he thought, but she hasn't guessed anything yet. When the hauls get a little bigger, she might suspect something, but that won't be anytime soon. Maybe I'll get a regular job first. Bigger miracles have happened. But by then I might not want it anymore.

He couldn't get the bloodstained clothes out of his mind. When he had stood and stared at them, they seemed to be beckoning to him, or screaming something for his ears only.

He would never know how he had managed to get the clothes back in the garbage bag, and he could only pray that he had left the bedroom in the same shape as he'd found it. Why hadn't the idiot just burned them? I haven't seen anything, he told himself.

4

THE MUFFLED SOUNDS OF WINTER FOLLOWED THEM INTO POLICE
headquarters and lingered in their clothing as they rode the elevator to
the fourth floor of the homicide division.

The corridors were lined with tile. For most of the year, noises that
made their way in from the street bounced dissonantly off the walls.
Now they just rolled by like loosely packed snowballs. A circle of silence
surrounds everyone and everything, Winter thought as he stepped
out of the elevator and turned the corner. Maybe January is my month
after all.

The investigation team gathered in the conference room. The massive effort of the first few days was winding down. Only the core group
was left. Just like always.

Most of the remaining fifteen inspectors were crowded in here, and
their clothes still smelled of raw cold and overheated engines.

Ringmar, who was acting as the assistant chief investigator, hadn't
slept the night before and had done his best to make sure that nobody
else had either. He hadn't bothered to comb his hair, which was his way
of saying how serious things were.

If we were at war and I was the platoon leader, Winter thought, I
would demand Ringmar for my assistant or threaten to hang out at the
mess hall all day long. He took the folder that Janne Möllerström, their
database expert, was holding out to him. If we were at another kind of
war, he corrected himself.

Möllerström was new and quite young. He had already done an

excellent job in a couple of difficult homicide cases, and Winter had insisted on having him again.

Sometimes there were two database guys, but Möllerström was all you needed. He kept track of everything, and the preliminary investigation database was his most prized possession.

Winter swallowed and felt the scratchiness he had noticed when getting out of bed that morning, a raw feeling way down in the left side of his throat. "Who wants to start?" he asked.

They looked around at each other. Winter was as disciplined as they came, and when he let go of the reins like this, it meant he was looking for some creative thinking about the murder. Or murders.

Nobody said anything.

"Lars?"

Lars Bergenhem shifted in his chair. His face has taken on real character since they made him an inspector, Winter thought.

"I've read the reports from London," Bergenhem offered.

"And?"

"I was thinking about the glove."

"Go on."

"The London team found the imprint of a glove in the bed-and-breakfast, and Fröberg found a similar one in the dorm here."

"Correct."

"The imprint is in the same place in both rooms."

"Correct."

"That's all I had." Bergenhem's features relaxed.

"There's another thing," Ringmar said from his favorite corner. He always stood there and fiddled nonstop with his mustache. It might look like he was vain about his appearance, but he simply thought more clearly when his fingers were in motion. "Those marks," he explained.

Winter looked at Ringmar, swallowed and felt the scratching sensation in his throat again.

Ringmar continued. "Is there anything in the latest report from INTERPOL and London about marks in the middle of the room?"

"No," Möllerström said, "but they're not even finished with half of the room yet."

"That means we're faster than they are." This from an inspector who would be leaving the core group soon.

"It doesn't mean a damn thing," Ringmar snapped, "until we get all the exact times down."

"Let's not turn this into a game of one-upmanship between London and Gothenburg," Winter said.

"My sentiments exactly," Ringmar said. "Where was I?"

"The marks," Möllerström answered.

"Right. The forensic specialists found these marks almost smack-dab in the middle of the room, and now they're sure what they are."

"They're pretty sure," Winter corrected him.

"Reasonably sure, let's put it that way," Ringmar went on. "They're working on the comparisons right now. I just talked with them, or rather with INTERPOL."

"It's time for some direct contact with London," Winter said.

"Are you planning to keep us in suspense all day long?" a woman's voice said. Aneta Djanali was one of the few women at Homicide, new to the division but never apologetic about it. Ringmar had talked to Winter about her, and they agreed that she would remain in the group as they prepared for the long haul.

"The marks were from a tripod," Ringmar said. "It might have been for a video camera or a regular camera—or a pair of binoculars, for that matter—but it's definitely a tripod."

"How the hell can they tell?" someone asked from the middle of the room.

"Say that again?"

"How can they be certain that it was a tripod?"

"They aren't certain, as we just pointed out," Winter said. "But the lab is in the process of eliminating everything else."

"So the bastard recorded the whole thing." The inspector looked around the room from his spot by the door.

"That's just speculation," Winter said.

"What we do know is that there are marks from a tripod base in the dried blood," Ringmar said.

"Can they tell when the marks were left there?" Bergenhem asked.

"What?" Djanali asked.

"Did he put a tripod there before or afterward?"

"Excellent question," Ringmar said, "and I just received the answer."

"Which is?"

"They think someone put it there before the murder."

"In other words, the blood is from later on," Bergenhem said.

No one spoke.

"So he was making a movie," Djanali said. She stood up, then walked out of the room and through the corridor to the bathroom. She leaned over the sink for a long time. Where are all the guys? she wondered. Isn't all this making anyone else sick to their stomach?

Winter had a lot to tell Karin and Lasse Malmström, but at first he just sat there with his hands in theirs. Nothing in here has a life of its own any longer, he thought. The grief has taken over and the shadows have crawled out from their hiding places.

"There's nothing worse than outliving your own child," Lasse said.

Winter got up and crossed the hallway to the kitchen on the left. He hadn't been there for years, though he had been a frequent guest at one time. The days fly by like wild horses across the plains, he thought, trying three cupboards before he found the jar of instant coffee. He filled the pot with water and plugged it into the socket by the sink. Carefully measuring the powder and milk into three cups, he poured the boiling water. He found a tray in a compartment designed for a pastry board and put the cups on it.

All this is keeping you on edge, he thought, but it's also making you more observant, which is probably good. Learning to sort things out and rearrange them will make you a better investigator. For whatever that's worth.

The sun trickled through the window over the counter and collided with the dim glow from the hallway, filling the kitchen with a light that revealed nothing and pointed nowhere. How will they find the strength to make it through the days ahead? he wondered.

He took the coffee back to the living room and sat down in the armchair. Karin had opened one of the blinds. The sun painted a long ashen rectangle on the north wall.

"So he had been gone for two days," Winter started off.

Lasse nodded.

"Did he know where he'd be staying?"

Karin and Lasse looked mutely at each other.

"Did he reserve a room before he left?"

"He didn't want to," Karin said.

"Why is that?"

"It wasn't the first time he's gone someplace on his own. He's never been in London by himself before, but he's been here and there."

Winter wasn't surprised that she spoke of Per in the present tense. Her son was still with her, a phenomenon he had observed many times before.

"He wanted to take things as they came," she continued.

The rectangle of light on the wall had moved, and Karin's figure was now illuminated. Her head was bowed, lending dark shadows to her face. Something glittered in her right eye, a reflection from far away. She was wearing washed-out jeans and a thick knitted sweater—the first clothes that caught her eye when getting out of bed after a sleepless night, Winter guessed.

"Teenagers don't like to plan so much," she added.

"Did he say anything about where he might be staying in London?" Winter asked.

"I think he mentioned Kensington," Lasse said. "He went with us a few times, and we always stayed at the same little hotel in that part of the city, but he didn't want me to call and make a reservation. I did it anyway and he was mad, but I never canceled it because I figured he'd end up staying there after all."

In his suit, white shirt and tie, Lasse formed an odd contrast to his wife. We all grieve in our own way, Winter thought. Lasse will go to the office for another day or two, and late one afternoon, or maybe early one morning, he's going to collapse over his desk, or into the arms of an unsuspecting client, and after that he won't be putting on any more ties for a long time.

"But he never made it there," Winter said.

Clouds swept by outside, erasing the rectangle of light that Karin had fixed her eyes on, and Winter saw them turn inward again as her head sank. I don't think she's listening anymore, he thought. "Were you ever south of the river?" he asked Lasse.

"What?"

"The south side of London. Did you ever go there? With Per, I mean."

"No."

"Did you ever talk about that part of the city?"

"No. Why would we?"

"Did he mention that he might want to go there?"

"Not as far as I know. Karin?"

She had raised her head again once the clouds were gone.

"Karin?"

"What?" She continued to stare straight ahead.

"Did Per ever say what part of London he was going to?" Lasse asked.

"What?"

Lasse turned to Winter. "Why the hell did he have to go there in the first place?"

"Did he have any acquaintances there?"

"Not that I know of. He would have told us, I'm sure of it. Do you think he met somebody?"

"It seems that way."

"I mean ahead of time, someone who lured him into that goddam jungle."

"We have no way of knowing at this point."

"I'm asking what you believe, for God's sake," Lasse said, his voice rising.

Karin still hadn't budged except to raise and lower her head with the passing shadows.

Winter started to take a sip of coffee but put his cup back down. When you've been a detective even as short a time as I have, he thought, you stop believing in much of anything. The worst mistake you can make during a murder investigation is to go around believing something that turns out to be wrong. But Karin and Lasse need something to put their faith in, an explanation of circumstances that can't be explained. "I don't think anyone lured him to that particular hotel," he said, "but he may have met somebody when he was in that part of the city."

"Thank you."

"You don't know of any other reason that he might have gone to London?" Winter's question echoed through the silent house.

Voices drifted in through the window. The school around the bend had just let out, and the children were on their way home. Their winter break was about to start. Karin stood and left the room.

Back in the car, Winter wondered why he hadn't asked Karin and Lasse the most obvious questions. Two or three of them were so important that the investigation depended on the answers. Even if they don't know, he thought, the questions have to be asked, and it's best to do it now. Take a few minutes to mellow out and then go back.

There are occasional moments in early February when spring whispers a message and then hastily retreats. This was one of those afternoons. As Winter drove down Eklandagatan Street, the city roared around him. The sun grabbed hold of Hotel Gothia Towers and jabbed at his eyes with its spiraling light as he came to the Korsvägen roundabout. Suddenly he knew where he was going.

The car behind him honked and he moved over to the right lane, heading west past the drowsy Liseberg amusement park. He hit all the green lights on the way to St. Sigfrid's Square and turned into the parking lot at the Television Building.

He coaxed the car into one of the spaces and leaned over the steering wheel. You've kept it together so far, he thought, but this is starting to get to you.

You have to talk with Hanne Östergaard, he told himself. Sit here as long as the sun is in your eyes and then go back and see Karin and Lasse. Put on some slow jazz now and try to make out your face in the rearview mirror.

5

SNOW HAD FALLEN AND CLOAKED THE BRANCHES, BESTOWING a solemn beauty on the city in just a few hours. From her fourth-story window, Östergaard could see people glide along the white surfaces, their breath like disintegrating cones in front of them. She ran her index finger across the windowpane to get a better view. The mist became clear and shiny. Rubbing her cold fingertip with her thumb, she turned to Winter.

"Too much all at once," he said.

"I hear you."

"At some point I can't hold it in any longer."

"Not even you?" She sat down behind her desk. It was big and cumbersome and she heartily disliked it. She had asked for another desk and another office, but she was stuck here while the wheels of bureaucracy ground away.

"Not even me." Winter crossed his long legs with difficulty.

I'm fond of him, Östergaard thought. He's too young for the job, too handsome, and he's a snob in his Baldessarini and Versace suits. His expression changes far too rarely. But he's a reflective man, and that's why he's here. He's not going to break down, even though it's occurred to him that he might.

"I'm not going to break down," Winter said.

"I know."

"You understand me."

"I'm listening."

"They say you're a good listener."

Östergaard shrugged. Listening was what pastors were supposed to do, and since she had started to divide her time between her congregation and police headquarters, she had gotten a lot of extra practice with the officers on the beat and the young inspectors who'd gone straight from the National Police Academy to the beltway around the Gothenburg tinderbox. If something really horrific occurred, they could go home for the day, but that wasn't nearly good enough. They were in the middle of an inferno, both witnesses and participants as society devoured its own children. Nobody could be weak anymore if they wanted to survive. Misanthropy was always on the brink of taking over.

Winter had done a good job convincing the members of his team to talk with each other, but Östergaard had something he couldn't give them. She wondered whether she could handle being here more than three days a week. If she wasn't careful, she'd end up being trapped in their nightmare.

"I'm so emotionally involved in this London murder that I don't know whether I'm the right person to be chief investigator," Winter said.

"Hmm."

"I thought I was getting over Mats's death, but that's going to take some time too."

"Of course."

"Maybe what I need is a family."

Östergaard studied Winter's blue eyes, or whatever might lie behind them. "Do you miss having a family?"

"No."

"You just said that you might need one."

"It's not the same thing. I made the choice to be alone, and I like being able to decide for myself when I want to talk with someone, but sometimes, like now . . ." He looked at her.

"Like now," she repeated.

"Yes."

Winter crossed his legs again. The scratchiness in his throat had coalesced into a tiny sore spot way down where he couldn't get at it.

"I don't usually stop to think about how it feels anymore," he said. "When I was a rookie and they put me out on the streets, I got my first glimpse of real violence and I actually planned to try something else for a while, but then it got better."

"What is it that got better?"

"What?"

"Did your feelings change? Did it all just start to swim past your eyes?"

"Swim past my eyes? That's a pretty good way to put it."

"Then they took you off the streets?"

"Sort of, but all the bad stuff was still there, though in a different way."

Östergaard thought back. She remembered a couple of twenty-five-year-old officers, only ten years younger than she, though they could just as well have been gnarled old men. The first ones to arrive after a neighbor's call on New Year's Eve, they had broken down the door and stopped short at the body of a ten-year-old girl. On the other side of the living room lay her mother, who was to live another three hours, and her husband, who had tried to slit his own throat afterward. "Chicken-shit bastard," one of the officers had said. Then they had come to her.

"Are there certain lines that can't be crossed?" Winter asked after half a minute of silence.

"Lines?"

"Yes."

"That's hard to say. I've always had trouble drawing lines between things—between some of them, anyway."

"Do you know what the hardest part of being an investigator is? It's trying to establish habits and routines as quickly as possible, and then doing everything you can to keep those habits and routines at bay. To approach every case like it's never happened before."

"That makes sense."

"As if the blood was dripping for the first time. Remembering that it could be yours or mine. Or, like this time, imagining the corpse before it went limp, before the soul left the body."

"So what do you do now?"

"I go to my office and read Möllerström's printouts."

<hr />

The burglar went back. For a moment he hoped that the apartment, or the whole building, wouldn't be there, that he had simply suffered a temporary blackout due to all the suspense, which gets out of control once in a while on your way to becoming a pro.

As usual, he kept track of the time and watched people leave the building—women, men and a handful of children, none of whom saw him. He didn't go in, though he knew that lurking about outside could get him in trouble.

He returned the next morning and saw the man leave the building at ten o'clock. Following behind, he watched him cross the road to his parking space and start an Opel that looked fairly new. Then the car disappeared into the distance. And now? Had he thought this far?

He was cold after standing outside for an hour and a half. He walked into the building, put his foot on the first step, and before he knew it he had his ear to the door of the apartment. Quickly entering, he went straight to the bedroom, his blood pounding in his ears. The floor was bare. No black garbage bags, no bloody clothing, nothing new to steal.

He heard someone in the hallway and realized that curiosity, or indecisiveness, or whatever had brought him here, had a breaking point.

It's the fault of the damn newspapers, he thought. If they hadn't written about the murder, you wouldn't be here trembling in your boots as the front door opens.

He fell to his knees and slid under the king-size bed. This is the punishment for all your sins, he told himself.

There was dust under the bed, and he had to hold back a sneeze as he wedged himself in. He put one hand over his mouth and the other around his neck to stifle the urge. You've always known you would end up in this predicament sooner or later, he thought.

The hall light went on and he saw a pair of shoes come into the bedroom. He was so scared that the tickling sensation in his nose let up and he held his breath. The glow of a lamp, apparently from the nightstand, spread beneath the bed. He slowly turned his head to see whether he was casting a shadow on the floor.

You can't just crawl out and lunge at him, he thought. He'll wring your neck before you're halfway out.

He heard a rattling sound and a series of cell phone beeps.

"I'm running late."

I can't bear this much longer, he thought.

"Right . . . Absolutely . . . No way . . . That's why I came back . . . Okay . . . Ten minutes . . . No . . . I had a little chat with him . . . Celluloid . . . Hmm . . . No . . . Hmm . . . Yep . . . Ten minutes."

The rattling sound again, and the shoes stood still with their toes pointing straight at him.

What next? he thought.

It was as quiet as it gets in an apartment building when all the tenants are away. He heard a car swish by and the streets fall silent again.

Is he thinking about something, or is he staring down at the bed? If those shoes come much closer, I'll throw caution to the wind and roll out on the other side.

He got ready, his body taut.

The shoes retreated toward the hall, then through the doorway. The light went out and the door closed.

He lay there for twenty minutes soaked in sweat.

He won't actually look under the bed when he vacuums, or is that just wishful thinking? What difference would it make if he realized that someone has been here? What do you do now? Besides never coming here again. What if he's still out there in the hall? How long can you lie here? Wait a little longer. Okay.

Covered with dust like a thin layer of dirty snow, he tumbled out and scrambled to his feet. He tiptoed out of the room, picking up the clumps of dust that fell to the floor as he moved. Leaving the apartment, he listened for any signs of life, took a deep breath and soundlessly made his way down the stairs.

———

There was a draft from the balcony door. Winter stood up from his desk to close it, but then opened it all the way instead and stepped outside. He shivered, catching a whiff of the city below. A patch of fog from beyond the channel drifted through the park and across Nya Allén Street. When the clammy air reached him, he went back inside and shut the door.

He had been poring over the terse memo from the London police. There was an eerie similarity between the two murders. He couldn't remember anything like it. Not only that, but there was something peculiar about the way the murders had been committed. The British investigators had found little marks in the dried blood that might turn out to match those in the dorm room here in Gothenburg.

He had come home from the office and immediately begun searching the Internet for similar cases, finding what seemed at first like clear patterns, but they were mostly in the realm of the imagination, an illusion. He saw photos that were evocative of his own case, yet they could just as well have been in a dream. He looked for clues in the depths of the electronic night and browsed through several American databases. A surprising number of these kinds of offenders came from Texas or California. Too much sun and sand drives people mad, he thought.

The cell phone on the desk began to ring. He extended the antenna and put the phone to his ear.

"Erik!" crackled a voice at the other end.

"Hi, Mom. You were just on my mind."

"I'll bet I was."

"I was thinking about the sun and sand and what they do to people."

"Marvelous, isn't it?" She mumbled something, and he saw in his mind's eye how she turned around in the little open-plan kitchen and fixed her fourth martini of the evening while glancing at her profile in the mirror. Dear old Mom.

"How was golf today?" he asked.

"We never made it to the course."

"That's too bad."

"It's been raining all day, but now—"

"Didn't you move there to escape all that?"

Her sigh echoed in the receiver. "The grass is always greener." She laughed and it reminded him of unoiled brakes.

"Erik?"

"Yes, Mom."

"I was planning on calling Karin and Lasse."

"Now?"

"It's not that late, is it?"

It's four dry martinis and half a white Rioja too late, he thought. Maybe mañana. "They're going through an awful lot right now," he said. "Wait until morning."

"You're probably right. I always said you had a good head on your shoulders."

"For a cop, you mean."

"That's what you had your heart set on." He heard her turn on a mixer with her free hand. "You're the youngest chief inspector in Sweden."

"If you'll excuse me, I've got a little work to do, Mom." He clicked past a report from Costa del Sol.

"We'll call again soon."

"I'm looking forward to it. Say hi to Dad."

"One more thing," she said, but he was already putting down the phone.

Winter got up and walked into the kitchen. He poured some water in the coffeepot, plugged it in and pushed the button. As the hissing sound grew louder, he filled a tea ball and dropped it in a china cup. He poured in a little milk and finally the water. When the brew was dark enough, he removed the tea ball, tossed it in the sink and took the cup into the living room. He put on a Coltrane CD and sipped his tea, watching the evening outside darken to night. A floor lamp by one of the bookcases bathed the room in a soft glow. He stood by the window to look out over the city but saw only his own reflection.

6

IT WAS SATURDAY. KAREN AND WINSTON HILLIER LIVED SOUTH of the river. Macdonald kept a respectable distance from the cars in front of him as he drove west on A236. The rest of the world was in a hurry, and the driver in the Vauxhall behind him gave Macdonald the finger even before they'd left North Croydon.

Make my day, Macdonald mumbled to himself, waiting. Go ahead and pass me, pal, so I can call in your license plate number. They were approaching a junction—he would have to take the left fork and watch his tormentor zoom by, honking his horn and screaming obscenities with his finger in the air.

We're a nation of hooligans, Macdonald thought. That asshole was no doubt on his way to Griffin Park—the place to be on a brisk day in early February, spending a few carefree hours with your buddies.

When he reached the Tulse Hill district, he parked outside a house on Palace Road. It looked to be newly painted. The people in the neighborhood were from the old middle class and had remained there as the battle lines were drawn all around them. Getting out of the car, he heard what sounded like gunfire coming from Brockwell Park.

The windows were dark, but he knew that the Hilliers were waiting for him inside. Thank God you're not breaking the news, he thought, although your belated arrival might prove to be a disadvantage if the shock has worn off.

Karen opened the door as soon as he knocked. Had she been standing there all morning long? She might have been mentally preparing herself, Macdonald thought, but she looks like you just broke into her house.

"Mrs. Hillier?"

"Yes. Inspector Macdonald, I assume?"

He nodded and pulled out his badge. She ignored it and motioned toward the living room. "Come in."

I'm like one of those prowlers who stalk people's nightmares, he thought.

They walked through the hallway. Illuminated as if by a spotlight, Winston sat in a wide couch at the far end of the living room. Macdonald heard a distant squeaking. Looking out the window, he watched a British Rail train go by, a hundred yards below a bare hilltop.

"We never take the train," Winston said.

Macdonald introduced himself, but Winston didn't seem to hear. "The railroad and tracks have spoiled this part of London," he said. "It's even worse than highway construction."

Macdonald saw some bottles to Winston's right and a glass in front of them. Winston picked it up and raised it unsteadily to his lips. He looked at Macdonald, who took a step closer. Macdonald couldn't tell whether the pale inscrutability of his eyes was the result of blindness or booze.

"I'm not blind," Winston said, noticing Macdonald's bafflement. "Just drunk. Since eleven o'clock this morning, to be exact."

"May I sit down?"

"Welcome to our happy little home." Winston's laugh turned to a hiss. "I told Geoff the program was a good idea." He got up to take a clean glass from the shelf behind him, then looked out the window. "It sounded exciting." His eyes were on a second train making its way below the hillside, which had become grayer in the light of dusk. "A fresh start for a young man with a bright future ahead of him. A chance for an education in this brave new world of ours." He gulped his gin and tonic.

"Why Sweden in particular?" Macdonald asked.

"Why not?"

"Did he have any special reason?" Macdonald heard footsteps behind him and turned around. Karen had walked in with the afternoon tea. He could smell warm scones. "Was there some reason for picking Sweden?" he repeated.

"No, except that he had a pen pal in Gothenburg a long time ago,"

Karen said, sitting down next to Winston. She laid out cups and little side plates.

"That's why he went," Winston said.

"How did he find out about the program?"

"Through his school here," Karen said.

"Geoff always wanted to be an engineer, and the curriculum appealed to him. The school had an English name. Chandlers or something like that."

"Chalmers," Karen corrected him.

"Chalmers."

Karen turned to Macdonald. "He received a letter too."

"From Chalmers?"

"No. Somebody wrote to him from Gothenburg, and that seemed to convince him that he should apply."

Macdonald could tell how hard it was for her to string so many words together all at once. "A personal letter?" he asked.

"What other kind is there?"

"Was it from his old pen pal?"

"We never found out," Karen said.

"He kept it to himself," Winston said, "which was perfectly understandable, but he didn't want to say who it was from either."

"Just that he had gotten a letter," added Karen.

"From Sweden?" Macdonald asked.

"Gothenburg," Winston answered.

Macdonald heard another train in the distance. The strident sound gradually filled up the house. "And he didn't mention anything about the letter after he got there and moved into the dorm?"

"Not a word," Winston said.

"Did he say who else he met there?"

"No."

"Not anybody?"

"He was killed just a few days later, for God's sake," Winston shouted. His gaze turned malevolent. Suddenly he slumped to the floor and lay there facedown. "Get out," he said, his voice muffled by the carpet.

Karen looked at Macdonald as if apologizing for their grief.

They've got no reason to apologize, Macdonald thought. I'm the intruder here.

He said good-bye and went out into the late-afternoon sunlight. Tattered clouds hovered in the western sky. Another hour and it would be completely dark. He turned on the ignition, made a U-turn and drove up to Station Rise, parking at the little depot where the trains took aim at the Hilliers and their anguish. The spot was barely legal, but he went into the Railway Pub anyway, ordered a Young's Winter Warmer and waited for the foam to evaporate, but not a second longer.

7

THE MORE THE CORE GROUP SHRANK, THE HIGHER THE STACKS of paper seemed to grow. Cartons and file folders filled up with bizarre evidence—hair, skin, a piece of a fingernail, impressions, marks, bits of clothing, photos that showed the same scene over and over from different angles, a watchcase echoing the cries for help that Winter had heard the last time he was in the room.

Winter had talked to Pia Fröberg, and she didn't think that all the blows had come at once. She was a top-notch coroner, meticulous. Now, with the remainder of his team gathered in the conference room, he took out a scrap of paper with his notes on it. Geoff Hillier had died of suffocation. The details of his long agony were familiar to everyone in the room.

"How long did it go on?" Fredrik Halders asked. The detective inspector had just turned forty-four. He had stopped combing his hair over his bald spot the year before and left the rest in a crew cut, which had relieved him of the need to smile awkwardly every time someone spoke to him.

"It was a long performance," Winter said.

"No intermissions?"

"Quite a few," Ringmar said.

"The first and last wounds were three or four hours apart," Winter explained. "That's the best estimate they can come up with."

"Fucking sadist," Bergenhem said.

"Yes," Ringmar said.

"Geoff's upper arms were uninjured," Möllerström said.

"That's where the bruises are," Djanali said.

"He must be a strong son of a bitch," Halders said. "How much did Geoff weigh?"

"Close to a hundred and eighty," Möllerström answered. "And he was six foot one, so dragging him around was no easy task."

"If that's what he did," Djanali said.

"That's what he did," Ringmar said.

"Something like it anyway," Möllerström said.

"Size ten-and-a-half footprints spinning around the room," Bergenhem said.

"The only place where he could get hold of him," Halders said.

"You didn't have to explain that," Djanali scoffed.

"Worn-down heels, but with a distinct pattern on the edge," Möllerström continued.

Winter had asked the group to keep talking. It was a kind of inner monologue turned up for everyone else to hear. Details, thoughts, analyses, day in and day out, new stuff and old, the latest evidence. Don't hold anything back, let everyone know. They whittled the facts down until the edges took shape and they could start putting it all together.

"How did he manage to sneak out?" Bergenhem asked.

"He changed while he was still there," Winter answered.

"Even so," Bergenhem said.

"He bided his time," Winter said.

"There was a bathroom in there," Djanali pointed out.

"But still," Bergenhem said.

"He might have run into two or three people on the way out," Ringmar offered.

"I've been reading some background material," Winter cut in, "and it seems like everyone looked the other way. Students don't want to stick their noses into other people's business these days."

"It was different back in my time," Halders mused.

"*You* went to college?" Djanali asked, her eyes wide open.

Halders sighed.

"Then there are those marks on the floor," Möllerström continued.

"I don't understand how they can know for sure that it was a tripod," Halders said.

"That's why you're here and they're there," Djanali said.

Halders sighed again. "A damn tripod."

A damn tripod, Winter thought. It didn't have to mean anything. When they had finished interviewing all the potential witnesses, knocked on a thousand doors, entered all known psychopaths in the database, recorded everybody's comings and goings down to the last detail, completed the inquiry into the victim's background, examined and compared the particles found at the scene of the crime, made a million phone . . . "Have we traced all the calls that were made from the phone in the hallway of the dorm?" he asked.

"We're working on it," Ringmar said.

"I want a list."

"Yes, sir."

"Okay."

"I'll take care of it. How about the Malmströms?"

Winter thought for a minute. "Yes, all the calls from their house too." The tripod. What was attached to the top of it? he wondered. And what had happened to the device after the murder? That's what would tell them all they needed to know. A videotape somewhere. Or several, or one with different segments, or . . .

"We've got witnesses from the Brunnsparken area," Möllerström said.

"Have you finished going around the neighborhood a second time?" Bergenhem asked.

"Almost," Ringmar answered.

"I want a report of everything the neighbors have to say by tomorrow morning," Winter ordered. "Something doesn't jibe here."

"I have something I want to show you," the man had said offhandedly, taking the items out of his duffel bag as they stood in front of Jamie's building. Then he had continued along Drottninggatan Street, and Jamie had gone to work.

Now he rang the doorbell just as Jamie was stepping out of the shower.

The anticipation was almost too much to bear. A thrill of expectation rippled down Jamie's back as the warmth slowly filled his groin. It was a pleasant feeling. This could be for real.

He's big, Jamie thought. He's putting the equipment together now. He sees the bottle of wine on the table. Now he's coming over and taking the glass from me. I don't understand what he's saying. What's this creepy mask he's putting on? He's going back and turning on the camera. Isn't it supposed to make more noise than this? There's the whir.

Jamie was spun around to face the black lens, and he opened his eyes in confused horror. A rag was twisted into his mouth and his arms were tied behind his back. He tried to say something but the words stuck in his throat.

The man brought him a chair from the kitchen. The whir grew louder and Jamie's eyes were glued to the lens. This is one sick motherfucker, he thought. I don't mind trying something a little different, but it's freaky that he's not saying anything. Some games are just too weird. I don't want to sit here anymore. He's standing there and staring at me. Get up and turn your back to show him that you want him to untie your arms. Here he comes.

Jamie felt a jolt behind his back and something that burned in the pit of his stomach. When he jerked his head down to see what it was, a pain throbbed under his belly button and it felt like his back was being slit open. The ache was so intense that he was afraid to lift his head back up, and he saw a pool form at his feet. The bastard is pouring wine all over the floor, he thought.

Now he was spinning around. There was the mask again, or maybe it was a new one. And when he saw what the son of a bitch was holding in his hand, he realized that he had let things go much too far. The fear sapped all the strength from his legs and he fell forward toward the object that glimmered in the light from the table lamp and the camera flashes. He tried to scream but nothing came out and he could no longer breathe.

He stood up again. He knew what was happening to him now. He tried to make his way toward the south wall of the room, but the gesture was mostly in his mind. He slipped and struck his hip as he fell. He slid along the floor.

He heard a voice. There's a voice inside me and it's calling to me, and the voice is me. I know what's happening to me. Now I'll go over to the wall, and if I stay calm, it's going to be all right.

Mom! Mom!

He heard a whir like when time freezes and the world stops before your eyes. He couldn't escape it.

Get away from me.

Go away.

It went on for a long time. He grew tired and was lifted up. He didn't think so much now. The wires and cables in his head had been clipped in two and his thoughts spilled out and careened around his brain. He was lifted up again.

8

WINTER FELT TRANSPARENT. THE LIGHT WAS POURING IN FROM
the left. He took his sunglasses off the dashboard and put them on, and
the city rearranged itself before his eyes. He stopped to let three men
stagger across the road on their way from Vasaparken Park to Victo-
riagatan Street. Their long hair flapped in the northwest wind.

The adrenaline coursed through his veins. He couldn't have been
more ready. It would never be more real than during the next few hours,
never more horrible or clear. He was drawn irresistibly to the scene of
the crime, and he knew from experience that he would feel ashamed or
frightened or both when it was all over. Maybe that came with the territory, getting so involved in a case that he couldn't imagine spending his
time on anything else.

Officers were keeping the sidewalk clear of onlookers, but a horde
of people stood just across the street on the other side of the cordon.
I would have been one of them in another life, Winter thought. How
many of them are there, thirty maybe?

"Call Birgersson and ask him to send five officers right away," Winter
said to Bergenhem.

"Now?"

"This instant."

Bergenhem dialed the number as they walked up the last flight of
stairs. He repeated Winter's request when the division chief answered.
"He wants to talk to you," he said to Winter.

Winter took the phone. "Sture? . . . Yes, we're almost there . . . Three more steps . . . He told you, right? . . . Actually, I thought they would be here already."

Bergenhem could hear Sture Birgersson's voice but was unable to make out the words.

"I want everyone on the other side of the street questioned. Call it an encirclement if you like . . . Yes, now . . . Thank you. Bye."

Winter had seen a crowd of faces but no expressions as he walked toward the front door. It must be cold standing out there. Who knows, one of them might be more than just a curious bystander. Someone who knew what Winter would discover in the apartment. Something that brought him back no matter how hard he fought it.

"Who was here first?" Winter asked as he stood outside the apartment looking around at a blur of uniforms.

"It was me." The officer was in his midtwenties. A faraway look shrouded his pale face.

"Did you arrive alone?"

"My partner was with me. Here he comes." He pointed toward the stairs.

The alarm had gone out from Skånegatan Street and reached Winter about the same time as the closest squad car. The officers had entered the apartment, turned pale and cordoned off the area.

Jamie hadn't shown up for his morning shift to do the dishes, mop the kitchen floor and tidy up after the gig the night before—a new band with obscure ties to the west coast of Ireland that hadn't packed it in until two o'clock.

Douglas was supposed to have the day off, and Jamie hadn't answered his phone. Annoyed, Douglas had gone to Jamie's apartment, rung his bell for what seemed like an eternity and pounded on the door until a neighbor stuck his head out and scowled.

He'd finally found the janitor. Jamie? The British kid? Yes, the one in the apartment with the makeshift nameplate on the door, Douglas answered, and he thought that something might be wrong with him.

The janitor, who had a hundred tools in pockets down the legs of his pants and around his waist, unlocked the door, and the rest was a dazed nightmare.

His ears buzzing and his eyes open wide, Winter was the first person to get a good look at the apartment. He stepped around a couple of footprints that pointed toward the door. No traces of violence on the walls. He heard the forensic team gathering by the stairs, and that's where they would stay until he gave them the go-ahead.

He knew he would be back at least once after the body had been removed, and what he looked for then would depend on what he found now.

The hallway was bright enough for him to see. The light was on in the bathroom. Had the officers turned it on when they came in? Surely no policeman was that dumb.

He stood in the doorway and looked down at the bathtub. There were streaks of blood on the tile, but fewer than he would have expected. He took his time, Winter thought.

Same story in the washbasin, plus three stains on the plastic mat by the tub.

Winter turned around and found himself at a twenty-degree angle from the kitchen door, which was partly open on the other side of the hallway. When he peered inside, he didn't see anything out of the ordinary except that the little table was missing a chair.

But when he turned his eyes to the middle of the main room, Jamie was sitting on the chair with his back to the door.

He was wearing socks and a pair of pants but no shoes or belt. A red and blue tattoo gleamed on his left shoulder. As Winter made his way between the stains on the floor to get a better look, he saw it was a car but couldn't tell what kind.

Jamie's upper arms were blue. His pants were bulging, about to burst. That's what's holding him together, Winter thought. His face is uninjured. So strangely aloof, it looks like it's floating above the chair.

On the table next to him was a bottle of red wine and two glasses, one half full and one empty. Winter leaned over and sniffed. There hadn't been any time for a toast.

The room was furnished simply, as for a transient guest: a couch for two; no armchair, bookcase or flowers; plain curtains that muted the sunlight between the half-open blinds; a CD player on a little whitewood bench; a hanging rack with twenty or twenty-five albums. Winter edged along the wall to the other side of the couch and read some of the

titles at the top: Pigeonhed, Oasis, Blur, Daft Punk, Morrissey. No jazz.
The player was open and he glimpsed a disc inside. Carefully, so as not
to graze the wallpaper, he leaned forward to see the name of the artist.

The oval of blood around the chair resembled the pattern in Geoff's
room. His eyes followed it toward the door and out into the hallway.

How many steps were there?

For about six feet inside the door, there were no patterns and hardly
any stains. Winter inhaled the room's odors. A bark sounded through
the west wall. If it could be heard here, he could be heard there.

It occurred to Winter that he never heard his neighbors, except when
they struggled to open the squeaky elevator door and rattled the cage.

Fifteen minutes in this apartment was enough. He went out and motioned to the forensic team, then walked down the stairs and into the
sunlight to question the onlookers across the street.

Hitchcock. He could never remember whether Halders or Möllerström
had come up with the name. Don't let the press get wind of it, he had
told them. He didn't like referring to a murderer like that but caught
himself doing it anyway.

By some odd coincidence, the investigators in London began calling
their man by the same moniker shortly afterward. And it wasn't long before the British and Swedish teams figured out that it must be the same
murderer and started working together, overwhelmed by a feeling of
powerlessness, as if someone were laughing at them from above.

The burglar looked out at Kalle and the other children. The snowman
was gone. The kids crawled through the barrel, chased each other around
the swing and climbed down the rope ladder from the playhouse.

He didn't know which way to turn. He read the papers and followed
the news on television, and he wasn't stupid, even if he was an idiot
when it came to certain other matters. He knew something that nobody
else did. There was no doubt in his mind about that. Or was there? He
needed time to think, maybe somewhere else.

"What is it?" his wife asked.

"What did you say?"

"You have that look on your face again."

"Hmm."

"Is it the job?"

"What job?"

"You know."

"Hmm." He looked out at the playground.

"Why don't you go out and play with Kalle for a while?"

"I was just thinking about that."

"He's asked about it."

"Asked about what?"

"If you two can do something together sometime."

"I've been thinking about it."

"You could do more than think about it."

"How about we all take a vacation together?"

"Sure, anytime."

"No, I'm serious, we could go to the Canary Islands tomorrow or the day after."

"Right."

"No kidding, I won some money."

"No you didn't."

"Yes I did."

"When? How much?"

"Three thousand. I didn't want to say anything until I got the money so it would be a surprise."

"And now you have it?"

"Yes."

She examined him, trying to see beneath the surface. "Can I take your word for it?"

"Absolutely."

"How did you win it?"

"At the harness track. Remember last week when I went out there a couple of times? I'll show you the coupon." He wondered how the hell he was going to do that.

She looked out at Kalle. "That wouldn't be a very smart thing to do."

"What do you mean?"

"We can't just pick up and go to the Canary Islands."

"Why not?"

"Just think of everything else we need the money for."

"We'd never go anywhere if we waited until all our bills were paid. When's the last time we took a trip?"

"Okay, you've got a point, but how much does it cost?"

"We can afford it. That's all that matters."

"But now that . . ."

"There's no time like the present."

"I admit it would be wonderful." She still sounded hesitant.

"Two weeks. And the sooner we leave, the better."

"How are we going to get tickets on such short notice?"

"Hard cash."

Winter got hold of Bolger late in the afternoon.

"We've got to stop meeting like this," Bolger said when he heard Winter's voice.

"This is strictly business."

"Got you."

"Even if I'm taking advantage of our friendship."

"Now you've lost me."

"There's something I need to ask you."

"Fire away."

"Not on the phone. Can you hang around until I get there?"

"Sure thing."

Winter was at Bolger's bar in fifteen minutes. Three customers at a table by the window gave him the once-over. Bolger offered him a drink, but he turned it down.

"Do you know an Englishman by the name of Robertson?" Winter asked.

"An Englishman, did you say?"

"British at least."

"What did you say his name was?"

"Robertson, Jamie Robertson."

"Jamie Robertson? I know who he is, although we haven't really been introduced. He's not English, by the way. He's Scottish."

"Okay, Scottish."

"It's sort of obvious when he talks."

"Has he ever worked here?"

"No."

"Do you know whether he's worked anyplace other than O'Briens?"

"No, but I don't think he's been in Gothenburg very long. Ask over at O'Briens."

"I will."

"Has something happened?"

"He's been murdered."

Bolger seemed to pale, as if someone had changed the bulb in the overhead lamp.

"This isn't confidential information or anything," Winter clarified.

"It's the first I've heard of it."

"In any case, I could really use your help."

"Since when did you ever need my help?"

"Don't be childish, Johan."

"Why the hell would you need my help? You're smart enough for the two of us."

"Would you please give me a chance to tell you what I want?"

Bolger glanced over at the waitress behind the bar as if he wanted another drink, then apparently thought better of it.

"You're in touch with guys in the business," Winter said, "and people who know their way around the city."

"So are you."

"You know what I'm getting at."

"Sure, you want a petty criminal to do some snooping for you."

"Cut it out, Johan."

"Do they let you use informants who've been hospitalized for depression?"

"It's like this, Johan. We're doing all we can, but I want you to try to remember what you know about Jamie. Who he knew, who he spent his time with. Girlfriends—or boyfriends, if it was that way."

"I understand."

"Think about it."

"Okay."

"Ask around if you need to."

"I promise."

9

WINTER SAT ON RINGMAR'S DESK, HIS JACKET HALF UNBUTTONED, his holster girded by the gleam of his silk shirt. Ringmar knew that he himself could never sit there with the same kind of elegant nonchalance. His legs were too short and his suits too cheap and his shirt didn't shine the same way.

"How many times have we talked to Geoff's parents in London?" Winter asked.

"Two or three."

"I'm still thinking about the letter someone wrote to him."

"Me too."

"He didn't give anything to someone else, did he?"

"Not that we know of."

"There was something in the witness statement of his pen pal. Geoff wrote that he would be coming to Gothenburg, and she answered right away. But that was the end of their correspondence."

"Right."

"Shouldn't he have responded eventually? Isn't that what pen pals are supposed to do?" Winter paused for a moment. "Englishmen don't waste their time."

"They get it right from the very beginning. Just look at their soccer teams."

"One of their officers calls the Malmströms every couple of days. But it's mostly to offer a little TLC."

"Hmm."

"That's their thing. He's called a family liaison officer or something like that."

"Uh-huh."

"The chief investigator picks one right away. At least some of them do."

"You did the same thing."

"If you're referring to Möllerström, I had no choice."

Before Ringmar could answer, the phone in his breast pocket started to ring. He pressed the green button and mumbled his name. "I'll see if I can find him," he said with his eyes on Winter. He put the phone on his desk and motioned to the corner of the room.

Winter followed behind him.

"It's your mother."

"Is she sober?"

"Getting there."

"What does she want?"

Ringmar shrugged.

Winter walked back to the desk and picked up the phone.

"Hello?"

"Erik!"

"Hi, Mom."

"We were so worried."

"Were you?"

"We read about the second murder."

"I'm a little busy right now, Mom. Was there something else on your mind?"

"Your sister called. I know she'd like to hear from you a little more often."

"She could have told me that directly without calling all the way to Spain." Winter rolled his eyes in Ringmar's direction. "I promise to give her a call," he continued. "Bye for now, Mom."

He pushed the red button and handed the phone back to Ringmar. "Women," he said.

Ringmar cleared his throat. "And where's your phone, may I ask?"

"It's charging in my office."

"Okay."

"I put it on call forwarding."

"That's what I figured."

"The cell phone is a monstrous invention," Winter said. "I've seen people standing on opposite street corners talking to each other."

"It's modern man's way of keeping himself company."

"Just imagine if lightning struck and zapped you back in time. There you are in exactly the same spot, but it's six hundred years earlier."

"Hmm."

"It's raw and chilly and there's nobody else around. The only thing you have with you is your phone. You duck behind a tree to hide from some knights that come charging down the path, or whatever it's called, and you realize that something crazy is going on. Do you follow me?"

"Perfectly."

"All you can do is try not to panic. When you've gotten a grip on yourself, you call home and Bodil answers. Still with me?"

"Keep going."

"Here you are in the Middle Ages and you've got your wife on the line. Pretty amazing, isn't it?"

"Fascinating."

"What a movie it would make."

"With me in the lead role?"

"That's not for me to say. But here's the best part of it—or the worst. There was no electricity back then, so you don't have anywhere to plug in your battery charger. You stand there talking to Bodil, and you know that as soon as the battery runs out, it's all over. You'll be alone forever."

"What a grotesque story."

10

A MASSIVE EFFORT WAS UNDER WAY.

Twenty men had rung every bell in the neighborhood, and Möller-ström was working overtime entering all the information they had gathered into the database.

A couple of days after Jamie's murder, rumors had begun circulating that Sture Birgersson was thinking about calling in the National Criminal Police Corps, and the issue resurfaced when Winter's team convened to discuss the latest murder. Halders, who had heard the scuttlebutt, made a grimace that changed his appearance only slightly. "I'd rather eat shit."

Winter laughed out loud, which was unusual for him, especially at meetings. "I believe Fredrik just summed up all of our feelings."

"Stockholm is a great city," Djanali mused, looking out the window toward Skövde and Katrineholm. She turned back and eyed Halders. "Nice people, cultured, easy to be with."

"Particularly in the Flemingsberg area," Halders said.

"Do you always get off the subway there?" Djanali asked. "Hasn't anyone ever told you that it goes farther?"

"I'd rather eat shit," Halders said.

"You could use a more balanced diet."

"Your irony is a little undernourished too."

"Irony? Who's being ironic?"

Winter discreetly shuffled his papers and everyone stopped talking. "We'll continue to work in teams of two. Djanali and Halders will be together today. They seem to be hitting it off just fine. The rest of you can go ahead like you have been." He glanced over at Bergenhem. "And I have something to talk to you about after the meeting."

Bergenhem raised his head. He looks like a schoolboy, Winter thought. "We've found something," he said to the whole group.

Ringmar flipped off the light and turned on the slide projector. He clicked back and forth between the rooms of the two British victims and finally stopped on Jamie's.

The police photographer had used a wide-angle lens, and the room bulged out in the center.

Winter nodded. Ringmar clicked to the next slide, Jamie's upper body, and Möllerström felt ashamed, like an eavesdropper who is privy to a forbidden act.

"Look at those uninjured shoulders," Winter said, nodding again. Ringmar clicked to a new enlargement.

"Do you see it?" Winter stared into the semidarkness. Nobody noticed anything. He nodded to Ringmar once more, and an even bigger enlargement appeared.

"Do you see it now?" Winter moved his pointer toward a spot on the bare shoulder that could have been a piece of dust on the screen.

"What's that?" Djanali asked.

"It's blood," Winter said. She saw the light from the projector reflected in his eye. "But it's not Jamie's."

Nobody stirred. Djanali shivered and raised her arm as if to keep her hair from standing up.

"I'll be damned," Halders said.

"Not Jamie's blood," Bergenhem echoed.

"When did you find this out?" Djanali asked Winter.

"Just a couple of hours ago, when I went through the photos in the morning light."

He was here when it was pitch black, Djanali thought, when everyone except this superman was fast asleep.

"Fröberg called me as soon as the test results came back," Winter said.

"And the lab has verified it?" Halders asked. "I mean, there was quite a lot of blood, to put it mildly."

"Yes," Winter said.

"Can it be used as evidence?" Bergenhem asked.

"If there's enough," Ringmar said. "They think so. They're working like crazy on it right now."

"Enough for what?" Möllerström asked. "If there's nothing to compare it with in the register, we won't have a thing to go by."

"That's negative thinking." Bergenhem looked at Möllerström as though he had broken a spell.

"It's realistic thinking, as long as we don't have a DNA database that starts at infancy."

"We all know your opinion about that," Djanali said.

"I for one am glad that we're finally getting somewhere," Halders said.

"This could be our breakthrough," Ringmar said.

Ringmar rolled in a VCR with an oversized television screen and put in the videotapes from the crime scenes one by one. They began discussing the patterns on the floor.

These tapes are horrible, Winter thought. It's like we're seeing everything through the murderer's eyes, and you can bet he taped it too and it's lying in a drawer someplace or playing to an avid audience. "There's a clue for us somewhere," he said.

The video camera zoomed to the oval pattern on the floor.

"We think it's a dance." Ringmar pointed to the screen. "The two rooms show striking similarities, as if the murderer acted the same way both during and after the crime."

"What kind of dance?" Bergenhem asked

"When we know that, we'll be in much better shape," Winter answered. "Sara Helander here will be working on it from now on," he continued, nodding at the person to Halders's right. "You all know Sara."

Helander lifted her hand in acknowledgment. She had been called in from the wanted persons group. Crossing her legs, she brushed back a lock of hair from her left temple and kept her eyes fixed on the screen.

"If it's the fox-trot," Halders said, "we can pick him up any night of the week at the King Creole Club."

Helander spun around. "What's that supposed to mean?"

"Forget it." Halders turned back to the video.

"How are we ever going to make anything out of all this?" Bergenhem asked.

"How do you make anything out of anything at the beginning of an investigation?" Helander retorted.

Winter nodded in approval. Police work was all about waiting until the impossible became possible. A dance? Why not? He had jotted down the name of the album in Jamie's CD player and given it to Helander. There's a tape somewhere with audio, he thought, and it might be music or it might be something else that only people with certain predilections can stand the sound of.

"What does the London team have to say about this?" Djanali asked.

"I've been trying to get hold of the chief investigator all morning," Winter answered.

"How about INTERPOL?" Halders asked.

"We need to be talking directly with London at this point," Winter said.

Winter stood where he had been during the meeting, while Bergenhem sat next to him and jotted down some notes.

"Try to be as discreet as possible," Winter said.

"How many strip joints can there be?"

Winter fingered the package of cigarillos on the table in front of him. When he opened the blinds, he saw a whole class of students crossing the street from Kristinelund High School, no doubt on a field trip to the upholders of public order. At the front of the pack was a man in his early fifties, a wrinkled Seeing Eye dog leading blind youth, none of them much younger than the victims of the murders Winter was investigating. He closed his eyes. "Any questions?" he asked, turning to Bergenhem.

"Can you give me a week?"

"We'll see. I know someone you can talk to right away."

Winter went home early that night and made an omelet. Cutting up the tomatoes, he thought briefly of the Mediterranean sun that watched over his vagabond parents.

A restless feeling chafed at him. He walked over to the stereo but stood there idly. He thought about opening a bottle of beer, then changed his mind and decided to go for a run in the Slottsskogen woods across Sprängkullsgatan Street. He'd pulled the jersey halfway over his head when he heard the phone ring. It was Angela, one of his girlfriends—the best idea of all.

He pulled her to him as soon as she walked through the door. In bed he bent down and lifted her by the thighs. He was in a hurry, and it felt like an eternity before his body erupted, his mind blissfully empty.

They lay on their backs in the silent room. "You needed that," she said.

"It takes two."

The phone on her side of the bed began to ring, and she rolled over to pick it up while he gazed at the smooth contours of her hips and thighs. "Hello?" she said, listening intently. "That's fine, go ahead and put him through."

How does she manage? he wondered. It's almost like she's my wife.

"Yes, he's right here." She looked over her shoulder. "It's a chief inspector calling from London—MacSomething," she whispered to Winter.

11

WHILE ANGELA HEADED FOR THE SHOWER, WINTER SQUIRMED HIS way across the bed to pick up the phone. She closed the bedroom door.

"Erik Winter here."

"Good afternoon, this is Steve Macdonald in London. I hope I'm not interrupting anything."

"Not anymore. I'm glad you called back."

"I got the message."

"We have some things to talk about."

"You can say that again. Somebody else was also . . . Sorry, I'm not talking too fast, am I?"

"Not at all."

"You Scandinavians speak excellent English. That's more than I can say of us in south London."

Winter heard the shower running. Soon she would come out and wave good-bye as if it had all happened in a distant, stormy dream. He felt the dried perspiration at the top of his forehead. "Your English is easy to understand," he said to Macdonald.

"Well, just tell me if I need to repeat anything. It's my own special blend of Scottish and Cockney."

Winter heard Angela turn off the shower. He pulled the sheet up to his waist, suddenly embarrassed by the stranger's voice. Or maybe I'm just cold, he thought.

"We've got to get down to the nuts and bolts of this," Macdonald went on.

"I'm with you all the way."

"I've been reading your reports, and the last one makes me feel like we're standing on some kind of stage."

"A stage?"

"Somebody's out to prove something."

"Isn't it always that way?"

"This guy is a little too clever," Macdonald said. "We're not talking about your everyday sociopath."

"You're right. He's a sociopath, but there's something more."

Angela slowly opened the door and threw him a kiss. He nodded back. She turned around and walked out. He heard the front door close and the elevator cage rattle.

"We just talked to Jamie's parents for the first time," Macdonald said. "Or rather his mother. They live on the outskirts of London."

"Our database expert mentioned that."

"I heard that he called his counterpart over here. He speaks good English and they had no trouble communicating."

Winter saw Möllerström in his mind's eye, the way he enunciated every syllable. Why doesn't everyone have an e-mail address? Möllerström had wanted to know. Is English easier to write than speak? Halders had asked.

"It's a strange investigation." Macdonald paused. "Actually, it's several investigations rolled into one. My boss has put our team on the case full time."

"Same here."

"Nothing new on the letters?"

"We talked to Geoff's pen pal, but she couldn't help us out very much. She didn't notice anything unusual in his last letter, only that he was excited about coming to Gothenburg. As far as the letter that he supposedly received from someone else in Sweden is concerned, we don't know anything yet. His pen pal had no idea who it might be from."

"I guess it's to be expected that he no longer had the letter when you found him."

"No new witnesses who saw Per?" Winter was still mulling over Macdonald's remark about being onstage.

"Yes and no, you know what it's like. Everybody has seen everything and nobody has the information you're looking for. To say that our phones are ringing off the hook would be an understatement."

"Nothing solid to go on?"

"Not at the moment, but that's how it always is. The good news is that the press has been unusually cooperative. A white European kid murdered in the ghettos south of the river is a real story, as opposed to the crack-related murders we usually deal with. Try to get the papers to write about them. I'm grateful for all the publicity and calls we can get, even if we have to weed out a bunch of nutcases. Croydon is England's tenth largest town—three million of us. So there's no shortage of loonies here."

"Gothenburg is Sweden's second largest, and that adds up to half a million."

"Any drugs to speak of?"

"More and more."

"Did you get the newspapers I sent by diplomatic pouch?" Macdonald asked.

"Yes, we did, thanks."

"Then you know what I'm talking about. When the *Sun* demands that a curfew be imposed until an arrest has been made, the public feels called upon to help us solve the case."

Winter was thinking to himself. "What did you mean by feeling like we're onstage?" he asked finally.

"Onstage?"

"What made you say that?"

"It's like somebody's watching us, somebody who's in orbit above us, just out of reach."

"I have the same feeling."

"Maybe it's the tripod. It could give anyone the creeps."

"What on earth did he need a tripod for?"

"Excellent question."

Winter thought out loud. "Maybe he wanted to have his hands free. That's one scenario at least."

"Who knows, maybe there's even a script."

"What makes you think he needed one?"

"Everyone needs a script."

Winter's cell phone began ringing on the other nightstand. "Hold on a second." He put down the receiver and lunged across the bed.

"Hello?"

"Erik? It's Pia Fröberg over at the coroner's lab. We've got a big problem with that blood on Jamie's shoulder."

"Yeah"

"There's been a terrible mistake. It turns out the blood is from somebody on the ambulance crew."

"How can something like that happen?"

"It can't."

"I understand," Winter said calmly, but he didn't know whether his effort at restraint came across over the phone. "I've got someone on the other line. I'll call you back in a little while."

He hung up and returned to Macdonald. "Sorry for the interruption."

"No problem."

"We need to go through all this from beginning to end, and there are a few things I have to see firsthand in London."

"When are you coming over?"

"As soon as I get the go-ahead."

"My boss and I are both anxious to have you here. It's a case for international cooperation if I ever saw one."

"I'll let you know the moment my plans firm up." Everyone needs a script, Winter thought. We're onstage and somebody is orbiting just above our heads. We're part of something bigger than ourselves. We make one mistake after another. Maybe we learn.

"The ambulance guy," Fröberg said.

"How could anyone be so careless?"

She had taken off her white jacket to meet Winter in her rectangular office, where the shelves were overflowing with books and file folders.

She's started to wear glasses at work, Winter thought.

"He had a day-old cut on his wrist in the opening just above his glove," Fröberg said.

"Unfuckingbelievable."

"He scraped it on the doorjamb when they came in with the stretcher and accidentally smeared the blood on Jamie's shoulder while they were wrapping him up."

"One little drop was all we needed."

"Actually, you should thank me, Erik. It takes just as much time to eliminate a possible clue as to verify it."

"Sorry."

"No need to apologize."

"So you've followed up on all the evidence?"

"Everything we could."

"And I was hoping that all we needed was one good suspect."

"What happened to all the ace interrogators?"

Winter thought about his best hope, Gabriel Cohen, who had been brought in on the second day of the investigation. Cohen was as methodical as Winter, reading all of Möllerström's printouts, waiting, preparing. "Cohen's ready to go," he said.

"Medical science can't always come to the rescue."

"You're right as usual. How about dinner tonight?"

"I can't." She smiled and reached for her jacket on the back of the chair, her blouse stretching against her breasts. "My husband is back."

"I thought he had left for good this time."

"So did I."

Waving good-bye, he walked out of the office and nearly rammed headlong into a stretcher that had come rolling past.

12

YOU HAD TO MAKE UP YOUR MIND HOW MUCH OF THE NEIGHBOR-
hood to cover—which buildings and which particular entrances. That
meant all the tenants who lived in the chosen locations had to be questioned, no matter how heavy an accent they had, or how much they
smelled of garlic, or how dirty they were—*what we in this country call
dirty*, ventured a grinning twenty-five-year-old investigator fresh from
the National Police Academy, his youthful cynicism intact. A seed of
racism that could only grow, Winter thought, making a mental note of
the man's name. You're far from enlightened yourself, he mused, but
little shitheads like him can go find somebody else to work for.

Jamie had died on the fifth floor while the cars passed by on Chal-
mersgatan Street below, and Winter thought about a possible connection
with Geoff's dormitory half a mile away. It was pure speculation at this
point.

The buildings in this part of the city clung to each other, massive as
cliffs carved out millions of years ago. The police walked up and down
stairways, knocked on doors, drew muttering replies, invoked vague
memories of incidents that nobody had paid any attention to when
they'd happened and couldn't say much about now.

Lasse Malmström had continued to put on his suit and go to work, and
on the afternoon of the third day it all caught up with him.

It wasn't only Per's body, which had just arrived by plane.

Time was like a stone wall. He was having gruesome thoughts. As the plane was landing, he had hoped for a second that one of the wings would fly off and the whole runway would go up in flames.

Then the world ceased to exist for him. No job, no suits, silence all around and almost nothing he wanted to remember. Everything he thought he knew was gone, his refuge a place deep within.

The last thing he needs to hear is that you feel his pain, Winter thought.

The morning light flooded the living room, adding a shimmering veneer to the silence. A two-day-old beard deepened the wrinkles on Lasse's face. He rubbed his chin nonstop, and it sounded like a nail file, or a rake unearthing frozen leaves. "What's the latest?" he asked.

Winter stalled. "Anything particular you want to know?"

Lasse stroked his chin even harder. "I read the papers until Per's body came back," he said. "It seems like a hundred years ago."

"The fact that two kids were murdered here in Gothenburg around the same time as Per might be due to any number of things," Winter began.

"Things?"

"I mean motives, however twisted they might be."

"I don't know if that's supposed to make me feel hopeful or discouraged."

"I don't follow you."

"I mean if more police are working on it, investigations are going on in different places, that's a good thing even if the murders turn out to be unrelated."

It occurred to Winter that he would have felt the same way in Lasse's shoes.

"The more people get killed, the harder you guys try, and then maybe the murderer will be captured, or whatever the hell you call it."

"You could be right."

"Here I'm talking like there was some kind of connection between the murders, but I don't know anything about it, and maybe you don't either."

"It's one of our theories, but we're working on some other threads too."

"You'll keep me informed of everything, right?" Lasse looked Winter straight in the eye for the first time.

"No matter what happens, I'll make sure to keep you posted. That's what we always do, and I'm not about to start changing things now."

"That's reassuring."

"We don't just sit around and twiddle our thumbs and wait for someone else to figure it all out. We're constantly coming up with new ideas. We have a good system that we stick to, and the investigation is always moving forward."

"Got it."

It's really true, Winter thought. You're not just saying this. He's listening to you now. The dog that's barking outside has jolted him back to his senses, and he's stopped rubbing his chin. Now's the time to spring the question. "There's something I need to ask you, Lasse."

"Shoot."

"You know we're trying to find out as much as we can about Per's habits—the people he hung out with, his girlfriends, all that kind of thing."

"Yes."

"All that kind of thing," Winter repeated. "We talked to his girlfriend, or that's what we thought at first."

"What?"

"She wasn't his girlfriend after all."

"You just lost me there, Erik."

"You or Karin told us that she was Per's girlfriend, but that's not how she described it."

"You know how it is at that age. They must have broken up or something."

"It's more like they had never gone out, not really."

"And here I thought that I was the one having trouble getting my words out. What are you trying to say—that they were only friends, or that Per never got it together to screw her?"

Winter didn't like either alternative.

"Answer me, for Pete's sake."

"More like the latter," Winter said finally.

"He never screwed her. Is that what you mean by keeping me informed?"

Winter started to answer, but Lasse interrupted him. "Is this some kind of newfangled interrogation method, Mr. Investigator?"

"Please try to understand, Lasse. This is the type of information that's absolutely essential if we're going to get the answers we need."

"What fucking answers?"

"We've got to find out as much as we can about Per and his . . . interests."

"Like whether he was a fag?"

"Was he?"

Lasse dropped his eyes and started rubbing his chin again. "Leave," he said quietly.

"Pull yourself together, Lasse."

"You ask me if my son was a pervert, and then you tell me to pull myself together?"

"I don't know a thing about Per's sexual orientation. That's why I'm asking."

Lasse sat with his head bowed over the coffee table and finally looked up at Winter.

"I wouldn't ask if it weren't important," Winter insisted.

Lasse muttered something indecipherable.

"Sorry, I didn't get what you said."

"Hell if I know."

Winter waited.

"I can honestly tell you that I have no idea. It's true that he didn't date a lot, but I never thought much about it. I was a late starter myself."

The dog continued to bark, as if it couldn't stop until Lasse's ordeal was over. It's not his dog but it's a kindred soul, Winter thought.

"Have you talked to Karin about it?" Lasse asked.

"Not yet."

"Ask her."

The dog stopped barking.

"I'm really sorry to put you through all this," Winter said.

"I'm telling you the truth. Even if I knew Per was gay, I wouldn't lie to you about it."

How would Lasse have reacted if Per had told him he was gay? Winter remembered the way Mats had been the last year of his life—so fragile and tormented by feverish dreams. "There's nothing for anyone to be ashamed of," he said.

"You mean that I was ashamed of Per."

"No."

"I don't have anything against gays, but this came a little suddenly, that's all."

"We don't know anything yet, I assure you. But we can't ignore any possible clues."

"Go ahead and talk to Karin and his friends. Do you need to search his room again to check this out?"

"No, but I appreciate your cooperation."

As he was walking out, Winter glanced over at his sister's house. He had spent part of his childhood there and come back to visit on occasion. After her divorce, she had grown a little too neurotic to be a general practitioner. Things got better when she bought the house from their parents and moved back in along with her children.

Nobody's home, you can call tonight, he thought.

13

THE FRONT HALLWAY WAS COOL AND DARK EXCEPT FOR A STREAK of white light from the other rooms of the apartment. Winter took off his shoes and picked up the mail under the slot in the door: a circular from Mercedes about their new rollout, the latest police newsletter, postcards from a girlfriend vacationing in Thailand and another one in the Canary Islands, a slip from the Kungsport Avenue post office that a package of books had arrived, and a letter with a Spanish stamp—he recognized his mother's purposeful handwriting and saw a little red blot in the bottom right corner of the envelope that could be anything but was probably a drop of wine.

He walked into the kitchen, set the mail on the table and the two plastic shopping bags from the Saluhallen indoor market on the counter. He emptied the bags: a halibut fillet, an eggplant, a yellow pepper, a zucchini, several tomatoes, a pint of kalamata olives and sprigs of fresh thyme and basil.

He sliced the eggplant, arranged it on a tray and sprinkled salt on the pieces. After pitting a few olives, he poured a little oil into a baking dish, turned on the oven and sliced the pepper, tomatoes and squash. He patted the eggplant dry and sautéed the slices in a large skillet. In the dish, he overlapped the vegetables along with minced garlic and the olives, scattered herbs on top, added a little more oil and finished off with a few twists of the pepper mill. Finally he put the dish in the oven beside two potatoes that he had cut in half and sprinkled with sea salt. He waited fifteen minutes and laid the fish on top of the vegetables.

He ate alone in the living room, looking out over the city and forgoing the distraction of music or a book. He drank half a bottle of carbonated mineral water. You should cook more often, he told himself. It calms you down. The doubting Thomas that has always tormented you about putting up a good front stops knocking on the door.

He smiled to himself and stood up. As he carried the glass and tray through the hallway, he heard the elevator jangle its way up to his floor. The cage opened and closed in rapid succession, followed by the ringing of his doorbell. He glanced at his watch—it was nine o'clock.

He went into the kitchen, put the glass and tray down, walked back to the hallway and opened the door. It was Bolger.

"Hope you're not getting ready for bed or something."

"Come in, pal."

Bolger closed the door behind him, removed his leather jacket and kicked off his shoes.

"Would you like some coffee?" Winter asked.

"If it's not too much trouble."

They went into the kitchen and Bolger sat down at the table while Winter fussed with the espresso machine. "Just in case we were planning on sleeping tonight." He smiled.

"Not that I have any information that would make you sleepy," Bolger said. "Or keep you up, for that matter."

"Maybe you just felt like talking."

"Hmm."

"You haven't been here in a while."

"I don't remember much about the last time. I was smashed, no doubt."

"You were pissed off about one thing or another."

"There's always something . . ."

"Anyway, I'm glad you came," Winter said. "I need you more than ever." He filled two small cups, put them on the table and sat down across from Bolger. He seems uptight about something, Winter thought. He hasn't aged much since high school—as long as you don't look too closely, that is. "What have you found out?" he asked.

"Apparently Jamie was a popular guy, but that's true of most bartenders."

"At least early in the evening."

Bolger sipped his coffee. "This tastes like melted asphalt."

"Then I succeeded."

"Am I supposed to chew on it or something?"

"You got it."

"When you work at a bar, you're surrounded by people who aren't your friends exactly but they think of you as one of them."

"I see."

"Casual acquaintances, but something more."

"Jamie must have had other friends too."

"A couple of boyfriends." Bolger took another sip.

"So it's true?"

"That's what they say. Or Douglas, rather, the guy who runs the place. No specific evidence or anything, but it's not the kind of thing you can hide. He gave me a couple of names. I brought them with me in case you need them." He took out his wallet, unfolded a slip of paper and handed it to Winter.

"Thanks."

"They're both around the same age as he was," Bolger said.

"Hmm."

"Fags, I would assume."

"Okay."

"I have no idea if they're the violent kind."

Winter committed the names to memory, put the slip of paper in his breast pocket and sipped his coffee like bitter medicine that you take for no apparent reason. "How have other restaurant owners been reacting to all this?"

"It's a rather unpleasant affair, of course, but nothing to get all riled up about."

"I understand."

"It's not like he went and got himself murdered because he was a bartender."

"No."

"Somebody has too little brandy in his Lumumba, racks his brain about how to get back at the barkeep and finally takes his revenge."

"Perhaps I chose the safer occupation after all."

"Or a martini that isn't dry enough, or shaken instead of stirred."

Or maybe as thick as this coffee, Winter thought. My spoon can almost stand straight up in it.

"At my place, we let some ice settle in the vermouth for a while," Bolger said. "Then we drain the glass and put the ice in the gin."

"Somebody might call that stinginess."

"Our customers call it style."

Johan has never been very good at wearing a poker face, Winter thought. Or maybe too good.

"Do you think somebody in the restaurant industry could have done it?" Bolger asked.

"You know I never speculate."

"But it's possible, right?"

"Anything's possible, and that complicates matters, doesn't it?"

"Do you want me to ask around some more?"

"Definitely; I need all the help I can get."

"Douglas said something about having seen a new face several times at his bar recently," Bolger volunteered. "He said that he usually notices when someone comes back a second or third time."

"Hmm."

"It's hard to remember entire groups, but if somebody shows up alone often enough, it tends to stick in your mind."

"Was there something unusual about this particular customer?" Winter asked.

"That's basically all he had to say."

"I've read all the witness statements, but Douglas didn't mention anything about that when we talked to him."

"I guess you'll have to ask him again."

"Right."

"A little footwork for the chief investigator."

Winter reached for the espresso machine. "More coffee?"

14

BERGENHEM HAD ASKED HIMSELF MORE THAN ONCE WHY HE had been assigned to the county criminal investigation unit. It wasn't his decision, or maybe it was, after all—they knew perfectly well what he wanted to do. He had no interest in the narcotics, technical or white-collar crime divisions, and larceny didn't have nearly the same appeal. Violence was tangible and concrete—dirty business committed by people who were settling private scores, however bizarre.

It wasn't until the victims were wholly innocent—when one side held all the power, when children lay on stretchers and faced a lifelong disability—that his job began to trouble him. Three-year-old girls who would never see again, six-year-old boys who kicked soccer balls one day and were beaten black and blue by their fathers the next.

He wasn't going to become thick-skinned. He wanted to be just the opposite, a warrior battling all the odds.

Bergenhem buried his face in Martina's hair until he could scarcely breathe. They had been married a year now, and she was eight months pregnant. Their child would be kicking a soccer ball before they knew it. Bergenhem would play goalie.

An inspector almost straight out of the National Police Academy. He felt as if he had won some kind of award but had no idea what for. He was promising material, someone had said. Material for what?

The first few weeks had been particularly lonely. He had been a little shy at the academy, and making his mark among forty other inspectors

at Homicide—or the thirty who weren't in the wanted-persons group—
was an even more daunting challenge. He didn't really understand why
they were keeping him on Winter's team as the investigation went
forward.

He had his assignment, and he knew that his position was secure
even if it took a while before things started to happen. Something always
happened, eventually. That was Winter's mantra. Nothing stands still,
everything flows—but better a deceptive calm than chasing your tail
without ever getting anyplace.

Loneliness. He recoiled from the jargon of his profession, and he
wasn't cynical enough to learn it—not yet, at least. He couldn't simply laugh off the misery he encountered, and that made him feel like a
square peg in a round hole.

He noticed that Winter rarely smiled. Winter wasn't a square peg in
a round hole, and he didn't laugh at the wrong times like Halders was in
the habit of doing, or even Ringmar every once in a while.

Bergenhem admired Winter and wanted to be like him but didn't
think it would ever happen. It wasn't Winter's style—his elegance or
whatever you wanted to call it—that Bergenhem craved for himself.
That quality ran deeper in Winter than in others, sure, but it was his
toughness that struck Bergenhem. An iron fist in a velvet glove. Winter
was surrounded by an aura of stern concentration, and when he worked,
his features shifted but his gaze remained steady. Maybe he let his guard
down when he was off the job, but Bergenhem didn't see him then.

There were all kinds of rumors about Winter and women, that he
used them to relieve the pressures of his job. He had a reputation that
would have been devastating if he weren't a man. But the rumors all had
to do with the past, and Bergenhem suspected that Winter had learned
to be more discreet in his erotic adventures. He didn't really give a damn
one way or the other. Winter meant something else to him altogether.

Where will you be in twelve or thirteen years? The aroma of Martina's hair filled his lungs. Will you be lying here and brooding over
the same thoughts about the world around you? Some people walk in
worn-out shoes. How many more will be destitute in twelve or thirteen
years?

"What are you thinking about?"

Martina turned over on her side, a little clumsily, supporting herself
on her right elbow and lifting her left leg. He ran his hand over her belly.

It stuck out like one of those orange cones they used during soccer practice. He didn't play soccer anymore. His coach had said that he hoped Bergenhem had learned his lesson and would be more careful in other areas of his life.

"Nothing special," he answered.

"Tell me anyway."

"Some people walk in worn-out shoes."

"What does it mean?"

"That's all. Some people walk in worn-out shoes. The phrase just popped into my head."

"It sounds like a song or something."

"Right, that's where it's from. I heard Marie Fredriksson sing it once with Eldkvarn. But Cornelius Vreeswijk wrote it a long time ago."

"Some people walk in worn-out shoes."

"Yes."

"That's a good title."

"Hmm."

"I can see them in my mind, all the unfortunate ones in their worn-out shoes."

"Right now?"

"They're not so unusual these days," she said, pointing vaguely at the world outside the bedroom window.

"Is that the kind of thing you think about?"

"Not that much, especially now, to be honest about it." She placed her hand on her belly. "Right there, do you feel it?"

"What?"

"Put your hand . . . No, there."

At first he didn't notice anything, but then there was a tiny movement, or the hint of one.

"Do you feel it now?"

"I think so."

"What does it do to you?" she asked, her hand on top of his.

"I can't really describe it. Give me a couple of hours and I'll come up with something."

"That's what you always say."

"This time I promise."

She closed her eyes, and he felt another flutter under his hand.

They lay there silently.

The egg timer went off in the kitchen.

"The potatoes," she said, not moving.

"To hell with them." He smiled.

———

"Do you think I'm too soft to be a police officer?" Bergenhem asked over dinner. "Like I'm not up to the job?"

"No."

"Be honest."

"How could I say you're too soft? The softer, the better."

"To be a policeman?"

"What?"

"Too soft to be a policeman?"

"It's a good thing."

"To be too soft?"

"It's the kind of job where you get hard too fast, and that's the worst thing that can happen."

"I don't know. Sometimes I doubt if I'll make it through the day."

"Don't let go of that doubt."

"What?"

"Don't let yourself get stiff and hard."

"So it's better to be soft?"

"It's much better to be soft like overcooked asparagus."

"But sometimes I'm more like raw asparagus, right?"

"What do you mean?"

"Not all of me."

"What part of you?" She reached across the table and squeezed his biceps. "Overcooked asparagus."

"I'm not talking about anything above my waist."

———

Bergenhem stepped inside Bolger's bar. He's just as tall as Winter, Bergenhem thought, but seems twice as big. It could be his leather vest, or his features. You've been here for three minutes and his expression hasn't changed. He's as old as Winter, but until people get past forty, their age is always hard to pin down.

"You don't strike me as a restaurant goer," Bolger said.

"No."

"Not much for nightlife?"

"It depends on the night."

"What's that supposed to mean?"

"I'm not at liberty to say."

Bolger turned toward the rows of bottles behind him. "Since Erik sent you, have one on the house. Even if you're not used to sinning in broad daylight."

"I'll take some juice, if you don't mind."

"Ice?"

"No, thanks."

Bolger found a carton of juice in the refrigerator underneath the bar and filled a glass from the hanging shelf above. "I'm afraid that I'm not all that familiar with the part of the industry you're after," he said.

The drink had a tangy sweetness over the orange flavor that Bergenhem couldn't place.

"Clubs have been sprouting up like weeds in this city over the past few years," Bolger continued, "and I'm not talking about restaurants either. It's all happened so fast I've pretty much lost count."

"Illegal clubs?"

"That may be an accurate way to describe them, but most have licenses these days. Which only goes to show that crime pays, right?"

"In what way?"

"You open an illegal club and a week later, bam, you're holding a license in your grubby little hands."

"I see."

"After two weeks, you close the joint down and start all over someplace else. But that's all old hat to you guys."

"Some of us, anyway."

"That's not exactly the information you were looking for, is it?"

"I'm grateful for anything you can give me."

"Like what's going on in the illustrious porn world?"

"For example."

"What does Erik expect to find out, anyway?"

Bergenhem took another gulp of his juice.

"The industry has grown," Bolger continued. "It's a different scene from back when I played a bit part."

"What's so different now?"

"It's a lot more than tits and asses, to put it bluntly."

"Hardcore?"

Bolger's teeth gleamed in his dark face and the windowless room. "More like supercore. From the little I've seen, what goes in isn't as important anymore as what comes out. Or both at the same time, if you catch my drift." He took down a glass, filled it with beer and sipped it once the foam had settled. "I got out of there just in time."

"Do they have illegal joints too?"

"Illegal strip joints? It depends on how you look at it."

"I'm not following you."

"There's the part that the general public sees—a magazine rack, a few books, sex toys, peep shows and a couple of large screening rooms."

"Strippers?"

"They're called exotic dancers."

"And?"

"What?"

"You said that's just what the public sees."

"Now, I'm going strictly by hearsay. But one or two of those places have a room where you can find things that are a little out of the ordinary. Magazines with a special twist, maybe movies."

"Movies?"

"Movies where the actors engage in unusual acts."

"Unusual acts?"

"Don't ask me what they are, but it's no Sunday school picnic."

"You know that these movies exist?"

"That's what they tell me, and also that there are a couple of small, anonymous joints that don't even pretend to be anything else."

"Where?"

Bolger threw out his hands.

"Can you look into it?" Bergenhem asked.

"Maybe. It might take a little time, though. I've got to watch my step."

"Who are the customers?"

"You ask as if I knew the answer."

"What's your best guess? As opposed to the customers you had, or the ones who look for the ordinary stuff."

The sunlight from the other room suddenly dimmed, and Bolger put on a pair of metal-frame glasses with thin lenses.

They add character to his face, Bergenhem thought.

"My best guess? I don't think there's that much of a difference. Interest breeds interest, like when you start with beer and move on to the harder stuff. Or from smoking grass to shooting up."

"You develop more of an appetite?"

"Some people just want more and more. It's hard to say where it all stops. Others are sexually aroused by the fantasy of being strangled or having a limb cut off. Who knows what kind of movies they like to watch?"

"Where can I find them?" Bergenhem asked.

"People who dream about somebody cutting off their leg?"

"All of these sick people. When they're not at a club, I mean, or at home, or in a hotel room."

"Since I drive a BMW, I'd say in Volvo's boardroom. Or in the boardroom of your choice. Or on the county commission. There are crazy people everywhere."

"Creepy." Bergenhem got up.

"Be careful out there. I'm not kidding."

Bergenhem waved from the doorway and walked out into the sunset. The wind swooped down from the rooftops and raised his collar. A glass broke somewhere behind him.

15

MACDONALD DODGED THE OBSCENITIES THAT THE FRUIT STAND vendors screamed at each other across the intersection. He was at the corner of Berwick and Peter streets in Soho. Just look at what they've done to our proud fruit market tradition, he thought. Covent Garden closed, everything driven out of downtown.

This was what has become of it: half-drunk men slipping on banana peels, a few pitiful stands for a handful of curious tourists and ten times as many junkies. Soho doesn't swing anymore, it crawls—at least here, where an empty lot is the most pleasant sight for miles around.

He turned up the collar of his raincoat against the drizzle and stepped over a crushed beefsteak tomato. Walkers Court was so short, unassuming and shoddy that it didn't even appear in the new edition of a *London A–Z* street atlas. Maybe they excluded it on purpose, he thought. It's not the kind of street you feel like bragging about to rosy-cheeked Italian and Scandinavian tourists straight from Heathrow and Gatwick.

Walkers Court was porn without silk sheets or the pink young models who show their pee hole in *Hustler,* Macdonald thought as he shook his head at a doorman who beckoned him into one of the theaters. It was more for sweaty junkies in rags—low-budget sex for the masses, books, magazines and videos for those who came to see themselves as they might have been in another life.

Maybe they bought the fantasyware in these sophisticated stores. Just what you need in certain situations. Or how about this leash or that noose? This is a free country. We're all entitled to a personal life. Some people light a cigarette in the privacy of their own home; others like to poop in the faces of strangers.

He passed by the biggest bookstore on the street. It looked out of place with its advertisements featuring the latest in fine literature for the educated middle class: V. S. Naipaul and Jonathan Raban, a new biography of Bruce Chatwin.

Macdonald knew that the owner was a complex character. The ground and upper floors were bright and cheerful, overflowing with novels, poetry, travelogues and cookbooks. The basement, which you got to by descending a stairway on the other side of a curtain, was a different world altogether. Magazines with titles like *Over Forty* and *Life Begins at Fifty* fearlessly defied the youth culture. The room was always full of customers. Just like that one, Macdonald thought as a man with a flat brown bag hurried out of the store.

Macdonald promised himself that he would read more as soon as he retired from the police force. He was thirty-seven, and he had served Queen and country since he was twenty-three. Only eleven years left. After that he could be a private detective and chase runaway teenagers from Leeds through the bowels of London. Or work as a security guard at Harrods and keep an eye on the Oyster Bar. Or arrange birthday parties for his grandchildren at his house in Kent, never more than ten steps from a malt. He'd let them pull on his ponytail as much as they wanted, he thought as he waited for a car to pass on Brewer Street. Crossing the intersection, he followed Rupert Street for a quarter of a block, nodded at a black man in a leather jacket and entered a theater under a flashing neon sign that said PEEP SHOW.

It took him a few seconds to get used to the shadows. Passing the cashier's booth, he knocked on a door to the left of the main entrance. He stood and listened to the moans that echoed in the darkness. Somebody was screaming, "Yes, yes, YES, YES," but it didn't sound very convincing.

The door opened a couple of inches and another black man stared out at him. After the door closed again, Macdonald heard a rattling sound and it was flung wide open.

The man stretched out his hand and nodded for Macdonald to enter. "Welcome, Mr. Investigator."

"You don't skimp on security here, do you, Frankie?"

"Not a chance."

They shook hands and Macdonald stepped into the office. No larger than a hundred square feet, the room was thick with humidity, along with the smell of vinegar and grease from half-eaten fish and chips on the pockmarked desk. A poster celebrating the pleasures of life in Jamaica was taped to the wall above, its bottom right corner curled, as if protesting the romanticism of it all. Next to the plate of leftovers was a notepad, a pen and a keyboard. The computer screen on the right side of the desk flickered more than it should. Cheap crap, Macdonald thought.

"Sorry I couldn't offer you my lunch," Frankie said. "But I'd be glad to order some more."

"Looks like it was pretty tasty."

"As English as can be. Should I send Johnny Boy to get another?"

"No thanks, the savory smells are enough for me."

Frankie flicked his shoulder as if he were brushing off a thank-you after having paid for a five-course meal at Wheeler's. "It's your call. So what can a hardworking businessman do for the guardians of law and order?" he asked, taking a chair from behind the desk. "Have a seat, I'll go get another one."

He returned carrying a big, clunky chair with red imitation leather upholstery and gray stuffing that stuck out through the loose seams.

Frankie followed Macdonald's eyes. "It might be ugly, but it's comfortable as hell." He sat down but popped back up when a young woman walked in with a tray. After putting a stainless steel teapot, two cups and saucers, a little pitcher of milk and a bowl of sugar on the desk, she smiled, bowed her head slightly and left the room. Frankie sat down again and poured a cup for each of them.

"Just what I needed." Macdonald leaned forward.

Frankie stood up a second time.

"What is it now?"

Frankie walked out and returned with a plate of cookies.

"Are the rituals just about over?"

"Now they are. Jamaicans are crazy about ritual. We come from a different world than you do."

"What the hell are you talking about? You were born in London."

"A zebra never changes its spots. Genes, you know."

"Genes have always fascinated me."

"Me too." Frankie picked up a nail file and inspected his left index finger. "But I don't expect that you came all the way here to talk about genetic code."

"You haven't given me much of a chance to explain why I'm here."

"I'm all ears."

"You aren't nervous, are you?"

"Me, nervous? Because I'm not used to such fine company, you mean?"

"Don't ask me why."

"Good-looking coat."

"Hmm."

"I like your ponytail too, but isn't it rather passé these days?"

"It's mostly to blend in here."

"Everybody's welcome in south London. We don't discriminate." Frankie filed away at the offending nail.

The computer beeped.

"An e-mail from the other world?" Macdonald asked.

"Didn't you know that there are more computers per capita in Jamaica than anywhere else in the Caribbean?" He read the message, which appeared to be quite short.

"Wrong," Macdonald said.

"What?"

"Brixton may officially be a suburb of London, but it has more computers per capita."

"Very funny, but this e-mail actually comes from your bailiwick." He quickly reread the message and closed the program.

"Since when did it stop being yours?"

Frankie's smile flashed in the semidarkness of the room. He picked up the file and moved on to another finger.

"Brixton," Macdonald repeated.

"Right, the e-mail is a confirmation that my subsidiary has just received a new shipment of top-quality magazines and videos."

"A new shipment?"

"That's what I said."

"Where from?"

"Is this an interrogation, Steve?" A jewel glittered in one of Frankie's front teeth.

Macdonald tried to remember what those gems were called, but couldn't. "You know me better than that, Frankie."

"I'm not sure twenty-five years is long enough, Paleface."

"Come on, now."

"We're from two separate worlds."

"Okay, you win. But that shipment you mentioned is what interests me at the moment. You've read about the murder in Clapham, haven't you? The kid who was cut up?"

"I saw something about it on television. But that was quite a while ago. Norwegian or Swiss, wasn't he?"

"Swedish."

"Oh."

"*Crimewatch* is going to do a reenactment of it any day now."

"It must be a big deal, then."

"It's a little different, that's for sure."

"Different? You can say that again. A white guy gets knocked off for once."

Macdonald sipped his tea.

"When's the last time *Crimewatch* did a show on a black victim?" Frankie continued.

"You know how it is."

"I know exactly how it is. When black people get murdered, nobody gives a shit." He put down his nail file. "How many murders did you say you had in southeast London a couple of years ago?"

"Forty-two or forty-three, I think."

"And how many of the victims were black?"

"Something like . . ."

"Hell, Steve, stop pretending like you're even trying to remember. I know that at least thirty-five of them were black. You don't have to be a mathematician to figure that out. And I also know that those murders have as much of a chance of appearing on *Crimewatch* as I do of being admitted to a gentlemen's club on the Mall."

"We're doing everything we can."

"To get me into a club?"

"To attract the attention of the press."

"I'm not blaming you for it. You can't help it if you're white." Frankie went at it with the file again.

"I'm looking for any clues I can get," Macdonald said.

"And so you come knocking on the gates of my kingdom."

"Right."

"What the hell for? What does this goddam murder have to do with my business?" Frankie put the file back down.

"Nothing in particular, but certain things happened while the crime was being committed that we're anxious to find out more about. Have you heard about the two kids from London who were murdered in Sweden recently? In Gothenburg?"

"No, that's news to me."

"One of them is from Tulse Hill, where your aunt lives."

"White boys."

"Yes."

"My heart bleeds for them."

"Not as much as theirs."

"Sorry, Steve."

"All three murders have certain things in common, and it's possible that one or more videotapes are lying around somewhere with a blow-by-blow account of exactly what happened. This is something that only the police have any inkling of, and you know what that means."

"I won't say a word."

"You understand why I'm telling you all this?"

"Murders on film. What makes you think something like that?"

"I can't give you the details, but certain indications point in that direction."

"You really think that's a possibility?"

"Yes."

"Not in my worst nightmares . . . It's the most disgusting thing I've ever heard."

Macdonald nodded.

"You've got your work cut out for you, Steve."

Macdonald raised his cup to his lips, but the tea was cold.

"This isn't your typical murderer on crack who waits patiently for the police to arrive," Frankie said. He stood up, rubbing his forehead with his fist. "And you think I can help you find your snuff movie?"

"I'm just trying to get a little information. Like how much of this crap is actually around."

"I stay away from that sort of thing." Frankie glanced at the poster. "I swear by the spirit of my Caribbean ancestors."

"If I had any reason to think otherwise, we would have taken our tea down at the Eltham police station."

"I assume you want me to make some discreet inquiries."

"As discreet as possible."

"That goes without saying."

"Do you know anyone who has an inner room that's closed to the general public?"

"Sure."

Macdonald got up.

"But not where they show snuff movies. Not as far as I know, anyway. It's revolting enough, shit that makes the stuff I show here look like family day at the beach, but not the kind of thing you've had the bad taste to talk about."

"See what you can find out," Macdonald said.

"You can always ask your usual gossipmongers, can't you? Like that pimp on Old Compton Street."

"I'll take care of that part, don't worry."

"Fine."

"Call me in a couple of days, no matter what turns up. And watch your step."

"Snuff movies . . ." Frankie shook his head.

"Give me a break. This can't be the first time you've heard about a murder being filmed."

"No, but you'll never see any of this in the stores, Steve. These movies are marketed through special distribution channels that run high above our smutty little lives."

"Shit flows downward. Or maybe in both directions and meets in the middle. Someplace in this paradise we call Soho is somebody who knows."

"I envy your optimism."

"Thanks for the tea hour, Frankie."

"I'll call you on Friday."

Macdonald gave a half wave and walked out. Turning right outside the theater, he crossed Wardour Street and continued east on Old Compton. The rain had stopped. People sat at outdoor cafés and pretended it was spring. I envy their optimism, he thought.

When he got to Greek Street, he went into the Coach and Horses pub, ordered a Theakston Old Peculier and wriggled out of his coat. It was the usual crowd of literary wannabes, has-beens and lethal combinations of the two. A couple of authors who had come close to making it big spent most of their time here drowning their sorrows in drink. The place was always half empty at this time of day.

An intoxicated woman three stools away was carrying on a conversation with two men at a nearby table. "You have no fucking idea what it means to be a gentleman," she shouted, then raised her glass to her lips.

16

STURE BIRGERSSON'S OFFICE WAS IMMACULATE. NOT A COFFEE
stain or piece of paper on his desk. Winter harbored a certain admiration
for the way the division chief arranged his world: concentration on one
thing at a time, no reminders of everything that was still unsolved, no
remnants of incomplete thoughts, no reports resembling books whose
authors had died in the middle of writing them.

They called Birgersson the Boss in the corridors of police headquarters, but that had more to do with his position than his personality.
Birgersson sat eternally in his office and waited. He read but drew no
conclusions. God knows what happens to all the reports after he's done
with them, Winter thought as he crossed and uncrossed his legs in front
of the desk.

Birgersson was a Laplander who had wound up in Gothenburg by
chance, not design. Unlike everyone else from northern Sweden, he
didn't go back and hunt in the fall. He always took two weeks off, but
Winter was the only one who knew where he went, and he wouldn't
have told anyone else if his life depended on it. In all the years Winter
had been acting division chief during those times, he had never needed
to call Birgersson. He couldn't conceive of a situation he wouldn't be
able to handle on his own.

"I have to admit you've got a healthy imagination." Birgersson had
the peculiar accent of someone who'd grown up in a mining district
near the polar circle and spent his adult life in the hustle-bustle of a European metropolis.

Winter brushed a speck of dust off his tie, leaned forward and tugged on the seat of his pants, which had gathered too tightly on one side when he'd sat down.

"Not so much in the way of results, but you compensate for that with creativity," Birgersson continued, lighting a cigarette.

"We're making progress."

"Shoot."

"You've read the reports."

"It wears me out to go back and forth between all the different styles." He pointed to the empty desk as if it were overflowing with stacks of paper. "William Faulkner one minute, Mickey Spillane the next."

"Which do you prefer?" Winter asked, lighting a cigarillo.

"Faulkner, of course. He was a small-town boy too."

"But you don't feel like you're seeing any results."

"No."

"I don't look at it that way. We're reading the witness statements, we're going through the files on our favorite jailbirds, not to mention some of the more obscure ones. I'm not the only one who's online from morning to night. And we've got all our sources working for us, and I mean all."

"Hmm, have you talked to Skogome?"

"Not yet."

"Why not?"

"Because it's too early, Sture. I don't want a profile by a forensic psychologist until we've got more to go on."

"That's exactly what I was talking about."

"What?"

"Not enough results."

"What you're talking about," Winter said, "is longer reports and more bullshit to feed the press and evidence so strong that it will reach out and grab the police bigwigs."

"Speaking of the press, I hope you're ready for them."

"Absolutely."

"A fresh planeload of British reporters has just landed," Birgersson said, "and they're not taking any prisoners this time."

"Not taking any prisoners? You've been watching too many Hollywood action movies."

"This afternoon I want you by my side, partner."

"So you're going to be there too?"

"Orders from the top."

"I see."

Birgersson put out his cigarette.

"I'm leaving tomorrow," Winter said.

"Remember that your trip is unofficial."

"Of course."

"Police force to police force."

Winter took a puff of his cigarillo and scanned the room for evidence that it had ever seen a piece of paper. Nothing.

"I have no idea what to expect from London," Birgersson said. "But their DSI seems to be on top of things. Their detective superintendent."

"I know what it means."

"He has nothing but praise for your contact, that chief inspector."

Birgersson looks like a dwarf birch, Winter thought. One that's made a heroic effort to straighten up and climb down from the mountain. Funny I never noticed it before. "Macdonald," he said.

"On his way up just like you."

"Right, on an eleven o'clock flight tomorrow morning." Winter put his half-smoked cigarillo in an ashtray that Birgersson had taken out of a desk drawer.

"Who knows, maybe you'll have the whole thing solved by the time you get back. Meanwhile, we'll do our best to hold down the fort."

"Now that's reassuring." Winter smiled.

"I suggest you go to your office and get yourself into the right frame of mind for the press conference."

"Wouldn't it be easier to take an extra beta-blocker?"

Birgersson broke into a hoarse laugh that could have been lifted from one of the action videos he guffawed his way through one night a week.

The press conference started off badly, staged a recovery in the middle and ended in chaos. Birgersson was exasperated before fifteen minutes had passed. Winter answered the questions that swarmed at them both.

The Swedish tabloid reporters were more restrained, taking the opportunity to pick up a few tricks of the trade from their aggressive British colleagues.

"Is this your first case?" This from the ugliest person Winter had ever seen. His face resembled five pounds of meat loaf molded by an arthritic potter. He acted drunk but was sober as a judge. Like the other Englishmen, he was wearing a threadbare suit, having landed in Scandinavia without a coat.

"Is the murderer Swedish?" somebody else asked.

"How many similar cases have you had?"

"Describe the murder weapon."

"What were the victims doing in Sweden anyway?"

"What kind of sex crime was involved?"

"Excuse me?" Winter balked, examining the reporter. She had blue eye shadow, blond hair with black roots, a narrow face and a spiteful mouth.

"What kind of sex crime?" she repeated.

"Who said that it was a sex crime?" Winter asked.

"Isn't it rather obvious?"

Winter looked the other way, hoping that someone would rescue him with a question about the weather in Sweden, what soccer team he rooted for . . .

"Answer the question," somebody shouted.

"We don't have anything that points to a sex crime," Winter said.

"Like what?" someone else asked.

"What did you say?"

"What is it that you don't have?"

"How about sperm?" Winter asked.

The room fell silent for a few seconds.

"What's that supposed to mean?" a reporter asked in Swedish.

"We didn't find any traces of sperm," Winter said, "which means we can't be a hundred percent sure that it was a sex crime."

"But it might be?" the reporter persisted.

"Certainly."

"Speak English," a British reporter shouted.

"What did he say about sperm?" somebody else asked.

"They found a shitload of sperm," the reporter with the pockmarked face explained.

"Whose sperm?"

"What did the lab tests show?"

"Was there sperm on only one of the victims, or both?"

"Was it on his body or his clothes?"

Winter could tell Birgersson was longing for the cool emptiness of his office. After he had straightened out some misunderstandings and asked the reporters to publish a few facts that would help the investigation, he fielded a couple more questions. The television cameras, both British and Swedish, whirred away.

"Have you checked out everybody who's come here from England recently?" a Swedish reporter asked.

"We're working on it."

"How about people heading the other direction?"

"We're working on it," Winter lied.

17

ANGELA CAME OVER TO HELP HIM PACK, BUT HE TRAVELED
light and insisted on saving space for some books he planned to buy in
London.

"If you ever get out of here," she said.

"The sky is clearing."

"Call the airport first thing in the morning."

"Excellent idea."

"What do you expect to accomplish—arrest this serial killer or something?" Angela ran her fingers over the collar of a white shirt on top of
the pile by the suitcase.

"He's no serial killer."

"What?"

"He's no serial killer," Winter repeated, folding two pairs of socks
and putting them in the suitcase.

"Is that so?"

"It doesn't look that way."

"Uh-huh?"

"It's even worse." He turned to her. "Could you hand me those pants,
please?"

"Take them yourself."

"Okay."

"Come and get them," she said, her eyes wide and misty as if she had
been walking through rain.

Winter lunged across the bed, grabbed the pants from her, smoothed out the wrinkles and put them on the chair. He took her hands and folded them behind her back as she leaned forward toward the bed.

"Now you've got me where you want me."

He doubled her long skirt halfway up her back, let his hand glide over her right hip and worked his finger under her panties. As she parted her legs, he moved his hand downward and felt how wet she was. His forehead was pounding and she gasped, raising her chin. He carefully squeezed his fingers further in, unbuckled his belt with his left hand and pulled down his zipper. All my blood is there and nowhere else, he thought, leaning against her thigh for a second. When she started to moan louder, he gradually entered her, stopping only for a moment when he couldn't go any farther.

After a few seconds they were in sync. He held her firmly by the hips, as though she were treading water above the bed.

He leaned forward, reached inside her sweater and cupped her breasts. Now she had dived into the water and was floating beneath him. He squeezed her hard nipples. She turned her head to the side and looked back at him. He caressed her cheek and lips with his left hand. Opening her mouth, she licked and sucked on his fingers one by one. Her tongue had the same rough texture as her sweater.

As they moved faster, he braced his left knee against the bed, grasped her hips with both hands and summoned all his strength to hold on as she trembled and then cried out, throwing her head back. His eyes dimmed. His power seemed to plunge him into unconsciousness as it poured into her. They clung to each other one last time, and he held her.

18

THE SNOW HAD STOPPED AND EVERYTHING HAD FROZEN OVER- night. The Monday morning sun had bleached the edge of the cold front.

Bergenhem shuddered in the kitchen, made some coffee and opened the blinds. The trees outside the window were wrapped in mist, which slowly dissolved as the colors of the day reappeared, coming back from their resting place, he thought, reinventing themselves and gliding back into the objects all around him. A juniper bush lost its transparence just after the clock struck eight. The fence emerged from behind its curtain of white, and his car glistened under its snowy blanket as if startled by the first dashes of sunlight.

He had the afternoon shift. Martina was asleep. He felt vaguely restless, a low murmur in his chest. He drank his coffee quickly and put the cup in the dishwasher, then went into the bathroom and splashed some water in his eyes. As he brushed his teeth, he probed the jagged edge of one of his canines and felt an icy coldness there when he rinsed out his mouth.

He tiptoed back to the bedroom and picked up his clothes from the Windsor chair next to the doorway. Martina stirred in her sleep, or half stupor. The sheet had slipped down and revealed her thigh, a spring hillside in the midst of a snowy landscape. Walking over to the bed, he ran his fingers over her bare skin and grazed it with his lips. She murmured something and moved again without waking up.

He put on his heavy sweater, boots, leather jacket, hat and gloves. The fresh snow was in the way, and he had to kick the door open.

He took the shovel that was leaning against the house and hacked at the frozen crust, plowing his way down the driveway to the car. This summer you are building a carport, he told himself. Assuming you can get hold of cheap wood.

He brushed the snow off the hood and windshield as best he could and tried to open the driver's door to get a scraper, but the key wouldn't go in. He stared dumbfounded through the window at the can of lock lubricant in the inside pocket of the passenger door.

He tried the other doors and the trunk, but they were all frozen shut. In the shed behind the car, he dug out a nine-inch length of wire, which he managed to slide through the crack in the door, and he was finally inside. He grabbed the lubricant, sprayed the lock, waited a few seconds and then worked the key in. Putting the bottle in his jacket pocket, he scraped the entire windshield. He was pleased with himself, as if this interlude had prepared him for the trials and tribulations of the day.

The ignition sputtered for a few seconds before turning over. He put the defroster and heat on high. A Phil Collins song was playing on the first station he came to. He flipped the dial for a while but soon tired of it and slid R.E.M.'s *Automatic for the People* in the tape deck instead. It had been number two on the *Billboard* charts in the winter of 1992, when he had taken a long field trip to London during his last semester at the Academy. He had gotten drunk at a pub in Covent Garden and found himself in bed with a party girl in Camden. He could never quite remember how they had wound up at her place. *Automatic for the People.* My automatic is for the people, he'd said, because that's a cop's job, and he'd gulped down some more wine while she giggled under the sheets.

He had met Martina the following spring.

As Bergenhem drove south, the open fields quickly gave way to glass and concrete. In Torslanda, smoke poured out of Volvo's main assembly plant on his right. Ahead loomed the Älvsborg Bridge. The glitter of oil tanks almost blinded him as he approached the abutment.

The second wave of the morning rush hour rolled across the freeways as commuters descended from the north into downtown Gothenburg.

Driving onto the bridge, he glanced quickly to his right, and when he reached the top, he saw a clear purple stripe below the rising sun. From this vantage point, the horizon changed according to the time of year.

It was impenetrable on most winter days, as if someone had built a wall over the water. But on mornings like this, you could see through the shimmering light as it slowly turned to blue. The city had pulled back its curtains.

Leaving the bridge behind him, he continued west with no destination in mind. This restiveness had whispered in his ear for as long as he could remember, though it had grown louder the last month or two. He wondered whether it had to do with the blunt little cone that stuck out from Martina's belly, and he felt ashamed of himself.

He drove to Frölunda Square, turned around and came back through Gnistäng Tunnel. His mind went blank in the darkness, and he had to blink and shake his head when the sky reappeared and the sunlight stung his eyes. Fear struck him suddenly, like a premonition. He was cold, but the heat was already as high as it would go. Driving back over the bridge, he stared straight ahead the entire length of it.

Winter's taxi swerved in and out near Mölnlycke, found a spot in the outer lane and zoomed past an airport bus. There's plenty of time, he thought. It must be a matter of professional pride for the driver to get you there as fast as possible.

The phone hummed in the inside pocket of his sport coat. He pulled out the antenna and answered.

"Erik!" His mother sounded slightly out of breath. No doubt she had just jogged from the kitchen table to the refrigerator and back. "Are you at home?"

"I'm on my way to the airport."

"You've always been such a smart boy, Erik."

Winter looked at the driver, who was staring fixedly at the road as though he were considering whether to veer over to the right lane and smash his way through the guardrail into the cliff.

"You're a traveling man," she continued. "They always need you someplace."

"I spend most days going back and forth between the Vasaplatsen subway station and Ernst Fontell Square," he said.

"Fontell what?"

"It's the square in front of police headquarters, on Skånegatan Street."

"I see."

"There's all my traveling for you. Sometimes I even ride my bike."

"So where are you going now? Not on your bike, I hope."

"London."

"It's a dreary city. But I'm proud of you anyway."

"That's what you always say."

Beneath the static on the phone line, Winter thought he heard fragments of words that clung to each other like the language of another planet. "What were you calling about?" he asked.

"Do I need a reason to call my son?"

"We're at the exit ramp now," he lied.

"Since you wanted to know, I called Karin Malmström yesterday. She said you had been very kind to them."

Winter looked out the window.

"She also told me that Lasse has taken it extremely hard. She was surprised to find out that she could handle it better than him."

The taxi slowed down and weaved its way over to the right lane toward the exit. Winter heard a rumble behind them and turned around. The airport bus had caught up, apparently poised to zip into the priority lane a hundred yards ahead.

"It's a tough time for them," Winter said.

"What did you say?"

"They've got a lot to work through before they can come to terms with Per's death."

"Fucking idiot!" the taxi driver screamed. His eyes, which suddenly turned wild, snapped to the rearview mirror. The bus had screeched to a halt a few inches behind them. "Those assholes are out of their minds," he said to Winter's reflection. "They drive like there's no tomorrow."

Winter put his hand over the phone. "They've got a schedule to keep."

The driver snorted.

"What did you say?" his mother asked.

"Nothing."

"What's going on?"

"We're at the airport now."

"Don't forget to call your sister."

"I promise. Bye, Mom."

"Watch out in Lond . . ."

But he had already lowered the phone and hung up.

At check-in, a murmur of expectancy ran through the long line to Winter's right; the Canary Islands were a popular destination. Handing his ticket and passport to the attendant, he requested an aisle seat, in an exit row if possible to leave more room for his long legs.

While the attendant prepared his boarding pass, he thought about all the passenger lists his team had received. It was a thankless task, trying to keep track of everybody who had flown from Gothenburg to London the past two months, mainly for the purpose of having something to shove in the face of the reporters and police honchos demanding signs of progress. When we've got three thousand more officers and two extra years to work on the case, he thought, we'll go through all the lists and hope that nobody was traveling under a false name.

Was Macdonald's group in the same predicament—staring at a pile of passenger lists, never knowing what they might show? After receiving his boarding pass, Winter watched his suitcase bounce away on the conveyor belt. He smiled at the attendant, then walked upstairs to security.

Djanali could see her breath. The cold shadows under the apartment building smarted after the sunshine at the end of the street.

"You're not so used to this kind of thing, are you?" Halders asked.

"What do you mean?"

"All this cold. It must come as quite a shock to you."

"What are you talking about?"

"They call it snow." He snatched imaginary flakes out of the air.

"You don't say."

"They've never seen it back where you come from, right?"

"And where is that, exactly?"

"You don't need me to tell you that."

"But I want to hear you say it."

Halders watched his breath drift away, turned his head and looked down at Djanali's face. "Ouagadougou."

"Excuse me?"

"Ouagadougou, the place you come from."

"Okay."

"The capital of Burkina Faso."

"Uh-huh?"

"Formerly known as Upper Volta."

"Never heard of it."

"Burkina Faso," he repeated.

"Is it anywhere near East Hospital in Gothenburg, where I was born?"

"The Ouagadougou branch."

They both burst out laughing.

They opened a gate just down the street from the scene of the murder. It was their second round of the neighborhood, and they were looking for people who hadn't been home before or had failed to return their calls. A little walkway ran from the entrance to the stairs that led up to Jamie's apartment.

The late-morning sun was like a forty-watt bulb, startling by its very existence after the long winter.

Ringing the bell on the second floor, Djanali heard a hissing sound from somewhere else in the building, a voice in the apartment above and finally someone approaching the door. A man opened it all the way. He was somewhere between thirty-five and forty, with bushy hair, wide suspenders over a white shirt and unbuttoned cuffs as if he were in the middle of dressing, maybe for a party. An unknotted tie was draped around his neck. Must be a party, Djanali thought, a midweek bash for the fast crowd. He looks rather elegant in a degenerate kind of way, his hands trembling slightly, his eyes watery. A drinker.

"Can I help you?"

"Mr. Beckman?" Halders asked.

"Yes?"

"We're from the police." Halders employed his usual bumbling swagger.

He's in his element here, Djanali thought, invading somebody's privacy like this. That's why he does the same thing year after year and never gets promoted. He doesn't understand his own mind, or else he understands it all too well and there's no longer anything he can do about it.

"And?" Beckman said, fiddling with his tie.

Italian, Djanali thought. Silk, could be expensive. Winter would know. "Do you mind if we come in for a second?" she asked.

"What for?"

"We'd like to ask you a few questions."

"About what?"

Halders pointed at the stairs to remind him that anybody could be listening. "May we come in?"

Apparently convinced, or perhaps feeling like a couple of burglars had threatened him at gunpoint, Beckman backed up. Closing the door behind them, he ushered his guests through the hallway into a room that was bigger than any they had seen in the other apartments. Djanali took note of the height of the ceiling, the stucco, the amount of space, everything that had been so hard to judge in Jamie's apartment. "You've got a big room here," she said.

"I knocked out a wall," Beckman explained.

"All by yourself?" Halders asked.

Beckman looked at Halders as if he were a comedian whose punch line hadn't sunk in yet. "Is it about the murder?" he asked, turning to Djanali.

Halders stared at the far wall while Djanali returned Beckman's gaze.

"The murder of the kid next door," Beckman clarified.

"Yes," Djanali said. "We have a couple of questions for you."

"Okay."

"Were you home around the time it happened? That would be about eleven-thirty at night."

"I think so. But I had a flight to catch early the next morning."

"When did you find out about the murder?"

"A few hours ago, as soon as I got back. It's all over the place. Not that I watch much television, but they talk about it constantly. I've seen the headlines too." He pointed at a pile of newspapers on the table.

Djanali walked over and saw the two most recent editions spread out on the floor. "So you just returned from a trip?"

"Early this morning."

"Where did you go?"

"What difference does that make?"

"If it doesn't make any difference," Halders said, "you might as well answer the question."

"I was on vacation in Grand Canary," Beckman said. "Can't you tell by my face?" All of a sudden he looked worried that he hadn't gotten a suntan and had wasted all his money. He went out to the hallway, came back with a little tote bag and took out a ticket envelope. "Here's the proof."

"Do you remember ever seeing the kid?" Halders asked, not bothering to look at the envelope.

"What kind of question is that?"

"Did you ever see him go in or out of the building?"

"Sure."

"You did?"

"We must have kept the same hours, because I caught sight of him a few times late at night. I'm a streetcar driver," Beckman explained.

That makes a lot of sense, Djanali thought. Late hours are what I associate with streetcars—sometimes so late they don't come at all. He looks more like a bank manager. She imagined Winter sitting calmly in a glass booth as his streetcar wound its way through the city. "Was he alone?" she asked, suppressing the image of Winter.

"What?"

"Was he by himself when you saw him?"

"Not every time."

"No?" Halders asked.

"When was the last time you saw him with someone else?" Djanali asked.

Beckman seemed to be deep in thought. Suddenly the scene he was trying to conjure up appeared before his mind's eye and the blood drained from his face. Taking a step to the side, he grabbed the table. "Gawd," he said.

Halders stepped forward to support him. "What's going on?"

He sees something very clearly, Djanali thought, and he's wondering whether it was the devil himself. Don't put words in his mouth. This is one of those precious moments you can't afford to ruin. "When was the last time you saw him with someone else?" she repeated.

"It must have been that . . ." Beckman stammered.

"What did you say?"

He cleared his throat and got his voice back. "I saw him and a man together." Then he fell to all fours. "Just a minute." He leafed through the newspapers on the floor. "There was a date someplace."

They could have told him the date but let him go on looking.

Beckman stood up with one of the newspapers in his hand. "Jesus Christ," he said, examining his copy of the ticket. "It was the same night."

"The same night as what?" Halders asked.

"The same night it happened," Beckman said, looking from Halders to Djanali. "That must be when it was."

"And you just figured that out?" Halders asked.

"My flight left early the next morning."

"Grand Canary?"

"Yes, Puerto Rico."

"Are you telling me there's a Puerto Rico in Grand Canary?"

"Yes, that's the name of the resort, I think." Beckman seemed to be second-guessing himself about where he had spent the past few weeks.

"Wherever you were, they sell Swedish newspapers," Halders said.

"I didn't read the papers," Beckman said. He looked like someone had knocked the wind out of him.

Djanali made a sign to Halders to ease up.

"This is the first time I suspected anything," Beckman continued.

"I understand," Djanali said.

"The first time," he repeated.

"Would you recognize the man who was with Jamie Robertson if you ran into him again?" Djanali asked.

Beckman threw out his hands. "I saw him mostly from the back."

"But you're sure it was a man, right?"

"Yes, and quite tall. They were going up the stairs when I passed by on the walkway. Or maybe they were waiting for the elevator."

Halders looked at Djanali, then returned his gaze to Beckman. "We'd like you to come with us so we can discuss this in a little more detail."

"More detail? Am I a suspect or something?"

"You have some very interesting information, and we want to give you the chance to remember as much as possible."

"I'm awfully tired right now."

Look, pal, Halders thought, don't make me say that we can hold you for six hours and get an extension for another six.

"Okay, sure," Beckman said after a slight hesitation. "If you'll just excuse me for a minute." He made a bolt for the bathroom, and they heard him vomit.

"What time does Winter's plane take off?" Halders asked.

"Right now, I think." Djanali glanced at her watch. "He said a quarter to eleven, and that's in ten minutes."

"Call him." Halders pointed to the right pocket of Djanali's jacket.

She took out her phone and dialed Winter's number. "No answer."

"He's already turned off his phone and started to think about ordering a drink and flirting with the flight attendants."

More retching from the bathroom.

"Call the airport," Halders said.

"I don't know the num—"

"941000."

"You're a walking phone book."

"Just ask me anything."

Djanali told the agent what she needed, and two minutes before the plane was scheduled to leave the gate, the woman who had just taken Winter's boarding pass announced his name over the loudspeaker. Half an hour later he stepped out of his car in front of police headquarters.

19

BECKMAN HAD SPENT HIS VACATION DRINKING ON THE TERRACE of the Altamar Aparthotel, gazing out at the northern horizon. He had been sober on the plane home. End of story.

He wasn't the first person they'd brought in for questioning. But this was something different, Winter thought as he took the elevator up, briefcase in hand. His luggage would arrive later.

Beckman was suffering minor withdrawal symptoms, far from delirious but with an unsteady gait that made him look like he was listening to funk.

Winter sat across from Beckman: what a homecoming for him, and to think *I* never even got off the ground.

The tape recorder hummed, registering a short, clear laugh that echoed through the corridor outside.

"I don't remember very much," Beckman said after they had dealt with the formalities.

"What time did you get home from work the night you saw Jamie Robertson with this man?"

"A minute or two after midnight. But that's not what actually happened."

"What didn't actually happen?"

"It's like this. I went out, and then I came back and thought I saw the man again."

"You saw him a second time?"

"I had dropped my scarf somewhere. It might sound weird, but I couldn't find it and I thought it must have fallen off while I was buttoning up my coat in the doorway, so I went back and saw him from behind as he walked up the stairs."

"Was he by himself then?"

"Yes, the second time he was by himself."

"Can you describe what he looked like?"

"That's not so easy."

"Try anyway."

"But there was something else about him too."

"Yes?"

"I don't know how to put it."

The laughter returned, a little softer as if it had bounced off the wall at the end of the corridor.

Maybe the laughter will calm him down, Winter thought. Or just confuse him even more. Right this minute we're ransacking his apartment. He killed Jamie and caught the first available flight. He's going to confess any minute, and then the other murders too. Maybe he went to London. Maybe tonight we can celebrate and hope for a decent interval before the next case. Everything depends on coincidence, a stroke of luck or a wide net that pulls in just the fish you're looking for. As long as we stick to our routines, if we've got our catch, it's just a matter of waiting until he stops flailing.

"There was something about him I recognized," Beckman said. "Now that I've had the chance to think about it a little."

Winter nodded. The central air droned like the murmuring of a heart, suffocating the room in its own odor of perspiration mixed with stale cologne from some other era. The afternoon radiance was waning, the fluorescent lights casting deeper shadows. Winter hadn't turned on his desk lamp yet. He nodded again to Beckman.

"It was his jacket. That must be what made me think about it now, or what I recognized then."

"You recognized his jacket?"

"Yes, I don't know why, but I flashed on something I'd seen on the streetcar."

"The streetcar?"

"When you sit in a booth like that all day long, you pick up on little things about people. Not as much now as when we had the same route every day, but still."

Beckman's hand trembled as he raised a glass of water to his lips, but he managed not to spill it. "You begin to notice regular passengers," he continued, putting the glass back down.

"So you remembered this guy?" Winter asked.

"I'm pretty sure I had a passenger a few times who wore a jacket like that, but nothing else comes to mind."

"What was so special about the jacket?"

"That's what I'm trying to figure out."

"The color?"

"It was a black leather jacket, but that's not it."

"The kind of leather?"

"No," Beckman said, drawing out the word. "I can't put my finger on it."

"The buttons, maybe?"

"The buttons . . . no."

Jesus, Winter thought. "The writing on the back of the jacket?"

Beckman shook his head. "It's completely slipped my mind."

"Was he tall?"

"I think so . . . Yes, he was."

"Taller than Jamie?"

"It looked like it. But it's hard to tell when two people are walking up the stairs."

"About my height?" Winter stood up.

"Yes, probably."

"How would you describe the way he walked?"

"Just like anybody else."

"He didn't limp or anything?"

"No, but walking up a staircase is a kind of limp. He had long, dark hair by the way."

"How long?"

"Shoulder length, I think."

"Are you sure?"

"It occurred to me at the time that you don't see many people with hair like that anymore."

He's calmer now, Winter thought, as if he had been given a hangover remedy. Or maybe the sound of his own voice and the scraps of memory have soothed him, the way music puts the mind at ease.

"Fifteen years ago, when you saw pictures from the sixties," Beckman explained, "it seemed like everyone dressed differently back then, especially with their hair. But now I guess they're pretty much the same as the photos that appear in the papers today."

"Soccer teams," Winter said.

"What?"

"Most photos of soccer players in the sixties could have been taken yesterday, at least when it comes to the hair."

"That's true."

"So this man's hair was long?"

"Like an Argentinean soccer player. There was something unreal about it, almost like a wig."

"A wig?"

"I'm not sure."

"A toupee?"

"He was wearing glasses."

"Glasses?"

"Heavy, with black frames, I think, but don't hold me to it."

"Horn-rimmed?"

"I guess that's what they're called."

"We're going to put together a composite sketch based on what you've told us."

Beckman looked past Winter as if he were getting ready to describe a face he'd never seen. "He was carrying a bag when he went up the stairs the second time."

"What did it look like?"

"A duffel bag of some kind."

"Could you tell if he noticed you?"

"I don't think so. I was worn out from work and didn't make much noise."

"He didn't look in your direction?"

"Not that I recall."

"Did you hear him say anything?"

"No."

———

Crossing Heden Park, Winter saw that the cold had left a blue sheen on the sky even though it was already dark. He felt displaced the way he always did when he had to cut a trip short. He didn't want to go home. His suitcase had shown up, finally, and though he'd deliberately left it at the office, he changed his mind and retraced his steps. A patrol car drove him back to his apartment. He rode the elevator up, opened the door, dropped his suitcase by the coatrack and leafed through the mail. None of it needed to be opened tonight.

Hungry and restless, he pulled off his clothes outside the bathroom door, took a shower and changed to a mock turtleneck and a soft gray Ermenegildo Zegna suit. He called his favorite restaurant and reserved a table.

His hair was still too wet for outside. Grabbing a towel, he rubbed his head as hard as he could and combed his hair. The phone rang, and he listened to his sister leave a message while he put on a pair of black socks. It rang again. This time it was Bolger, who apologized and said he had just realized that Winter was in London.

Winter's scalp, still not dry, tingled in the subfreezing air. He pulled his black knit cap down over his forehead and headed west on Vasagatan Street, through Haga Park and across Linnégatan Street to Le Village Restaurant on Tredje Långgatan.

He made his way through the bistro, hung up his coat in the restaurant and walked over to the host.

"Table for one. I have a reservation. Winter."

"This way, please." The maître d' led him to a table at the far end of the room. "Care for something to drink?" he asked once Winter was seated.

"Mineral water, thanks."

He ordered blue mussel and basil soup, followed by grilled codfish, lightly salted. He drank half a bottle of Sancerre with the entrée. Afterward he lingered over two cups of coffee, lost in thought.

20

BOLGER WAS AGHAST. "I THOUGHT YOU'D BE PAINTING THE TOWN in Soho by now."

"Another time," Winter said.

"You obviously weren't grounded by the weather."

"Something came up."

"Have one on the house."

"Mineral water in a glass, please, with ice and a slice of lime."

"Sure you don't want something more daring?"

"Bring me a mineral water and tell me what you think of Bergenhem."

Bolger fixed Winter's drink by the rack under the mirror behind the bar.

"He seems a little green." Bolger put a glass down in front of Winter. "But he's got a pair of eyes that could serve him well if he learns how to use them in the dark too."

"What do you mean by that?"

"What I mean is that he needs to get his act together."

"He's young, but that's not always a disadvantage."

"It usually is."

"But not always."

"No."

It was almost midnight. Three of the seven tables were taken, and the voices of the customers seemed muffled by the smoke.

Two women sat at the far end of the bar with cigarettes between their fingers and expressions on their faces that suggested they had finally discovered the meaning of life and concluded it didn't make any difference.

One of the women gazed at Winter out of the corner of her eye. The lines on her face tightened. She said a few words to her companion, put out her cigarette and lit a new one. She fingered the package in front of her as if to assure its dwindling contents that she hadn't forgotten about them.

"I'm not sure Bergenhem wants to get his act together," Bolger said.

"Depends on who explains it to him."

"Who else but you?"

Winter felt like lighting up a cigarillo, but a glance at the chain smokers to his right made him think better of the idea. The woman who had eyed Winter earlier motioned to Bolger. He walked over and took her order. After fixing her drink at the bar, he put the glass down in front of her. A look of disappointment passed over her face as she drank.

"She asked for the same thing the gentleman over here was drinking. I'd bet she was expecting a gin and tonic."

"I could have been living it up in London tonight."

"You're married to your job."

"My theory is that there are things just beneath the surface that we don't know are there." Winter broke down and lit a cigarillo.

"Absolutely."

"Sometimes all you have to do is blow away a little dust and it appears."

"And that's Bergenhem's job. Is that what you're saying?"

Winter smoked and glanced at the women but turned his head away when they reciprocated. "Maybe more than a little dust," he said. "I have a feeling you know a few things that you haven't told us and maybe don't want to talk about."

"What kinds of things?"

"About the industry."

"What industry?"

"Give me a break; I'm a little tired."

"Okay, okay, the industry."

Winter took another sip of water. Sinatra's voice came over the speakers. That song is from the fifties, he thought. I hadn't even been born.

"The restaurant and porn industries aren't one and the same," Bolger insisted. "They're light-years apart."

"Of course."

"I know a little about the porn scene because of the late hours I stay open."

"It doesn't sleep during the day, I assume?"

"No, but it thrives under the cover of darkness."

"You know your way around the city pretty well. How has it changed the past few years? It's not the same, right?"

"Colder and more callous, but I can't say exactly how."

"It's all society's fault."

"No doubt."

"I'm not being totally facetious. People are moving to the cities like never before and that creates problems."

"Let me tell you a little story." Bolger leaned forward. "More and more girls are coming here from the countryside, and it's not to go to school. There aren't any jobs for them on the west coast or wherever the hell they come from, and it isn't long before they find out that things are no better here."

"But they come anyway?"

"Yes, and guys are waiting for them on the platform with open arms—literally. An innocent little farm girl steps off the train and there he is."

"Sounds like something out of the former USSR."

"These girls hardly have time to put their suitcase in a locker, much less settle in with their aunt or get a cheap hotel room, before the guy springs his proposal on them."

"Hmm."

"And it's not just girls."

"Why is that?"

Bolger's gesture suggested that Winter may as well have asked about the key to eternal life or the path to inner peace. "But I can give you some names," he offered.

"Names of whom?"

"Names of people who know more about this kind of thing than I do."

"Good." Winter flicked his cigarillo in the ashtray that Bolger had slid across the bar.

"I don't want anybody to get hurt." Bolger went over to the women, who had begun to wave again. One of them said something and Bolger returned to Winter. "They're wondering if they can buy you a drink."

Winter swiveled around on his bar stool, bowed gratefully, gave a little shake of his head and pointed at his glass of water as politely as he could.

"Might be worth a go," Bolger said. "Happy-go-lucky girls, but not fresh from the countryside."

"It's more the other kind who interest me right now. The ones you seem to know something about."

"The whole thing's innocent enough if you ignore a few details. A girl is offered a job as a hostess at a strip joint, which means she keeps the Coke glasses of the customers filled and gets up on a table, or a little stage, and gyrates to the music."

"Or in a glass booth in one of the inner rooms."

"Right."

"Are we talking about prostitution?"

"Eventually. Not for all of these little angels, but some of them."

"Boys too?"

"Yes."

"Dancers?"

"A dance for angels," Bolger said.

"Dance with an angel."

"That's one way of looking at it."

"When it comes to murder," Winter said, "there are lots of ways to look at it."

"You know more about that than I do."

"What can you tell me about the movie business?" Winter considered ordering another glass of mineral water but remembered the women at the end of the bar—he didn't want to seem like he was snubbing them.

"Not much."

"Think harder."

"Not a hell of a lot more than you do," Bolger said. "You know so much about everything."

"It's no secret there's more than appears on the racks when you walk in."

"An awful lot can appear on the racks, we're so permissive now-adays."

"But not child porn."

"Where do you draw the line?"

"Somewhere in the deep dark recesses of a store or a warehouse is a line that somebody can step over."

"Let me ask you something, Erik. Have you ever rented a porn video?"

"No."

"Seen a porn flick at a theater?"

"No."

"So you really don't know what you're up against."

"What do you mean?"

"I mean that you've never had the slightest urge to rent or buy a movie that shows people engaging in various kinds of sex acts. You don't know what it feels like."

"So it's a different kind of feeling from what somebody like me might have?"

"I don't know. You've always been fascinated by sex. But you've been able to satisfy your needs the way God intended."

"Interesting theory."

"I'm serious. The point is that the second or third choice takes over, and pretty soon they're just as satisfying as what you can't have."

"Hmm."

"Physical gratification isn't what's most appealing—maybe just the opposite, in fact. It's more pleasurable without physical contact, because nobody is making any demands on you." Bolger brought him another glass of mineral water. The women had left without looking their way. "Some of the poor bastards who hang out in the screening rooms would be scared to death if they could get their paws on a living man or woman."

"That makes sense."

"But their appetite grows and grows—a naked body or ordinary sex isn't good enough anymore. And I'm not even talking about the most extreme customers."

"So there aren't any limits—is that what you're trying to say?"

"What I'm trying to say is that some people want to get as close to reality as possible without actually being part of it. Their need for entertainment can grow to monstrous proportions. Monstrous—do you know what I mean?"

"You said you had some names."

"Not when it comes to what we're talking about now."

"You never can tell."

"True enough. Not when it comes to you."

"I've never been able to figure you out either."

The customers at the table in the middle of the room had gone, waving briefly to Bolger. The place was empty.

Bolger put on an album. The tones of a tenor sax filled the room like a watchful spirit. *New York Eye and Ear Control*, Winter thought. Albert Ayler, Don Cherry, John Tchicai, Roswell Rudd, Gary Peacock and Sonny Murray recorded it on July 17, 1964. I was four years old.

"We didn't know what you were up to when you started that jazz club at Rudebecks," Bolger said.

Winter had arranged little concerts for jazz aficionados at the private high school they'd attended. The whole thing came to an abrupt halt when he graduated.

"Do you hear John Tchicai's alto sax?" Winter asked.

Bolger closed his eyes. "I never understood what made you tick. All that money went to your head."

Winter smiled and glanced at the clock. "Do you think about those days very much?"

"High school? Only when I see you."

"Liar."

"Could be."

"I never miss it."

"Depends on what part of it you're talking about."

"I'm talking about all of it. Everything was unpredictable, and you didn't know from one day to the next what the hell was happening all around you."

"Hmm."

"You had no control over your own life."

"And now you do?"

"No."

The walls and tables vibrated with the music. The smoke had swirled to the floor once the last customers were gone.

"Knowing what's happening all around you," Bolger said. "That sounds like a good description of your profession."

"It's only a job."

"Like hell it is, not for you." He reached back and dimmed the overhead light. The dishwasher clattered in the kitchen.

"Somebody always slips up," Winter said.

"The homicide division, for example?"

"Sooner or later, it comes to our attention and we do what needs to be done. That's what we're trained for."

"But by that time it might be too late."

"What are you trying to say?"

"Too late to do anything about it."

"Too late for whom? The victim, the police or the public?"

Bolger shrugged.

"We discover every blunder eventually," Winter said. "Not only our own, but other people's. That's how the police work—at least that's how I work. One little mistake and you can bet that we're going to find out about it."

Bolger clapped his hands at Winter's spiel. The sun had been up for a long time. He yawned and looked at his friend. "You ended up in the career you'd always dreamed about."

"I guess you're right."

"So what happens now?"

"What do you mean?"

"When do you go to London for real?"

"Day after tomorrow, I think."

"I haven't been there in ages. Longer than I care to remember."

"I've heard you say that before. Why don't you just pick up and go?"

"You're there pretty often, aren't you?"

"Not as much as I used to be."

"You're always buying tailor-made shoes on that exclusive street. Don't tell me you're not different, Erik."

"Everybody's different."

21

BERGENHEM HAD TIPTOED AROUND ONE OF THOSE PLACES A FEW times long ago. The only thing he remembered was pink flesh everywhere he looked and a sheepish feeling that clung to him afterward.

He parked half a block away and crossed the street toward Riverside. It was the fourth strip joint he'd been to. He had also stepped inside a couple of others that didn't flaunt themselves as openly.

The entrance to Riverside was discreet enough—a steel door in a nondescript brick wall and a sign next to it showing the hours. He immediately found himself in a large room with magazines along the wall like the browsing room of a library. A handful of men were hanging around the racks. Overcome with the feeling that invisible eyes were watching him, he walked over to the left wall, glanced at the men and continued on.

At the far end of the room was a doorway with a curtain hanging down and a man in a little booth. Bergenhem paid the cover charge and ducked through the drape. He hung up his coat in an untended cloakroom and sat down at one of the tables. Four other men were there, each seated alone. A young woman came over and asked him what he wanted to drink. He ordered a light beer. She walked out through a swinging door and came back with a bottle and an empty glass. "Welcome to Riverside." She smiled.

Bergenhem nodded and felt like an idiot, just the way it had been at the other clubs. Should I invite her to sit down? he asked himself. Isn't she supposed to make the first move?

"The show starts in five minutes," she said, smiling again.

Bergenhem nodded once more. Does she wonder why you're here? Is she a student working her way through college who thinks you're repulsive?

What difference does it make? You're just doing your job. People can probably tell you're a cop as soon as you walk in the door.

The show began. Tina Turner's voice blasted over the speakers. Two women danced at either end of a little dais that served as a stage. They moved their hips faster and faster. Bergenhem couldn't help but think of an aerobics class.

The show was over in fifteen minutes, and he had seen about all there was to see. One of the women's nipples had been big and brown, seeming to cover half her breasts.

The other woman was younger and didn't follow the music as well. Maybe she was new at this. Her slender body seemed to shiver under the floodlights.

She had sat on a stool with her back to the audience, spread her legs and looked over her shoulder with feigned coquettishness in her eyes. She wasn't a very good actress yet. Compassion, maybe shame, swept over Bergenhem. She's an outsider, he thought, just like me. She's not used to being gawked at through a red glare.

Nobody feels any better after watching this, he thought—or horny, not even when they make those little circular movements with their breasts. All I feel is a longing for fresh air.

She looks wounded, he thought. She's hiding inside her skin, and something even more frightening is waiting for her when she steps off the stage. Performing for strangers is her only refuge.

He stood up and walked through a door on the left side into the movie section. Riverside had thirty private screening rooms, each with a remote control device, a wastebasket and a roll of toilet paper. It also featured three rooms with large screens that showed the same kinds of movies as the other clubs he had been to.

The sounds and the writhing bodies were all alike. The first time Bergenhem had sat in one of these rooms, he'd hoped to be turned on, but he'd simply been exhausted after a little while, the tightness in his groin gone slack.

Just like the other times, he felt like a Peeping Tom even though the spectacle didn't really interest him.

He'd browsed through the racks at all the clubs but found nothing out of the ordinary. Tucked away among the inner aisles were various scat magazines, but that wasn't so unexpected. Somebody was always standing around the rack pretending he just happened to be passing by. It was an odd sight, as if the man were about to break away in every direction at once.

The movies Bergenhem had seen were provocative but not violent in any way. At a couple of clubs, he'd asked about the kind of stuff he was looking for and got only a puzzled look in return. No surprise there either.

It was necessary preparation, even if it didn't yield any results, and now he was ready for his next move.

Winter sat in his office examining the composite sketch Beckman had reluctantly helped them create, but he knew what a chancy proposition it was. A front view based on what Beckman had seen from the back and side wasn't much to go on. He stared at the sketch for a long while, but nothing registered.

They had told Beckman to spend some time thinking about his streetcar routes, when he had driven and what he had seen. Ringmar had said, "Good luck," prompting incredulous glances from both Winter and Beckman.

Winter removed his coat from the hook by the door, then walked through the corridor to the elevator. Rain lashed against the window in the entryway.

It's the worst kind of rain, Winter thought. This damn shit does nobody any good. The snow is already shoveled away, there's plenty of groundwater, and all it does is seep under your collar and make everything colder until your mood is subfreezing as well. And I was so happy just a week ago.

Winter took the shortest route to Douglas Svensson's Kobbarnas Road address and parked next to a handicap spot.

Standing in the fourth-floor living room, he could see police headquarters off in the distance.

"I already talked to the cop . . . police once," Svensson said.

"Once isn't always enough."

"What?"

"Sometimes we need to follow up with more questions." Winter pondered whether Svensson was the right type for a bar owner. He looked like somebody who'd been shoved up onstage and forced to talk. Winter had never been to his bar. Who knows, maybe he was more cheerful when he was in his element.

"Okay, have a seat," Svensson said.

The police had talked with the two acquaintances of Jamie whose names Svensson had given to Bolger, who in turn had passed them on to Winter. The officers hadn't turned up very much, other than that the kids might be gay but didn't know whether Jamie was or not. It would have become obvious soon enough, they had said, and Winter had wondered what they might mean. That was all they were willing to say on the subject. He had the impression they were afraid.

Something was missing.

Svensson sat down uneasily and waited for him to begin.

Finally Winter slipped the composite sketch out of his briefcase and handed it to him. "Can you tell me whether you recognize this face?"

"Who is it?"

"I just want to know whether there's anything in the face that's familiar to you."

"Anything? Like the nose or the eyes?" Svensson looked down at the picture, turned it at different angles and glanced up at Winter. "It looks like a Martian."

"It's a computer image based on what a witness told us."

"A computer—you're putting me on, surely."

"No."

"Amazing."

"So you recognize the face?"

"No."

"Not at all?"

"Not even the nose."

Winter's next move had to be decisive. "What was Jamie like?" he asked.

"What?"

"Did he get along with people?"

"What people?"

"Let's start with you and his coworkers."

"It's just me and one other person," Svensson said. "Plus someone who's been working part-time since Jamie was murdered."

"I know."

"Then why did you ask?"

"My question was how well you got along."

Svensson seemed on the verge of answering but apparently changed his mind. A shadow flitted across his face as if the reality of Jamie's death had struck him for the first time. His features turned gray and his gaze wandered off in a new direction. "We always got along. Everybody liked Jamie, and his English—or Scottish, I should say—was a drawing card."

"Did he ever get into arguments?"

"With one of us? Never."

"How about with anybody else?"

"What about?"

"It's fairly common."

"At my place?"

"In general."

"Those are places that hire nutcases as bouncers. We don't use bouncers, so we don't have to worry about nutcases. I don't even have a cloakroom."

"Fine," Winter said, "but let me ask the question a different way. Were there any regular customers Jamie talked to more than others?"

"I don't have the slightest idea."

"You've got regulars, right?"

"Lots of them, more than the city jail, I'd guess."

Winter remembered Bolger's account of something Svensson had recalled—an unfamiliar face, someone who'd shown up a few times, not a regular customer, maybe a new one. Careful to avoid mentioning Bolger's name, Winter worked his way around to the subject, steering the conversation a little closer as naturally and purposefully as he could. "No new regulars?" he asked.

"What?"

"You don't remember anybody who liked to hang out at the bar and talk to Jamie?"

"Everybody and his brother confides in a bartender," Svensson said as if coining a new expression. "People pour their hearts out, he stands there and listens and they feel a little better."

"Well put."

Svensson nodded, an Aristotle with his disciple: the purpose of tragedy is catharsis, my son.

That's what faith is, Winter thought. The Big Bartender in the Sky. The tones of Coltrane's "The Father and the Son and the Holy Ghost" echoed in his mind. "So you're telling me Jamie was a good listener?"

Svensson raised his arm as if to say the question answered itself.

"Was there anybody in particular he listened to?"

"That's a tough one. I have my hands full when I'm working behind the bar."

"You can't remember anybody at all?"

Svensson didn't answer.

"Try to think."

"There was somebody I hadn't seen before but who suddenly came in several times, maybe a few weeks before Jamie was murdered."

Bingo. The ball rolls into the cup on the thirtieth putt, Winter thought, and suddenly you remember why you became a detective. "So there was a face you recognized?"

"I wouldn't go that far. At least I'm not sure I would recognize it now. But there was someone who sat at the bar a few times, and I hadn't seen him before."

"Did you ever talk to him?"

"I don't remember."

"But Jamie talked to him?"

"He sat or stood there occasionally during Jamie's shift, or during happy hour when each of us worked half the bar."

"So he could have talked to Jamie?"

"He must have ordered something, at least."

"Would you recognize him now?"

"I told you I don't know."

"But he didn't look like this?" Winter pointed to the image on the table between them.

"Not in the least."

"Then we'll have to do a better sketch."

Ringmar helped Winter keep the investigation moving, making sure nobody let up. He had a mild case of the flu but didn't show it; he coughed up all the phlegm early in the morning and tried to get plenty of fresh air during the day. A word with Birgersson would have suited him, but he held back.

They ran into each other on the stairs between the fourth and fifth floors—a welcome change from their wordless encounters in the elevator. They shook hands.

"I hear the investigation is going well," Birgersson said.

"Very well."

"Thanks to you, Bertil. Just don't let Winter get too far ahead of himself. Wise old heads like us have to pick up the pieces when upstarts like him charge off in every direction."

Fighting words, Ringmar thought. "Yes, that's the way it goes," he said.

"What's the way it goes?"

"Our job. Clearing away the smoldering ruins of the Swedish welfare state."

Birgersson stared at him.

"It takes wise old heads like us to understand that," Ringmar continued.

"We need to talk. I want to pick your brain about this case."

"How about this afternoon?"

"I have a meeting but it might work anyway. I'll give you a call."

Ringmar nodded and smiled affably.

"See you," Birgersson shouted. He disappeared around the corner.

The moment Ringmar stepped into his office, the phone rang as if it had been connected to a tripwire in the doorway. "Hello?" he grunted.

"There's a call I think you should take," Möllerström said.

"Why me?"

"It's Geoff's pen pal, the second one."

"Who?" Ringmar asked, but then just as quickly understood. "Put him through, dammit."

After a click a new voice came on the line. "Hello?"

"This is Bertil Ringmar."

"I . . ."

"Who's calling, please?"

"Do I have to tell you my name? I have . . ."

"What are you calling about?"

"I read in the paper the other day that you were looking for someone who had corresponded with that British kid who was murdered."

"Yes?"

"That's me."

The man sounded young, Ringmar thought, but you could never tell for sure. Sometimes he guessed someone was no older than twenty when they first talked on the phone and then had to add fifty years when he connected the voice with a face.

"Hello?"

"Sorry, so you corresponded with Geoff Hillier?"

Silence.

Ringmar repeated the question.

"Yes, I did."

"This is very important for us. I need to talk to you about it in person."

"Talk about it?"

"Just an ordinary conversation. Not an interrogation or anything like that."

"Can't we do it on the phone?"

"Unfortunately not."

"I don't know if . . ."

"We need help, and you could be the one who determines whether we succeed or fail." Pretty soon I'm going to say that this call is being traced and we're going to be at his place in ten minutes flat, Ringmar thought. "We can pick you up if you like," he said.

"No, I'll come on my own."

22

BERGENHEM RETURNED TO THE ROOM. THE SHOW HAD STARTED up again. Two women he didn't recognize were onstage. After a while he realized that one of them was the older woman from before and that the younger one was gone.

He sat down at the same table. The air was thick with cigarette smoke and the room seemed to have shrunk. More men sat around the tables, devouring the dancers with their eyes. Tina Turner was singing again, asking what love had to do with it.

Bergenhem spotted the younger woman now. She was sitting at one of the tables talking with two men, and he didn't like what he saw.

He didn't want her with those fucking pigs, and the feeling surprised him. It's not moral indignation that's got me riled up, he thought. I know this is none of my business, so what is it?

She's my age, he told himself. She's not a fourteen-year-old who grew up too fast. The men are forty-five and beyond help. And I shouldn't have an opinion about any of this.

She got up and one of the men followed her. They walked through a door on the right side, by the stage. He kept his eyes on them the whole time.

"Inspector Bergenhem?"

Something stirred to his right, and he looked up at a man with his blond hair in a ponytail and a suit that was lusterless against the colors of the stage. Bergenhem straightened up a little. "Yes?"

"I'm the owner. You wanted to see me."

"Oh, right." Bergenhem stood up. "I had a couple of questions . . ."

"How about we go to my office?" The owner scanned the room and the stage, then looked back at Bergenhem. "This way," he said.

His office was just to the left on the other side of the curtain. It had a window—the first one Bergenhem had seen at Riverside—with a view of the alleyway. The owner halted as soon as they were inside the door, apparently waiting for Bergenhem to do or say something. "I'm glad you're playing it straight," he said finally.

"What?"

"I'm grateful when a policeman doesn't sneak around and pretend to be someone he's not."

"It wouldn't work anyway."

"Not after a while, no."

"There you have it."

"It's annoying when the police treat us like we're not capable of taking care of ourselves or running a respectable establishment."

Bergenhem heard strains of Tina Turner through the south wall, mostly the bass lines. It sounded like she had a barrel over her head.

"I heard you were looking for me," the owner said.

"You didn't have to bring me all the way in here."

"We don't have anything to hide."

"I didn't think you did."

"So what can I do for you?"

Bergenhem explained as much about the case as he was authorized to, hinting at the police's suspicions. He acts like he's wearing earplugs, Bergenhem thought, but it's obvious he's soaking it all up. He understands everything and he will answer the questions he admits to having heard.

"Snuff movies? In Gothenburg?" The owner sat down in an armchair, crossing one leg over the other. His cigarette smoke swirled through the barely open window and out into the night air. Two train signals sounded through the gap. There was a railyard a couple of blocks away, deserted and windswept and sparsely populated by freight cars that jostled each other in the dark. "Never heard of anything like that. What made you come to me?"

"We're talking to everyone who owns this kind of establishment," Bergenhem lied.

"Never heard of it."

"You must have."

"You don't believe me?"

"I mean you must know that such movies exist."

The owner frowned. "Are you putting me on?"

"What?"

"If I heard you right, you wanted to know about snuff movies in Gothenburg. Not Bogotá or Los Angeles or London, or wherever the hell they're a box office hit."

"Haven't you ever seen a snuff movie?" Bergenhem realized he'd made a mistake before the words were out of his mouth.

"God knows why I'm sitting here and putting up with all these idiotic questions of yours."

Bergenhem wasn't sure what to say next. The wind magnified the sound of two freight cars bumping, iron against iron.

"But what the hell," the owner continued. "Okay, I've never seen a snuff movie. Have you?"

"What?"

"You're an inspector. I assume you've seen most everything."

"No, never."

"And why not?"

Bergenhem slumped down in a chair. The bass lines were heavier and deeper. Maybe they had put on a new set. No voices came through the wall and the door was soundproof.

Extinguishing his cigarette, the owner went over and opened the window a few inches more to let the foul air out.

The railyard sounds disappeared, as though the fact that the window had been open just a crack was what had made them audible. An open window evokes silence, Bergenhem thought. It's like the new high-speed trains. The faster they go, the less you hear. Finally you don't notice them at all until they're about to run you over.

The owner closed the window and turned to Bergenhem. "You haven't seen anything because there's nothing to see. Gothenburg may not be the innocent place it once was, but there's no market for snuff movies here."

Bergenhem could tell the owner was considering how to complete his thought.

"You probably think I'm naïve about the people in this city. But you've come to the wrong person if you believe I would be involved in that kind of thing. It wouldn't have a chance here even if I were. We aren't depraved enough yet."

"Yet?"

"Even though it's bound to happen eventually."

"You seem pretty sure of yourself."

"Do you know why I'm even bothering to talk to you about this stuff? I'll tell you why—it's because we club owners have our ethics just like everybody else."

"And what are those ethics, exactly?"

"What?"

"Where does love of your fellow man stop and the profit motive begin?"

The owner looked Bergenhem over as if trying to figure out where he was going to dump his body afterward. "There are limits to everything," he said.

"Just in Gothenburg, you mean?"

The owner picked at a seam in his jacket, then rubbed the bridge of his nose. Bergenhem could tell that he was about to get up and thank him for a pleasant visit. All his talk about ethics had a bombastic hollowness to it, like the low rumble of bass through the wall. Which had just stopped—intermission time.

"You've never received any requests from customers who are interested in something different?" Bergenhem asked.

"Just from you."

"Nothing beyond the visible selection?"

"The visible selection? That's a new expression."

"You know what I mean."

"No."

"Come on, now."

"What I'm trying to say is that we don't get any requests like that because we have everything our customers could possibly want. I don't know how familiar you are with the movie industry, Inspector, but it might surprise you to discover how much is legal these days."

"Okay, I got you."

"Anything else on your mind?"

Not right now, Bergenhem told himself, but I'll be back. Something the owner just said doesn't make sense. I should have brought a tape recorder. Better to go someplace where I can jot down my notes. "No, that will be all for today," he said to the owner, rising from his chair.

They walked out of the office together. Bergenhem heard the music start up like rolling thunder and made his way over to the curtained doorway. The younger woman was dancing to Tina Turner, her eyes staring into another world. For a couple of minutes, Bergenhem stood transfixed, and when he finally left, the owner followed him with his eyes.

It was late afternoon and the sun had already set. Winter sat in Ringmar's office reading the interrogation report.

"What do you think?" Ringmar asked.

"Not so much to think about."

"It's like he was embarrassed."

"For not having called us about the letter sooner?" Winter asked.

"You know I'm talking about something else."

"It's outrageous that people still have to keep this kind of thing secret even though society professes to be so tolerant."

"Maybe there's another letter somewhere."

"Another letter that tricked Geoff into coming to Gothenburg? I'll believe that when I see it."

Ringmar pointed to the report. "Meeting somebody online—is that common these days?"

"That's what I've heard."

"He couldn't really explain why they had switched to regular mail."

"Yeah, I noticed that."

"Maybe they thought it was safer."

"Could be," Winter said. "It lent the whole exchange an old-fashioned air of secrecy."

"We'll have to keep this guy in mind and hope something else turns up."

"I've been thinking about why we didn't find a letter from him in Geoff's dorm room. He had no reason to throw it out, did he?"

"No."

"Where is it, then?"

"Maybe he wasn't the kind who saves letters."

"A letter from a boyfriend who was one of the main reasons he came to Gothenburg? I'd bet anything he kept it, but somebody else got their hands on it."

"Why would anyone else be interested?"

"Because something in it was incriminating."

"Incriminating about what?"

"That's what I'm trying to figure out."

"So Hitchcock took it?" Ringmar asked.

"Right."

"Because something in it would give us a lead?"

"I don't know." Winter reached for his cigarillos but remembered where he was. Ringmar hated it when the smell of smoke filled his office long after the culprit was gone.

"We'll talk to this guy again, but not right away," Ringmar said. "I was thinking about the flights between London and Gothenburg the other night. The passenger lists we requested have started to arrive now, and we need an extra office to go through all of them, not to mention more staff."

"Lists for the past three months?"

"Right."

"How long do the airlines keep them?"

"Two years for the flights out of Gothenburg."

"Two years?"

"It's a shot in the dark, Erik."

"How many daily departures between London and Gothenburg?"

"Five round-trips on weekdays. The first is Scandinavian Airlines at 6:10. A.M. and the last is British Airways at 5:45 P.M. Then there's an extra Scandinavian Airlines flight out of Gothenburg at 5:50 on Sunday morning."

"Not all go to Heathrow, do they?"

"British Airways has a 7:15 A.M. flight to Gatwick."

"That's right, I was on it once."

"You have one of those travel passes, don't you?"

"I used to."

"Every flight between Gothenburg and London carries a hundred to a hundred and twenty passengers."

Winter nodded.

"Guess how many that makes in a year."

"I don't have my pocket calculator on me."

"Somewhere around four hundred thousand."

"That many?"

"Yep."

"But we're limiting ourselves to three months," Winter said.

"That's still too much work."

"Any period we choose is going to be too much work."

"Assuming we find the time," Ringmar said, "I suggest we start with the flights the victims took. Then go backwards week by week. But we still don't have the lists from London for the departures to Gothenburg."

"I guess we'll have to do it the way you suggest."

"We're still talking about a hell of a lot of passengers."

"The lists show each passenger's final destination, right?"

"I don't know yet."

"I hope so," Winter said. "That way we can cross out those who left from Gothenburg but had connecting flights to Blackpool, Cape Town or wherever."

"Assuming they weren't pulling a fast one."

"I'm trying to be a little constructive here. We both know what an impossible task this is."

"Sorry."

"So that leaves the passengers who flew round-trip between London and Gothenburg."

"On their own passports."

"Right."

"The airlines check each ticket against the passenger's passport, but if you have a fake one . . ."

"So all we have to do is identify everyone who flew on a valid passport. It's a simple process of elimination. Then we nab the others." Winter smiled.

"We can start with those who flew back and forth within a few days—say, a week or so."

"Now you're being constructive."

"Constructive idiocy."

"We'll rule out as many passengers as we can. Somebody's got to do it."

Ringmar scratched his arm. "Maybe it's constructive to track down the murderer this way," he said finally, "but I'm not as convinced as you are."

"I'm never convinced."

"We have no evidence that the murderer commuted between Gothenburg and London. We don't even know how many murderers we're looking for."

There was nothing for Winter to say. The role of investigators was to try out different theories one by one, occasionally several at a time. They didn't let go of a hypothesis until they ran into a dead end, and even then they didn't discard it entirely.

"All three murders were similar," Ringmar said, "but there are plenty of possible explanations other than that it was the same guy." They had already hashed this out a hundred times.

We have no choice but to plod along, Winter mused. We think out loud, and suddenly somebody comes up with something that hasn't yet been said and we pounce on it. "They were paid to do it, is that what you mean?" he asked.

"Could be."

"But what was the purpose?"

"The profit motive. I could be wrong, but I really think someone was out to make a movie."

"We haven't found any link between the three kids," Winter said.

"Except that they might all have been homosexual or bisexual."

"But we can't even be sure about that."

"Perhaps they never had the chance to find out themselves."

"But at least it's something they had in common."

"Maybe."

"And it might have been the cause of their deaths," Winter said. "Indirectly at first, and then as directly as could be."

"What do you mean by that?"

"Curiosity about something that was secret or forbidden got the better of them, and that's what made them let a stranger into their apartments."

"There might have been another reason."

"Like what?"

"What could persuade you to let a stranger in?" Ringmar asked.

"Lots of money?"

"No."

"A movie contract?"

"Try again."

"A case of whisky?"

"You're getting warmer."

"Somebody I knew."

"Bingo."

They sat there silently.

An angel flitted through the room.

"You're giving me goose bumps," Winter said.

"Somebody they knew."

"It's certainly possible, but I'm skeptical somehow."

Ringmar tried to weave together the various strands of the conversation in his head.

"I'm pretty sure there's only one murderer," Winter said. "He's been here and there, and he's here or there now too. Gothenburg or London."

"We look for this person in the victims' past. If he's there, we grab him."

"That's not where we're going to find him. Not in their past."

"The past and the present, where do you draw the line?"

Winter had no answer.

23

HE WAITED WITH THE OTHERS. EVERYBODY WAS SILENT, LOST IN
their own thoughts. When the sliding doors opened, he walked through
and onto the airport bus. He was tired, and apparently so was everyone else.

The bus made its rounds of the downtown area. New passengers
got on. They shivered outside the Park Avenue Hotel. A few airport
personnel boarded at Korsvägen Street, the crisp creases of their uniforms belying their weariness, as if only their clothing were holding
them upright.

Out on the expressway, the driver did his best to break the sound
barrier. But the sonic boom could never have reached him, drifting as
he was between sleep and waking, Ijahman Levi's reggae blasting in his
headphones.

The bus finally stopped outside the international terminal. He
grabbed his bag and got off. It was snowing again. Travelers jogged with
their carts from the parking lot.

Voices drifted to the ceiling of the terminal like sleepy bees. The
Scandinavian Airlines attendants finished their check-in preparations
and the long line began to move. He glanced at his watch: six o'clock.
The flight to Heathrow was scheduled for ten after seven. He had
skipped breakfast and was planning to grab a cheese sandwich and a
coffee before takeoff.

When his turn came, he held up his bag for the blue-uniformed attendant to see.

"Is that all your luggage?"

"Yes, it's small enough to carry on, isn't it?"

She nodded, checking his ticket and passport. "Do you have a seating preference?"

He shrugged. It didn't make a bit of difference to him.

"A window seat in the middle of the aircraft. Will that do?"

He shrugged again and she smiled, printing out his boarding pass and handing it to him along with his return ticket and passport. "Have a nice trip."

He nodded and stuffed everything into his right breast pocket, then strolled over to the escalator and rode up to security.

His sandwich and coffee finished, he watched people wander around the duty-free shops. He had promised to buy some perfume for his mother on the way back. The name was in his wallet somewhere. They must sell it in London too, he thought. Otherwise it was crap.

Someone he recognized walked up to him, and he turned off Dr. Alimantado, who was standing outside a hovel in a Kingston slum dissing the police. The music stopped with a long backbeat. He pulled the headphones out of his ears.

"So you're off to see the world."

He nodded. "London."

"Same here, but just for the day."

"Just for the day? Is it really worth it?"

"They want me to pick up some papers."

"There's always the mail."

"Some things are a little sensitive."

"I guess."

"How long are you going to be there?"

"A week, I think."

"Haven't you decided? It's enough to make a man jealous, anyway. Been in London before?"

"Only once."

"Do you have a place to stay?"

"Hell no."

"Have you gotten any tips?"

"My parents mentioned a place in Bayswater, so I guess it will be there. Or maybe I'll stay at a couple of different hotels."

"Don't you have a job to go to?"

"I haven't graduated yet."

"I see."

"I've got some brochures and I want to check out a few schools."

"Colleges?"

"Yeah."

"What are you going to study?"

He folded his napkin into smaller and smaller squares. He looked up at the departure board. The plane had arrived at the gate. "Maybe English. Or design or photography—that's the school I have the best feeling about."

"Is it hard to get in?"

"I don't know, but we'd better go now if we're going to make the plane."

"Relax, we've got plenty of time."

"Then there's the music." He took his bag and started to get up.

"What music?"

"I'm into the new reggae, so I thought I'd go down to Brixton and buy a few CDs, plus some of the old stuff I can't get here in Sweden."

"Hmm."

"I found a bunch of places online."

"Record stores?"

"Stores, discos, clubs—seems like a pretty cool scene."

"Brixton? Isn't that a long ways from Bayswater?"

"A few stops on the tube, that's all. 'The Guns of Brixton' by The Clash. My dad's got it. Have you heard it?"

"No."

They walked over to Gate 18, showed their passports and tickets, then boarded the plane. He shoved his bag into the overhead rack and squeezed his way over to the window seat.

He fastened his seat belt and looked out. Bare trees lined the edge of the airport. The runways were a shimmer of concrete.

Snowflakes stuck to the window and melted. He listened to the first part of the safety instructions, put his headphones on, closed his eyes and tapped his right foot to Dr. Alimantado.

A while later he was thrust backward in his seat. He opened his eyes and saw the blur of the runways like gray speed lines against a transparent background.

Then everything turned to white. They rose straight through the clouds and were soon cruising far above the earth. He tried to remember the last time he had seen a blue sky. Whenever it was, it had been nothing like this.

24

THERE WAS THAT RESTLESSNESS AGAIN, LURKING IN THE PIT OF his stomach like a predator.

Are you mature enough to be a father? he asked himself. Is it too big a step, or is something else bothering you?

He had felt the baby kicking earlier that evening, and his hand was still throbbing hot and cold.

"What's going on?" Martina asked, squinting at him.

"Nothing."

"You just had an expression like something horrid had crossed your mind."

"It's just the job."

"What about the job?" she persisted.

"The late hours are getting to me, that's all."

"Haven't you got the afternoon shift all week?"

"Yes, but they should call it the evening shift."

"Or the night shift. You come home smelling of cigarette smoke."

Bergenhem took the road that led from their row house to the bridge. The sunlight over the bridge had worn a different aspect the last day or two, like a promise. Will you have the same feeling fourteen years from now? he wondered. Will your heart still leap when spring is on the way? In fourteen years, the trees will tower over the house and you'll be a detective inspector and your kid will be starting high school.

Then we'll hole up in some secret hideout, like Birgersson, for the last week in February when the whole world is waiting out winter's last gasp. Birgersson is never tan when he comes back. Where the hell does he go, anyway?

Chunks of ice floated below the bridge. The setting sun struck the water and turned the river into a trail of broken glass.

A cutter cleaved the surface on the way to the sea as if it had diamonds in its propeller. West of the bridge, it met the *Catfish*, soaring above the water on its way in from Denmark. He heard nothing, the hovercraft a burst of movement without sound.

He left the bridge behind and found himself surrounded by the silence that wafted through the city from the sea.

It must be possible to get hold of a sailboat at a decent price, he thought. Martina would be glad for some time alone, wouldn't she?

He put a tape on and turned up the volume until it was just short of unbearable. The traffic flowed soundlessly outside the window.

The sign was lit up, just like the last time. He parked in the same spot. The door looked different now that he knew what it was like inside. He walked quickly past the racks of magazines, through the curtain and into the club proper. There were men at all the tables except the one closest to the door, and that's where he sat down.

A woman was dancing on a table next to the stage at the far end of the room. The customers clapped every once in a while. No music was playing this time.

Tina Turner deserves a break, he thought. A waiter in a white shirt and dark bow tie came and took his order, returning a couple of minutes later with his Coke. He raised his glass and sucked an ice cube into his mouth to chew on.

"Back already?" The owner stopped halfway through the curtain.

"You don't waste any time."

The owner didn't respond.

"I had a couple more questions for you."

The owner stayed where he was, cigarette in hand.

"This is fine right here. We don't have to go into your office."

"Fire away."

"Isn't the curtain bothering you?"

"Is that the first question?"

"I was just wondering."

"It's a great curtain, exotic, just like our dancers."

"It looks like something out of a silent movie."

The owner held up his hand in resignation and sat down across from Bergenhem. He peered over at the glass on the table. "We can spike your drink if you like."

Bergenhem asked himself what Winter would have done in this situation. He sipped his Coke, feeling the icy cold on his tongue. "With what?" he asked, though it was obvious he was being offered any substance of his choice. "How about rum?"

The owner went off and talked to the bartender, then returned, and soon the waiter appeared with a couple of drinks. "For our friends only," the owner said, lifting his glass once the waiter was gone.

This is an innocent enough game, Bergenhem thought. He's testing me, but for what? "I just remembered I'm driving," he said.

"A few sips won't hurt you."

This is pure strategy on my part, Bergenhem thought, raising the glass to his lips.

"Was there something you wanted from me?" the owner asked.

The music started to pound like a pile driver through rock. The low bass made Bergenhem's forehead throb. Is this another test? he wondered.

The owner studied him. The volume was lowered and the treble turned up. Two women climbed onto the stage. Tina Turner again.

The owner leaned over the table. "I'm still waiting."

"Is Tina Turner the only thing you've got here?"

The owner glanced over at the stage, then fixed his eyes on Bergenhem once more. He was wearing an open-neck plaid shirt, suspenders and dark pants with cuffs. The painted floodlights along the wall lent a red tinge to everything in the room. "It's the best music to dance to," he said after half a minute.

"That doesn't answer my question."

"Are you trying to make me angry?"

"Hell no."

"Then what did you come for?"

"Last time I was here, I forgot to ask you about the kinds of customers you have, whether there's any difference between them and the ones who patronize other clubs."

"I couldn't begin to tell you."

"Are you sure? Every club's got its own little specialty, right?"

"I have no idea what you're getting at."

Bergenhem eyed the stage. He recognized both women. The younger one looked even thinner than before. Her lips were crimson. He suddenly wished the owner weren't there.

"You're mistaken if you expect to find anything here," the owner said. "Just take a look around. I see you're already checking out the show."

Bergenhem managed to take his eyes off the women. The song ended, and another one started up after a few seconds. You're simply the best, Tina Turner thundered, better than all the rest.

"This isn't a gay club," the owner said.

"You've had a drag show or two in your time."

"Is that so. Were you here?"

"That's not the question. We're not prejudiced against anyone."

The owner shook his head in bafflement and stood up. "Feel free to finish your drink." He rustled his way back through the curtain.

The show continued for another ten minutes. The women left the room. Bergenhem sat quietly, sniffed his drink once but didn't touch it again. He didn't want to leave the car outside overnight. He'd assumed the owner would hang around for a while if he was drinking, but that had turned out to be a miscalculation. Perhaps just as well, he thought.

The younger woman stepped out of the doorway by the stage and walked to the closest table, where three men got up and pulled over a chair for her. Her black dress glistened in the red light. She took a cigarette out of her purse. One of the men flicked open a lighter even before she could put the cigarette between her lips. He said something and she laughed. Bergenhem studied their every move.

The woman stood up and went back out through the door, followed by the man who had lit her cigarette. Other women sat at a number of the tables, but there were more men. Bergenhem waited.

25

WINTER TOOK THE ELEVATOR UP FROM THE UNDERGROUND AND passed through the gates with his London Regional Transport ticket. Out on Earl's Court Road, he was assaulted by the odors of the city: gasoline fumes, deep-fried fish, rotting garbage and that pungent blend of cobblestone and dusty streets you encounter only in truly old places.

Spring was lurking somewhere. The sun shone through the fog, making it warmer here than in Gothenburg. Along the Piccadilly Line—which stretched eastward through Hounslow, Osterley, Ealing and Acton—the maples were about to sprout, the gardens wakening. Children were chasing balls across Osterley Park. Children chased balls all year round, but never as when spring flirted with them like this.

He had seen it all before. He was a stranger, but less of one each time he returned. London was his city too.

The mood in the train had been the usual mixture of anticipation and jadedness. The passengers who'd boarded at the airport were backpacking teenagers, middle-aged couples and a few solitary travelers who studied their maps for the entire forty-five minutes to Kensington and beyond. He heard Italian, German and something he thought was Polish, not to mention Swedish and Norwegian.

As they approached downtown, Londoners got on. White men in chalk-stripe suits and briefcases, the *Daily Telegraph* under their arms. Black women with children who stared wide-eyed at all the foreigners. Thin young women with skin as translucent as the hazy sky shivered in their short skirts, and he had suddenly felt awkward in his camel hair coat.

When the walk signal appeared, Winter crossed Earl's Court Road with his suitcase rolling behind, turned left and then right onto Hogarth. He continued a couple of blocks to Knaresborough Place. Crossing the quiet intersection, he heard the low rumble of traffic on Cromwell Road to the left. Just a stone's throw farther and you could actually stand still and listen to the birds sing.

He rang the bell next to a door with a big 8 on it. Arnold Norman, the manager of the little apartment hotel, opened the door with his hand already outstretched.

"Inspector Winter! It's a pleasure to see you again."

"The feeling is mutual, Arnold."

"Where have you been all this time?"

"I was wondering the same thing."

When Norman stepped aside, a younger man who had been standing behind him took Winter's suitcase. He walked quickly toward a stairway that cast a long shadow across the lobby.

Winter had stayed here often over the past ten years, whenever he was in London. The location was superb, a little way from the din up in Piccadilly and walking distance to King's Road in Chelsea, not to mention Kensington High Street and Hyde Park.

They took their seats in Norman's tiny office. "I've held suite T2 for you."

"Perfect."

"You look terrific."

"But older," Winter said.

Norman was a survivor, his rustic establishment a mere half block from Cromwell Road. "All our worries will soon be over," he said.

"You're only ten years older than me."

"That's not what I mean. I'm talking about a bunch of crazy Scots who have started to clone sheep up in the Highlands."

"Isn't it against the law?"

"To clone sheep?"

"To clone at all."

"I don't think they bothered asking."

"What does that have to do with old age?"

"They're going to create an immortal race, and what bothers me is that every one of them will be a Scot. It's bad enough they're all going to look alike, which they already do, but now the world will be stuck with them forever."

"So it would have been a different story if the experiments had been conducted in England?"

Norman eyed him with feigned incredulity. "You're not implying I'm a chauvinist or something, are you?"

Winter smiled and got up. "Take me to my rooms."

The suite was on the second floor, its windows overlooking a tranquil courtyard to the east. It consisted of a bedroom, a living room and a large kitchenette with a dining alcove. The bathroom actually worked, a rarity in England—you could turn on the faucets without attending a crash course in the aqueducts of ancient Rome.

He took off his jacket and shirt and was about to splash some water under his armpits but decided to shower instead. It could be a long day.

A towel around his waist, he lifted the wall phone off the hook and dialed, opening the drapes while he waited. It was one-thirty, and the sunlight that flooded the room was unlike anything he'd ever seen in this hotel. Maybe spring had arrived after all. A patch of blue sky framed the sooty buildings in the distance.

"Four Area Southeast, Major Investigation Pool, Detective Constable Barrow," a woman answered.

"Chief Inspector Erik Winter from Sweden here. May I speak to Steve Macdonald?"

"Hold on, please," she said flatly.

There was a murmur at the other end. The constable was talking to somebody seated nearby. Winter heard a shuffling sound.

"Macdonald."

"It's Erik Winter."

"Ah, Winter. Delayed again?"

"I'm in London."

"Good to hear it. Where exactly?"

"At my hotel on Earl's Court Road."

"I can send someone to pick you up, but it will take a while."

"Isn't British Rail just as fast?"

"Depends."

"If you're down in Thornton Heath, I know how to get there. My timetable says the train leaves from Victoria Station."

"It takes twenty-five minutes, and you'll see some of the most beautiful scenery in the world."

"That clinches it."

"Take the District Line from Earl's Court to Victoria Station. It's only a couple of stops."

"I know."

"Why doesn't that surprise me?"

Winter could tell Macdonald had already made up his mind: Mr. Scandi-know-it-all has arrived.

"You're starting to figure me out."

"Call when you get to Thornton Heath Station and I'll send someone for you," Macdonald said and hung up.

Victoria Station felt like the center of the world. If only I could get on the Orient Express right now, he thought. A quiet investigation onboard, all suspects assembled in the bar car.

The city never felt so close as at this station. Winter was standing by the southern exits, looking up at the information that flapped onto the departure board. The train to Tattenham Corner, which stopped at Thornton Heath, had just arrived.

There was hardly anyone else in his car as the train jolted its way out of the station. The sky was incandescent behind the chimney tops that hovered over the river. They crossed the water and stopped at Battersea Park Station: red brick, graffiti, but less than he would have imagined. People waiting on the benches. Not a sound to be heard. There's a wall of silence around people who are traveling, Winter thought. They're in a state of suspension, not at home and not somebody else's guest either—a no-man's-land whose chief occupation is waiting.

The purpose of the trip, even the altered slant of the sun at this latitude, saddened him. He had come to London, and to the south side of the river specifically, because death was his constant companion. The premonition plaguing him from the start of the investigation continued to nag—that they had seen only the beginning, that evil was preparing its next inscrutable assault. Whatever direction he took, menace was his journey and his destination. He was alone, and he had no faith in anything.

South London—never described in guidebooks, rarely visited by foreigners—stretched out to his right. He had been on this side of the river only a couple of times, and then no farther than the Putney and Barnes areas to take in some jazz.

Buildings of medieval brick composed an eternal city in which nothing rose above two stories as far as he could see. A man in shorts jogged across Wandsworth Common. When the train pulled out of the station again, he watched some schoolchildren playing soccer on a little gravel field. Their jackets were bright green like the buds of spring.

This part of the city was lusher than he'd expected, with more open fields than north of the river, as though the buildings had sprung up in total ignorance of the metropolis.

At Streatham Common he saw the tower of a mosque. Veiled women sat and waited on rough-hewn benches. Two black men, both wearing leather jackets and knit caps, entered the train, the music from their headphones an audible murmur.

He got off at the next station. Thornton Heath was immersed in shadow; the platform itself was below street level. As he climbed the stairs, a newspaper flapped by his ankle on its way down.

The station building was untended. Three black girls stood in a corner waiting for something to happen. Cars swished by outside the open entranceway, and when he came out on Brigstock Road, he felt as though he were in a faraway country, light-years from London. The passersby were Indian, Pakistani, Caribbean, Chinese, Korean and African.

He walked down a little hill, continued on High Street to an intersection and followed Whitehorse Lane for a block or two. He knew if he went another couple of blocks, he would come to Selhurst Park, a refuge for the ragged soccer fans in the poor sections of Croydon. He had seen a few matches in London, but only at the large stadiums on the north side.

He turned before the viaduct and passed Mame Amisha's Foreign Foods, which advertised "new puna yams" on a handwritten cardboard sign. The yams lay in plaited baskets outside the store. Bananas hung on poles in the window. He walked by the Prince George pub and was back at the station. He took out his phone and called Macdonald, who answered on the first ring.

"I'm by the flower stand outside the station."

"If you go down the hill and turn left again at Woolworth's, you'll find yourself on Parchmore Road. I feel like taking a stroll myself, so if

you stay on the right side of the street, you'll run into me in ten minutes
or so."

"Okay."

It occurred to him that Macdonald hadn't bothered to ask him what
he looked like. He'll know you're a policeman by the way you walk, he
thought.

He headed back toward the intersection and was just about to turn in
front of Woolworth's when he saw a white man grab a young black guy
by the scruff of his neck outside the main entrance.

"The little shoplifter is back, I see," the man said. Winter noticed a
badge on his chest. Several black men stood in a circle around the security guard and his prey.

"I didn't do anything," the young guy said.

"What's this, then?" The security guard held up an electric shaver.

"I didn't take it."

"Let's go." The security guard shoved his way through the circle,
hulking over the culprit.

Winter crossed Parchmore Road, turned left and weaved his way
north between the gravel heaps and the road workers.

Macdonald walked down the stairs, through the garage and out onto
the street, the sun warming his head. He let his leather jacket hang open
and left his gloves in his pocket. London is putting on its best face for its
Swedish visitor, he thought. He's going to get the wrong impression.

He headed south. He was stiff after a morning bent over witness
statements, and his eyeballs felt like they'd been glued to their sockets.
His body was too heavy, his spirit too anxious.

Half a block before him was a man in an unbuttoned camel hair coat.
The suit underneath was somewhere between blue and steel gray, with
trouser cuffs.

It must be him, Macdonald thought. He walks just like he talks. It's
a miracle he hasn't been mugged. Has he held his badge out in front of
him the whole way from the station?

The man's hair was blond and appeared to be parted in the middle
like that of a fifties actor. As they approached each other, Macdonald
saw that he was tall, maybe his own height. There was a fussiness beneath his sartorial élan and a touch of arrogance in his step. He was

clean shaven, his ears stuck out a little, his face was wide and a bit too handsome and Macdonald wasn't looking forward to this at all.

Winter was startled to hear his own name. The man could have been an inch taller than he was, maybe six foot four. His dark brown hair was in a ponytail and he had a day-old beard. He was wearing a tattered leather jacket, a blue-and-white plaid shirt, black jeans and pointed boots. He should have a holster on his hip, Winter thought. He looks lethal.

"Inspector Winter?"

He had an enigmatic smile and a few wrinkles around his mouth. There were no bags under his eyes but they were awash in a weariness that lent his gaze a dull fixity. At least he doesn't have a ring in his ear, Winter thought. "Inspector Macdonald?" He stretched out his hand.

"I thought we'd have a beer down at the Prince George," Macdonald said. "It's calm and peaceful there this time of day. Much more relaxing than the police station."

They retraced Winter's steps across the intersection and onto High Street. He noticed that Macdonald had a slight limp.

"I play on the pub's soccer team every Sunday," Macdonald explained before he could ask. "I'm always like this at the beginning of the week. People around here think it's an old gunshot injury and that suits me just fine."

"I quit a few years back."

"Wimp."

The pub was empty. Dust danced in the sunlight that poured through a lone window. The bartender nodded at Macdonald.

"Let's go in there," Macdonald said, pointing to a small, oblong lounge on the other side of the bar.

Winter draped his coat over the back of a chair and sat down. Macdonald went off and came back with two glasses of ale, still cloudy from the tap.

"Would you rather have a lager?" Macdonald asked.

"I always drink ale when I'm in London." Winter hoped he didn't sound too urbane.

"This is Courage Directors. They also have Courage Best here, which is pretty unusual."

"Directors is one of my favorites."

Macdonald studied him. Definitely a snob, he thought, but he might have good taste anyway. "Do you come to our proud city very often?" he asked.

"Not so much recently. And I've never been to this pub before."

"We rarely see new faces here. For some reason, most tourists stick to the area around Leicester Square."

"They miss out on Mame Amisha's yams."

"What?"

"She sells fresh yams down the block from here."

"There's Thornton Heath for you."

"I walked around for a while before I called."

"That's what I figured."

"But not all the way to Selhurst Park."

"Have you ever been there?"

"No."

"Crystal Palace is a lousy team, but the fans love them."

"Are you a fan?"

"Of Crystal Palace?" Macdonald laughed, drank his ale and looked at Winter. "Just because I work in this district doesn't mean I have to be as loyal as all that. If there's any English team I root for, it's Charlton. They'll never make it to the Premier League, but when I moved here a very long time ago, I ended up in Woolwich around the Valley, so that's where my allegiance lies."

"I would have taken you for a Scot."

"That's because I am."

Two men walked into the lounge and nodded at Macdonald. He nodded back, and they moved to the other room.

"Like I said, not so many new faces. But they show up occasionally, and sometimes things get out of hand."

"I knew Per Malmström. That's one reason I was anxious to come to London."

"I understand."

"Do you?"

"We'll drive down to the hotel in a while. We've left the room just the way it was."

"You do understand."

"I was planning to go to Gothenburg, but I wanted to wait until you had been here first."

"Has a foreign investigator ever come to see you before? Or vice versa?"

"An American cop was here a couple of years ago," Macdonald said, finishing his ale. "It was also a murder, up in Peckham, which is our northern border, more or less. And I went to Kingston on a case once."

"Jamaica?"

"For two weeks. A murder here that led straight to Kingston. Not so unusual for our part of London. If we scent a trail, it often goes to the Caribbean, Jamaica in particular."

"What happened?"

"The police down there weren't particularly thrilled to see me, but I learned enough that we managed to solve the case once I got back."

"Let's hope we have the same luck this time."

"One more?" Macdonald pointed at Winter's glass, which was almost empty.

Winter shook his head and took out his cigarillos.

"Those things are deadly," Macdonald said, standing up. "I'll go get another one anyway and let you poison yourself in peace."

Winter lit a cigarillo and inhaled its fragrance. There were more customers now, but they had all stayed in the outer room. Macdonald must have some kind of say-so here, he thought, but how many pints of Directors did it cost him?

"I made it Courage Best this time." Macdonald had returned with two more cloudy glasses. He sat back down.

Music was playing in the other room. Winter could tell it was reggae, but heavier than the kind he'd heard now and again.

Macdonald broke a minute's silence. "So you knew him?"

"Not exactly, but he grew up on the same street I did. I saw him mostly when he was a young child."

That child never got much older, Macdonald thought. Can I stand to hear the shrieks in the walls of that cursed room another time?

"How did you feel when you stood in his room?"

He gets it too, Macdonald thought. "I heard cries and screams."

"That's exactly the way it is." Winter drank from the new glass. "I hear your kids and you hear mine."

26

MACDONALD TOOK CROYDON ROAD NORTHWEST THROUGH
Mitcham, Morden and Merton, then headed west on Kingston Road
through Streatham to Wandsworth and Clapham. Mile upon mile of red
and gray brick row houses were interrupted by parks, schoolyards and
stores clumped earnestly together. Thruways had become cross streets.
Double-decker buses peered out over the other vehicles and lurched around
corners. Cars as far as the eye could see, drivers sitting on their horns. More
stores with flower and vegetable stands out front. It went on and on.

"London is more than just Soho or Covent Garden, and all this is my
territory." Macdonald gestured to the world outside.

All that's living, dead and everything in between, Winter thought.
"It's a big place," he said.

"It's more complicated than that. Did I mention that Croydon is the
tenth largest town in England?"

"Yes, the first time you called."

"I should be keeping my hands off Clapham. I'm invading the turf
of my colleagues on the southwest side. But it's my old district and the
bigwigs thought I was best suited for this investigation."

"What did your colleagues on the southwest side have to say about
that?"

"The murder of a white foreigner? They pounded me on the back
and then laughed behind it."

"So you're a popular guy."

"More than ever." Macdonald swerved to avoid a fruit cart that had
just rolled out of an alleyway to the left. He glared at the black man who

emerged behind it, clinging to the handle as if he were being pulled along.

"Did I tell you that this so-called thoroughfare is named Kingston Road?"

"Yes."

"It's no coincidence."

They drove through Tulse Hill. Winter heard a whistle and saw a train pass on a viaduct above them, then clatter to a halt in front of the station building.

"Karen and Winston Hillier live in this neighborhood," Macdonald said.

Winter nodded. "I want to meet them."

"I'll do what I can, but Winston just got back from the hospital after a nervous breakdown. It happened when I was at their house."

Macdonald drove west on Christchurch Road and crossed the intersection. "The street on the right is Brixton Hill," he said. "Follow it and there you are in the Caribbean."

"Ah, Brixton."

"Have you ever been there?"

"No, but I've heard about it."

"'The Guns of Brixton.' The Clash."

"What?"

"The Clash."

"Is that a band or something?"

Glancing over at Winter, Macdonald laughed and hit the brake to let a taxi pull away from the curb.

"The Only Band That Matters."

"Not my kind of music."

"I knew right off there was something wrong with you."

Macdonald's police radio chattered constantly with names of districts Winter had never heard of. He could hardly make out the words. The woman at the emergency hotline coordinated the calls as if she were reciting from a script.

"Brixton is a fascinating place," Macdonald said. "Lots of my friends live there."

The traffic was backed up on Poynders Road.

"I was thinking about the passenger lists on my way to London."

"Hmm."

"It's a hell of a job."

"That Jamaica case I told you about before? We went through three weeks of passenger lists, and that was bad enough."

"We asked for them anyway."

"Same here, but if—I'm saying if—you go to another country to kill someone, you're hardly going to fly under your own name."

"Unless the murderer is actually looking to get caught."

"So all we have to do is eliminate the names on the lists one by one until we reach the murderer's, and he'll be sitting there waiting for us to knock on his door?"

"Something like that."

"It's an idea. Have you talked to a forensic psychologist about it?"

"Not yet. It's just one possibility."

"Let me tell you a story."

The traffic began to move again, forming a semicircle around a car that had been pulled over to the shoulder and was being hoisted onto a tow truck.

"It was a Ford Fiesta too, did you see that car?" Macdonald nodded at the side of the road.

"Of course."

"There was a murder in Peckham last Christmas, and all we had to go on were a few witnesses who saw a man drive away from the scene of the crime around the time it was committed."

"Okay."

"Some witnesses said that the car was silver, another that it was brightly colored. One guy swore that it was a Mark 1 Fiesta. He didn't see it but he heard it drive away in the night and said, 'I've owned Ford Fiestas all my life, and I know one when I hear it.'"

"Was he trustworthy?"

"As far as we could tell. So we decided to check all Mark 1 Fiestas. First we concentrated on southeast England. We identified ten thousand cars. No way. We didn't have anywhere near the staff to track all of them down."

"So you decided to go by color?"

"Good thinking. We settled on silver and narrowed it down to eighteen hundred cars. Still an impossible task, considering we only had ten people and they were following up other leads at the same time."

"Hmm."

"So we zeroed in on Peckham—East Lewisham, to be exact. That left us with about a hundred and fifty cars. We didn't get very far, because some other information came to our attention that solved the case. As it turned out, the car was green. But, sure enough, it was a Fiesta."

"In other words, you can trust what people hear more than what they see."

"Yes, but my main point is that burying yourself in a bunch of lists isn't necessarily the way to go. Still, we keep them on hand in case we need them."

Winter nodded.

"Once we have a suspect, we can check the lists and say, Aha, he flew the day after his victim."

Winter heard voices from the hallway but not a sound from the adjacent rooms. A car zoomed from Cautley Avenue onto Clapham Common South Side. The afternoon sun sliced through the window and lit up the opposite wall, adding a luster to the dry blood that made Winter close his eyes and see Per in front of him. He had walked through that door over there, and the remnants of his life were now splattered on the walls and floor. Winter was sweating. He loosened his tie. He had a sour taste in his mouth from the cigarillo and the top-fermented ale.

"Do you want to be alone?" Macdonald asked.

"Yes, if you don't mind."

Macdonald turned to leave.

"Close the door, please," Winter said.

He shut his eyes again and saw the photographs. Macdonald had shown them to him at his office just a few minutes earlier. The similarities to what he had encountered in Gothenburg were frightening. Per was sitting in the same position, slumped against the chair with an eerie nonchalance, his back to the door as if he were reading a book. Opening his eyes, Winter walked over and stood behind the chair. Macdonald had left it exactly where it was when Per had sat in it.

Had Per been placed here for a reason? Had he been tied to the chair so that he could watch something enacted on the wall? Was he still alive at that point?

All of the victims had rope marks on their bodies, but it was as if the rope was there to keep them from falling off the chair, not to prevent them from escaping. No bruises or wounds to indicate a struggle, no signs that the thin strands had frayed.

Had Per been forced to watch another murder? A movie? Geoff had been killed at around the same time in Gothenburg. Could the murderer really have made his way from one city to the other that quickly? Maybe. Assuming it was the same person. Were there more murders that they didn't know about? Was Per watching a video of one of them just before he died? Did it matter which way he was facing?

Winter looked at the floor. There were traces of blood that would have thickened even while the murder was taking place, sticking to shoes, footprints swirled across the linoleum as in a dance.

He closed his eyes again. Was music playing? Macdonald hadn't found a CD in the room, or anything to play one on. Nobody had heard music coming from the room, no screams. All that was left was this deafening roar from the walls and floor that almost made Winter stagger backward. When he opened his eyes, the sun was gone. The walls were dull and unseeing, and if it hadn't been for the shrieks, he would have thought that they no longer remembered what they had witnessed.

He went out into the hallway. Macdonald was waiting by the stairs.

"It's going to happen again," Winter said.

They stood outside the Dudley Hotel. Clapham Common pulsated with activity on the other side of the street, animating Battersea, Clapham, Balham and Brixton. Winter saw schoolchildren scattered around a pond and playground, their uniforms merging into large blue and red rectangles as the teachers lined them up.

People just home from work were walking their dogs. The wind was still gentle in his face, and the scents of spring, more powerful here than north of the river, quickened his senses. The sun painted flames on the clouds between the trees in the park.

"Much of Clapham is upper middle class," Macdonald said. He had followed Winter's gaze. "There's money here, and you're likely to find most of it around the Common. I worked the area for several years as a detective inspector, and I'm reaping the rewards now. Or paying for my sins."

Two teenage girls passed by. Their backpacks, half as big as they were, wobbled a foot above their heads as they turned left and vanished behind the buildings.

"And we still don't know what Per was doing in London," Winter said.

"Unless his parents have come up with something new."

"Not a thing."

"Maybe he wanted to spend a few days checking out the music scene."

"Music?"

"From what I understand, reggae is in again. Which makes Brixton the place to go. That might be what he had in mind."

"We found some reggae in his room at his parents' house but no evidence that he was a big fan."

"It still could have been one of his reasons for coming here."

"In that case somebody should have remembered seeing him when you made your inquiries after the murder."

"People around here don't admit to having seen anyone."

"They're scared?"

"Yes."

"Even in such extraordinary circumstances?"

"Nobody's behavior changes just because something like this happens. People are genuinely afraid of each other. Brixton and parts of Clapham are rife with drugs. A lot of the crime is tied to crack."

"So no one admits to having seen a white kid who went around looking for music?"

"No, but it's always possible that they actually don't remember him. Whites, mostly teenagers, pour into Brixton every day on the train from Victoria Station. It's the music that brings them."

"And having once spent so much time here hasn't done you any good?"

"Not yet anyway."

Winter ran his fingers across his forehead. The sweat had dried, matting down his hair. All the new impressions had compounded his exhaustion from the flight, and the fear he had felt in Per's hotel room lingered in him like a chill.

He was hungry, which felt inappropriate somehow. He hadn't eaten anything besides some chicken salad and a jelly roll on the plane, and the ale had given him a headache. Or maybe it was just weariness.

"Have you had anything to eat, by the way?" Macdonald asked.

"Only on the plane. A little snack wouldn't be such a bad idea."

"I know just the place."

Macdonald drove east on Clapham Common South Side and onto Clapham High Street. After a minute or two, he turned left, continued another block and a half and squeezed his Vauxhall into a parking space by a restaurant with awnings and three outdoor tables.

"It's called El Rincon Latino. The owner is one of my old contacts— friends, I should say."

They walked up half a flight of stairs and through the open glass door. The restaurant curved past the bar on the left.

The whole place was lit by glass walls facing Clapham Manor Street. Fresh flowers were everywhere, but the aroma was of herbs and chili. The only other customers were a handful of people at the bar.

They sat for a long time over grilled salmon, broiled shrimp with garlic, queso fresco, olives stuffed with anchovies and chili peppers, steamed cornbread, cuttlefish in black sauce, wild mushrooms and grilled eggplant with potato wedges. The food was served in small clay pots.

"We investigators have an easier time of it these days," Macdonald said, putting his glass down.

"How so?"

"About a year and a half ago, they set up permanent teams, and I'm in charge of one of them. The way it used to be, if there was a murder in Clapham, they'd put together a team from around the city, but then some of London was suddenly undermanned. Investigators were sent back and forth to different stations to try to cover all the bases. It was a big mess."

Winter heard voices clamoring at the bar.

"Now they've divided Greater London up into four quadrants, and I work the one called Four Area Southeast. It has a hundred and three inspectors assigned to eight different teams, each with three detective inspectors and nine assistants, not to mention civilian backup for index cards, computer runs and that kind of thing. I head up one of the teams, and we work together on every case that comes our way."

"Then the trick is to have the right people."

"I've made it my business to have the best. Inspectors from the south side, a couple from the Yard."

"Murders only?"

"Yep. When you're covering an area with upwards of three million people, that's more than enough to keep you busy."

"Makes sense."

"There were seventeen murders in the southeast area last year and we solved every one of them. Probably because we were able to take our time. It was rougher going the year before—forty-two or forty-three murders, I have no idea why so many."

"Did you solve all of them too?"

"All but one. We're batting a thousand for the past twenty-one months, not counting the present case. The victim was notorious for breaking into houses in his neighborhood. Everyone who knew him, or had come home to find their bedrooms ransacked, was glad to see him dead."

"No witnesses?"

"Nope."

"And now you've got another case on your hands."

"This one isn't going to get away from us. We've dropped everything else. My detective superintendent also oversees another team, and he's put them on the case too."

"Twenty-six people altogether."

"Twenty-seven if you count the detective superintendent, but I'm basically running the investigation."

"Great, that should shake things up a little."

"More than you might think. Just wait until the reporters show up tomorrow."

"You're an optimist."

"What do you mean?"

"You said that you wouldn't let this case get away from you."

"We're realists, but we also have faith in what we're doing, right?"

"It's a good combination."

"I'd say it's a necessary combination. And if you're finished with that little snack of yours, I'll drive you back to the station."

27

HE HAD FOUND A ROOM AT THE NEW DOME HOTEL ON CAMBER-
well Church Street for twenty-five pounds a night, and the best part was
that it was within walking distance of Brixton Station if you followed
Coldharbour Lane. He had already made the trek, shoulder bag in tow,
from the station to the hotel.

He knew that a bus ran down Coldharbour Lane but preferred to
walk. The sun was out, and with Sugar Minott jamming on his headphones, he felt like he was experiencing life for the first time. Maybe
he'd run across some good weed. He would take it easy if he did. He was
here for the music.

As he approached the station, he saw a sign on the right: COOLTAN
ARTS CENTRE. LIVE MUSIC FRIDAY NIGHTS. That was only a few more days.
He would still be in London.

The scene around the station was mesmerizing—the narrow streets,
the market wagons that came rolling through, not a white face in sight.
Reggae blared from the stores. Some posters lying on the sidewalk dis-
played the names of various groups. He had found the right place.

He walked into Blacker Dread Music Store and saw everything he
could imagine asking for. I'm in heaven, he thought, or at least reggae
heaven. Or maybe I'm in Jamaica.

He browsed through the CDs. A number of the customers could
have been Swedes or Danes or Germans, but he didn't want to talk to
anybody or even try to figure out what language they were speaking.

He found *Natty Dread Rise Again* by the Congos and their double album *Heart of the Congos*. And "Scalp Dem" by Super Cat. The box set

Acid Jazz Roots Selection. Beenie Man, Lady Saw, Wayne Wonder, Tanya Stephens, Spragga Benz.

There was the new Bounty Killer—*My Xperience.* It would be three years before the album made it to Gothenburg, and then only by special order. He checked out the titles: "Fed Up." "Living Dangerously." "War Face (Ask Fi War)" remix. "The Lord Is My Light and Salvation."

He saw *Guns Out* by Beenie Man Vs. Bounty Killer.

He was drawn to the lyrics, the swagger—especially the Bounty Killer titles: "Kill or Be Killed," "Deadly Medley," "Mobster," "Nuh Have No Heart," "Off the Air Bad Boy." No compromise.

And here was Sugar Minott. *International* on RAS Records, produced by Hopeton "Scientist" Brown.

I could easily spend five hundred pounds here, he thought.

He leafed through the booklet that came with *History of Trojan Records, Vol. 2.* He would buy it.

Finally a pair of the store's headphones was available and he handed his stack to the guy behind the counter, who had dreadlocks with blue ribbons dangling from the ends.

He began listening: Shaggy, *African Revolution* by Trinity, Chaka Demus & Pliers; and a classic by Culture that he hadn't heard since some asshole borrowed it and never returned it—*The Dread Flimstone Sound,* an old Gregory Isaacs hit.

He listened to "Sodom and Gomorrow" by the Congos.

The best album was *Somma I (Hooked Light Rays),* and he knew he wanted it as soon as he heard the vocals. Nothing but voices, like a black Gregorian chant, or African slaves down in the hold of a ship bound for America.

He decided to be choosy the first day so he could look forward to coming back. If he bought all the albums now, he'd be forever switching back and forth between them. Plus somebody could rob him on the street. He'd never be able to relax and concentrate on the music.

He bought *Somma I* and his hands trembled as he put it in his Discman. His earphones were back on before he'd even left the store. He walked down Atlantic Road toward the station and Brixton Market. The voices rose and fell, then snapped into a frenzy of sounds, as if a madman were loose among pots and pans. The music pierced his ears. It was alive, like someone in a long corridor with the instruments in front of him and the choir behind.

He stood outside the underground station. The viaduct on his right was green and burgundy. Red Records was directly across Brixton Road. Take it easy, he told himself. You can come back another day.

He saw a newspaper stand with black customers and black magazines: *Ebony, Pride, Essence, Blues & Soul.*

He was surrounded by unfamiliar smells. People came by with cuts of meat that he had never seen before, strange fruits and vegetables. Suddenly he was hungrier than he'd been his entire life. On Coldharbour Lane, there had been a place that looked outstanding. Auntie something. Auntie's something Cuisine maybe. He went back and turned onto Electric Avenue. It was the best street name he'd ever heard of.

28

EARLY THE NEXT MORNING, WINTER WALKED THROUGH THE
underground garage and up the narrow staircase to the investigation
room. He passed two heavily armed men wearing bulletproof vests.
The walls in the stairwell were colorless, as if the everyday world had
receded behind him when he came in from Parchmore Road. He heard
the drone of a fan and telephones ringing nonstop.

Stepping into the corridor, he saw women and men moving in and
out of a maze of rooms. The chart covering the wall to the left of the
stairs was more suggestive of a sci-fi space laboratory than a regional
criminal investigation center. Spokes of a big wheel shot out in a thousand different directions, like a diagram of the solar system with the
earth in the middle instead of the sun.

Macdonald had explained the chart the day before. Each line represented a call from the murder victim's phone in the center. This was for
a big drug case that led to the West Indies. The calls had been traced all
across London, Britain and the entire Western Hemisphere.

The offices of the detective inspectors lined the corridor. The other
investigators worked in two rooms, as well as the open space farthest
from the stairs. Desks had been moved together to enlarge the work
surfaces.

Everywhere Winter turned, he saw computers, typewriters, file
cabinets, phones, stacks of paper, witness reports, handwritten notes
that had been retyped. Photographs stuck out of the piles like awnings
against the white and yellow paper. Old-fashioned efficiency. Computers

aside, this was how Swedish police headquarters had looked back when he had started.

They have a more intuitive way of working, Winter thought. There's a feeling here of anarchy and freedom and participation in decision making that we don't have in Sweden. We don't sit close enough to each other at our fortress on Skånegatan Street.

Macdonald's office was no exception: a hundred square yards, stacks of papers, phones. Heavy protective gear was crammed behind the door, impossible to reach in an emergency. His service pistol lay in a worn-out leather holster on the desk. A very English sun filtered through the venetian blinds and drew stripes across his face. "Tea?" he offered by way of greeting.

"Please."

Out in the corridor, Macdonald said something Winter didn't catch to someone he couldn't see. Macdonald came back, sat down and motioned to the visitor's chair, which was wobbly but had held out for the few minutes Winter had sat there the day before.

"Tea's on its way," Macdonald said.

"We have to make it ourselves in Gothenburg."

"England is still a class society. The weak make tea for the strong."

"We're on our way back to that time. The world-renowned Swedish model is out of date."

"You don't give the impression of being a working-class hero, exactly."

A young woman dressed like a waitress in a white blouse and tight black skirt slipped in with a tray. On it were perched china teacups, a white pot, a sugar bowl and a carton of milk. Macdonald thanked her, pushed a pile of forms out of the way and asked her to put the tray on his desk. She did as he said, smiled at Winter and left the room.

"Do all Swedish inspectors dress like you?" Macdonald asked, raising a cup in Winter's direction.

"Only when they're on the road."

"In England we come as we are, and that's probably the best idea if you work this area. This station is perfectly located. As you see, we don't go out of our way to make our presence known. We're by ourselves here, out of sight, and we come back as fast as possible after a hard day. This is where all the computers are, where we do our thinking and chew things over with each other."

"And answer the phones."

With these words the phone on the desk began to ring. Macdonald lifted the receiver, mumbled for half a minute and hung up. "The Hilliers can see us tomorrow."

"That's good."

"That remains to be seen."

"Can you describe the area you work—the southeast quadrant of London? Is there a general tenor to the place?"

"No, except that the farther you get from London, the more pleasant it is. Less crime, more attractive buildings, nicer people. It's not so bad in Croydon. There's a big town center here that's rolling in money, but the poor neighborhoods have quite a bit of trouble. It's even worse to the north: Brixton, Peckham. Lots of crime, little or no money, a large ethnic population that has never been given a chance."

"Hmm."

"I've been a policeman for all these years down here on the south side," Macdonald said. "If there's one thing I know for sure, it's that those who had a little chance before don't have a hope in hell now."

"And that means plenty of crime."

"It means plenty of crime, and it means plenty of silence. The way it used to be, the rich were a trifle discreet. Now there's nothing but open contempt. Those who have something to protect are arrogant and make it clear they don't give a damn about anyone else. I see it every day."

"But poverty isn't the only problem, is it? Or the color of people's skin?"

"How so?"

"It's the pervasive sense of alienation. Of being ostracized in every conceivable way."

"Right."

"We're starting to see signs of that in Sweden too."

"You must be kidding."

"No."

"Sweden? God forbid."

"Is it the cynical policeman in you that's talking?"

"I don't know." Macdonald slurped a mouthful of tea.

"But it's not only the fact of being a policeman that makes you cynical," Winter said. "It's this feeling that you're all alone, that nobody else gives a shit. You discover that people lie so damn much, all the time. Not only the suspect, the criminal whose testimony doesn't hold up against the evidence, but others too."

"And the real culprits, whoever they are, go free. Those are the kinds of thoughts that can really make you cynical."

"And all the other horrible stuff."

"What?"

"So much exposure to violence. That makes you cynical too."

"Yes."

"The most important thing is the daily contact with people. That's what keeps us going."

"We do everything we can to sustain that," Macdonald said. "If somebody has been murdered or has simply disappeared, we put up notices everywhere and we get thousands of calls from people who have seen something and want to help. As you can hear right this minute." He gestured toward the corridor. Phones were ringing, softly but relentlessly, in room after room. "We had a case a few years ago. A boy, twelve years old at most, was brutally raped and murdered, and we were all stunned. What the hell were we dealing with here? What kind of evil was on the loose?"

"I know the feeling."

"We got a call from a guy who said he'd delivered newspapers when he was a kid in the neighborhood where the boy was found. A man lives there who used to molest me, he said. There were plenty of stories about him, but nobody did anything. I'm thirty-two now, he said, but I've never forgotten that pig."

"Did he know the man's name?"

"He knew his name and address, and sure enough the man lived there and he wasn't an old codger exactly. All we had to do was ask him a few questions and he crumbled."

"That doesn't happen so often."

"No, but it's not simply a question of luck, not if you look at the big picture. If we hadn't made ourselves available, or if people hadn't known we were here, even if we're a bit out of the way, that guy would never have called."

"We're waiting for a phone call like that now." Winter had forgotten to drink his tea.

"Do you want a refill?"

"No thanks."

"It's no hassle."

"Not for you, no."

Macdonald looked at him and rubbed his knee.

"How's the soccer injury?"

"It'll be gone by Sunday and back on Monday. Do you want to get in on it?"

"In on what?"

"A match with the pub team?"

"Where?"

"Out toward Farningham. It's in Kent, fifteen miles down the road. That's where I live. The pub is nearby."

"If I'm still here."

"You don't have to worry about that."

Winter wanted to change the subject. "I guess I'd like another cup after all."

Macdonald got up and went out to the corridor. After a while he came back carrying the tray. "Our maidservant is busy at the computer."

"So the son had to do it."

"What?"

"*The Son of a Servant*. It's an autobiographical novel by Sweden's most famous author."

"August Strindberg."

"Who's Mr. Know-It-All now?"

"I have the translation at home. It's on my list of things to do after I retire."

Winter tasted the tea. It was strong and sweet. The sun warmed his back through the closed window. Macdonald had lines in his face, and they weren't from the blinds anymore. His clean-shaven skin had a bluish tint, and his black eyebrows were almost joined. Next to the stacks of paper on his desk lay a pair of frameless reading glasses. When Macdonald fiddled with them, they disappeared in his hand as if they had been made for children.

He must be a terror on the soccer field, Winter thought. Worse than me. "Do you have any witnesses who saw that man with Per?" he asked.

Macdonald let go of his glasses. The lines in his face deepened as he leaned forward. "Yes, several. And the best one thinks that the man looks like me."

"Like you?"

"That's what he said."

"What did he mean?"

"As far as I could tell, he meant that the guy was big and had long, dark hair."

"That's what we came up with too. Big and dark."

"He could be one of Per's acquaintances and nothing more."

"No, I don't think so."

"No?"

"Do you really believe that?" Winter asked.

"No."

"The man who walked through the park with Per is the guy we're looking for. Surely he would have contacted you otherwise."

"There are other possible reasons—if he's a closet gay, for example."

"You mean he's afraid that his family will find out?"

Macdonald shrugged. "A few people have turned up of their own accord, but they're the usual crackpots."

"I saw the notices you put up."

He couldn't have missed the notices when Macdonald dropped him off at Clapham High Street Station the night before—the photo of Per they'd sent from Sweden, information about the murder, the scene of the crime, the park, the facts that the investigators wanted the public to know. An appeal to call the police if you had seen anything at all.

The notices looked like zany posters, a parody out of a horror movie. Winter had felt a wave of nausea, which caught him by surprise.

Frayed at the bottom, they had already acquired a pale veneer that said everything was too late. They were stapled to three different poles and were in identical condition, apparently put up at the same time. The trains came and went, and some people read the notices and called the Thornton Heath police, but that hadn't yet led to any breakthroughs.

When he'd reached Victoria Station, the lower right corner of a notice flapped from a pole by the exit as the trains passed—as if someone had torn off a map of London and left only the southeast side.

It was an odd coincidence, like an encrypted message meant for Winter's eyes.

29

BERGENHEM WAITED OUTSIDE IN THE SHADOWS. MEN WALKED in and out. A bolt of electricity darted into the night every time the door opened.

The trains rattled behind him, their hydraulics sighing after a long day out on the rails. The freight yard was lit by a handful of bulbs attached to posts that stuck up between the walls. A train pulled in somewhere and broke the somnolent mood. He heard a shout and a voice that answered, the squeaking of brakes followed by the impact of something blunt and heavy.

The door opened again and she came out. She was alone. She hurried onto Odinsgatan Street toward Polhemsplatsen. He followed her. After waiting for a streetcar to pass, she crossed the street and the parking lot. He felt the cold air rising from Fattighusån Canal as they walked over the bridge. She continued along the moat. Nobody was coming from the opposite direction.

The Horticultural Society's park was on the other side of the moat. She didn't look around, and he had to quicken his pace not to lose sight of her when she turned the corner at Bastionsplatsen Square.

When he caught up, he saw her figure illuminated by the Kungsportsplatsen Square streetlights. She raised her arm at a right angle, apparently glancing at her watch. She crossed Kungsport Bridge, passed the Storan Theater and waited for the light to change at Nya Allén Street. He checked the time. It was just after midnight. He walked toward the crossing and waited with a group of four or five others. There was a lot of traffic for this time of night.

She clung to the shadows of the Vasastaden district. The buildings blocked out the sky. He followed her around the Röhsska Museum, but suddenly she was gone.

He turned and looked back. None of the cafés were open. He spotted a restaurant down the street, but she couldn't have gotten that far. And it was obviously closed, lit up only by a fluorescent bulb above the menu on the wall next to the window.

A car came to a halt fifteen yards away. Its inside lights went on when one door opened. Bergenhem glimpsed a blurred face above the steering wheel. The passenger got out, bowed his head through the open door and said something. Finally he closed the door and the car sped downhill toward Vasagatan Street. Turning around, the man seemed to disappear straight through the wall of the building before him.

What the hell? Bergenhem walked over and saw a door in the base of an old manor house. It was coarse as stone, like the stairs to an earth cellar. It has to open inward, he thought. He hadn't seen a light when the man went in. There weren't any signs, nothing to attract the attention of a passerby. No sound came through the wall.

Now he noticed a button on the right, almost indistinguishable from the hinge. He pushed it and waited. He pressed a second time and the door opened.

"Can I help you?"

He saw the outlines of a face and a body in the dim light from a stairwell ahead.

"Is there something I can do for you?" the voice repeated.

"Are you closed?"

"What?"

"Isn't there a show tonight?" Are we going to stand here all night and ask each other questions? he wondered. She definitely went in here. Why didn't Bolger say anything about this joint? Did it just open? Questions and more questions. "One of your clients mentioned this place. He said nonmembers were welcome."

"Nonmembers of what?"

"Hell if I know. Can I come in and see the show, or is it some big secret?"

The figure stepped out onto the sidewalk and Bergenhem finally saw a face.

"What do you want, anyway?"

"I just want to have a little fun."

"Are you drunk? We don't let drunks in here."

"I don't drink."

Another man appeared to Bergenhem's right and the bouncer nodded to him. He walked inside. Bergenhem watched him go down the stairs.

"Okay," the bouncer said, "but I'm going to keep an eye on you."

"What for?"

"Our customers are all respectable citizens," he answered, as if Bergenhem had shown up wearing a cardboard box.

"May I come in now?"

The bouncer looked around and took a step to the side so Bergenhem could squeeze by. He followed behind and closed the door. The light from the stairway grew brighter. Bergenhem heard soft music. It sounded Middle Eastern, or maybe the twists and turns of the cellar had distorted the tones.

A woman sat at the foot of the stairs behind an old-fashioned cash box. "Two hundred fifty crowns," she said.

He paid and hung his jacket on a plastic hanger in a little nook to the right.

"The cover charge includes one drink," the woman said, handing him a tag, also plastic.

———

She was dancing on one of the tables, and he sat down there. Her ribs were visible, but she was beautiful. Her breasts were bigger than he remembered from Riverside. She seemed to recognize him.

Soul music was playing, but it wasn't Tina Turner. Her movements followed the music upward. There were dark crescents under her black eyes.

The other two men at the table drank and watched. Women were also dancing on three other tables. Bergenhem felt like he was sitting in a cave.

He smelled alcohol, sweat, perfume, anxiety, fear and something inside himself that he couldn't identify. It was what had brought him here.

He didn't know where the investigation ended and this other quest began.

She stopped dancing as soon as the music died down, and her smile wilted to an even line. Suddenly she looked even more naked than before, as if the music had been her garment. He held out his hand and she gave a start.

"I just wanted to help you down," he said.

She looked at him and stretched out her arm, and he supported her as she stepped onto the chair. She left the table without saying anything or looking at him. One of the other men made a comment but Bergenhem didn't catch the words. Despite her high heels, she walked gracefully across the room and through a door behind the bar. The bouncer stood there looking at him. Bergenhem averted his eyes and sat back down.

He waited for a long time. A woman approached from the bar. She lit a cigarette, and he suddenly noticed a dank soreness in his throat from all the smoke in the room.

"Aren't you going to ask me to sit down?"

Bergenhem stood up and pulled out the chair next to him. "Please."

The other men at his table had gone over to the bar.

"You're allowed to buy me a drink," she said. She rested her chin on her right hand. Her wide face was hidden under the makeup, and her hair was blond.

Bergenhem didn't recognize her at first. "I didn't realize it was you," he said finally. "What do you want to drink?"

"This," she said, holding up the glass that a man from the bar had placed in front of her. "Obviously you don't know the routine here." She peered at him over the rim of her glass.

"How much does it cost? A thousand crowns?"

"Almost." She put her glass down. "I can dance for you in a private room if you want."

"No thanks."

"Isn't that what you're here for?"

"What?"

"Didn't you come for a private performance?"

"No."

"Then what do you want?"

"Want?"

"From me. What do you want from me?"

"From you? Nothing."

"Nothing? Don't you think I recognize you? I don't know how many times you've been down at Riverside now."

"Just a couple."

"I know your kind." She released a billow of smoke from her mouth and extinguished her cigarette in a cup on the table. "And I don't like it when people stalk me."

"Stalk you?"

"I saw you wait for me outside Riverside and follow me here."

Bergenhem drank his beer slowly.

"What do you want?" she pressed.

"Nothing, I told you."

She lit another cigarette. "I know you're a cop. Am I right?"

"Yes."

"I haven't done anything, and if you're trying to bust this joint, be my guest, but they'll open again in a few days."

"That's not why I'm here."

"It's not?"

"We're investigating a couple of murders." Or more, he thought.

She looked at him, smoking but not touching her drink. "I know."

"What?"

"You've been asking a bunch of questions at Riverside, haven't you?"

"Yes."

"They show movies here."

He held on to his glass, wishing he could lean toward her.

"It's no secret to our customers or people around town. But it's not the kind of thing you'll see at other places."

"What kind of movies?"

"BDSM. If you know what that is."

"Of course."

"It's not against the law."

He let that pass because he wasn't really sure.

"No child porn; otherwise I wouldn't work here."

"Where is it?"

"Where is what?"

"The screening room."

"Why do you ask?"

"I want to see it."

"It doesn't start until later, and I'll be gone by then."

"Why?"

"That's none of your business."

Sweat trickled down Bergenhem's back. He hoped it wasn't too obvious on his forehead. His groin chafed and his boxer shorts felt like sandpaper. He drank some more beer and saw that his hand was trembling. He could tell she had noticed it too.

"Do you even know what you're investigating?" she asked.

He put his glass down and wiped his lips with the back of his hand. "It was important for me to follow you, but not for the reason you think. We're trying to get a sense of what goes on at these clubs. If you're so much in the know, you understand why."

"There's something I want to tell you, but buy me another cocktail first. Otherwise I have to get up."

"Okay."

She must have made a sign that he missed, because the man from the bar brought her another glass and took away the old one, still untouched.

"You strike me as a nice guy, so I want to warn you about something," she said softly, her jaw clenched.

He watched her through the smoke from her cigarette.

"Both Riverside and this place seem peaceful enough, but looks are deceiving. They're strictly business and they'll smash anyone who pokes his nose in too far."

"Did anyone tell you to say this to me?"

"Believe whatever you want," she said, turning toward him and smiling for the sake of appearances.

It's like she's talking about something else, he thought. "What is it that I shouldn't poke my nose into?"

"You're a sweet boy. Stay away from me if you know what's good for you."

"What?"

"I don't know if you're having problems with your wife or what it is." She eyed his ring finger. "But I doubt that your boss is going to approve overtime for this little night shift of yours."

"I'm just doing my job."

"Am I your job?"

"No."

"Why are you sitting here talking to me, then?"

"I don't know. What's your name?"

She didn't answer.

When he crawled into bed, Martina shifted in her sleep, then glanced up at him and murmured that it must be late. He didn't respond, and she sank back into her deep breathing.

The smell of smoke lingered in his hair and the pores of his face. The roof of his mouth against his tongue was like the wall of a cave. Martina lay on her back, her belly like a little tent above her. He longed to put his hand on top of it but held back.

He heard the freezer rattle. Unable to sleep, he tried to concentrate on the night sounds in the air and walls.

He slipped out of bed and walked downstairs to the kitchen. Opening the refrigerator, he stood without closing the door and drank an entire carton of skim milk. It did nothing to quench his thirst. His gut was on fire. He poured a glass of orange juice. It tasted sweet and tangy after the milk.

What's with you? he thought.

"Can't you sleep?" Martina asked when he got back in bed.

"I'll be okay now."

"Mmm."

"Good night."

"Mmm." She was already half asleep.

He had scrubbed himself a second time with heavy-duty soap but the smell of smoke refused to go away. The scent of her perfume had made its way into the bedroom. It doesn't matter what her name is, he thought. What made you ask her that?

He listened to the gulls as they tore at the newspapers. It's like they're laughing at human folly, he thought. Every morning a helicopter division of gulls arrived at dawn from their base on the outskirts of the archipelago.

30

THEY WERE RIDING THE NORTHBOUND TRAIN. IT WAS EARLY afternoon, and nobody else was in their car. Winter saw someone jog across Wandsworth Common wearing shorts and a light sweatshirt that puffed out in the wind and flapped against his back. He thought he recognized the man from yesterday and from the morning train. Maybe he was a lunatic who ran back and forth hour after hour.

The Hilliers had changed their minds at the last minute. Winston couldn't handle talking to them. Maybe another day.

The south side was flashing by again. He had become a commuter. "When does Jamie's mother get back?" he asked, watching a station come and go.

"In two weeks," Macdonald answered.

"And you can't find his father?"

"No. That's quite common."

When they got off at Victoria Station, Winter pointed out the tattered notice. Macdonald tore it off and threw it in a trash container.

"Are you going to put up a new one?"

Macdonald shrugged. "Probably. Worn-out pictures are like worn-out memories—nothing to go by."

"There's a poet in you."

"The poet laureate of crime detection."

They took the underground to Green Park and made their way through the catacombs to the escalator. The daylight stunned their eyes.

"The Queen lives over there." Macdonald nodded toward the

park. "The humble servant of all her subjects, the Scots as well as the English."

"What about the Irish and the Welsh?"

"Them too."

They took a cab east, up Piccadilly and into Soho.

Frankie sat in his office by a blank computer screen.

"It crashed," he said after Macdonald had introduced him to Winter.

"Cheap crap," Macdonald said. "Didn't I tell you to steer clear of English hardware?"

"As if the Scottish were any better."

"No doubt about it."

"Give me an example."

"Macintosh."

"I've heard that one before. May I offer you some exclusive Caribbean tea?"

"Give me a break. Tea from the Caribbean? May as well make me some coffee grown in Sweden."

Frankie glanced over at Winter, who threw up his hands in disavowal. "I've asked around a little, as discreetly as I could."

Macdonald nodded.

"I was amazed at how low people can stoop."

"Cut out the hypocrisy."

"Here I am, walking the straight and narrow, and I ask myself every now and then what happened to all those customers who used to beat down my door."

Winter heard a shout in the hallway, a plea for help. Someone else laughed and said something he couldn't make out.

"I'm not talking about child porn or anything like that," Frankie continued.

"Stop with the crap," Macdonald said.

"I'm talking about outright torture."

"Torture?"

"Torture."

"What kind of torture?"

Frankie started to rock back and forth as if listening to music.

"Frankie," Macdonald pleaded.

"I don't want to talk about it anymore."

The back of Winter's head felt numb.

"Frankie," Macdonald said again.

"I'm just telling you what I heard, that somebody in London sells movies that contain torture scenes, and they're the real thing."

"Any names?"

"Forget it."

"You could be in danger here. Keep that in mind."

"I realize that. But that makes it even more important for me to ask questions. You've been around the block a few times, Steve. You know I can't reveal my sources to you and this pretty Swedish boy of yours. They don't know any more than I do, and they'd never breathe a word to you if they did."

"But you can't go back to your sources and ask more questions? Or start poking around somewhere else?"

"If we're going to do this, it will have to be my way."

Winter heard sounds all around him again, as if the world could no longer hold its breath.

"Believe me," Frankie said. "This isn't anything I want to see in my city or my industry. But people start getting nervous when the police barge in and disturb our peaceful lives, not to mention the lives of our law-abiding customers."

"And someone can die in the meantime," Macdonald said.

"That's less likely to happen if you let me take care of it."

"I need some cold facts by tomorrow."

"As soon as I can."

"Tomorrow." Macdonald turned to Winter. "Any questions, Erik?"

"These movies you were just talking about—they aren't shown in Soho theaters, I assume."

Frankie didn't answer.

"They're for private consumption," Winter said.

"That's correct."

"Just be careful."

"Thank you, O Great White Savior." Frankie's teeth sparkled. "Your assistance is humbly appreciated."

Macdonald saw the embarrassed look on Winter's face, but Frankie held his smile.

"How about some of that tea you mentioned?" Macdonald said.

"I have the Scottish kind, extract of dried oats."

"Yummy."

They separated at Piccadilly. Macdonald walked down to the underground and Winter looped back west past Charing Cross Road and continued half a block to 180 Shaftesbury Avenue, Ray's Jazz Shop. He'd been coming here since he was a teenager. If there was an album you couldn't find anywhere else, it would definitely be here.

Winter took in the walls, the old LP covers—dust, ink, brittle paper—a wispy, sweet-and-sour odor from the vinyl inside.

There were more CD racks than the last time he had been here, but the place was identical otherwise. The young black clerk behind the counter in the middle of the room put on an album. It was *New York Eye and Ear Control* again, sweeping back over him like an erotic memory.

He had also heard it in the walls of the hotel room where Per was killed. Not the kind of music you run across every day, he told the clerk.

"There aren't many copies left." The clerk straightened his dark glasses. "We sell them as fast as they come in."

"I seem to have lost mine."

"Then you're in luck."

"I'm here all the way from Sweden, and this is my reward."

"As far as I can remember, we've had only one other copy the past few weeks, and somebody else from Scandinavia snapped it up."

"Really?"

"It's hard to mistake the accent. I actually lived in Stockholm for a while, so I always recognize it straightaway. I had a girlfriend there." He smiled. "But it doesn't really show when you talk."

"That's because I'm a perfectionist," Winter said. It's because you're such a damn snob, he told himself.

"Sounds like you've come to the right place. Scandinavians are all in love with this album."

"Is that right?"

"That's what the other guy said, anyway."

"He did?"

"If a blue-eyed Scandinavian walks in, play it for him and you've got yourself a sale, he said."

"Interesting."

"Or he'll just come in and ask for it right off the bat, he said."

Winter decided to buy the album, plus the Julian Argüelles Quartet's latest, Django Bates's *Human Chain* and some other modern British jazz. The CDs became heavier as he carried them around the store.

31

WINTER HAD OPENED HIS POWERBOOK ON THE ROUND TABLE in the kitchenette and was leaning over it. The light was better by the window in the living room, but the table wasn't high enough. He had tried for fifteen minutes and decided he didn't want his back to permanently warp into the shape of a bow—a hazard of being tall and thirty-seven, he thought, listening to his tendons and ligaments crack as he stood up.

He summed up the day, his impressions. The city was exhausting, overwhelming in its heaviness. He had to let it die down in his brain before he could think about why he had come to London in the first place.

As he stared at the screen, he saw the faces of the victims. As long as he was able to do that, he could still accomplish something. After that there was nothing but fatigue. He drank his tea. London murmured from beyond the courtyard outside the window, but he had managed to narrow the city down to this suite on Knaresborough Place.

He had created a little diagram consisting of three poles, each of which represented a face. He added a brief account of the final minutes in each victim's life. He was thinking about Frankie—and his Swedish counterpart, Bolger—when the cell phone on the counter behind him rang.

"Winter."

"Are you in your hotel room?" It was Bolger.

"I'm in my suite."

"Alone?"

"Yes."

"Can you find your way around the city these days?"

"Some of my old hangouts are still here."

"I can't remember the last time I was there."

"Didn't you have an aunt in Manchester?"

"Bolton. Dad borrowed the first syllable of the name. No doubt you're on the prowl for rare jazz albums?"

"Of course."

"Do you know which stores to go to?"

"Ray's Jazz Shop, and a new little place in Soho."

"Back when I used to go to London, there was a good store in Brixton called Red Records."

"Brixton?"

"Yeah, give it a try."

Winter saved his document. The screen stood out more distinctly as the dusk descended on the back courtyard. Darkness slowly invaded the suite, starting in the far corner where Winter sat.

He heard the clatter of suitcases going up the stairs outside his door.

"I didn't want to bother you," Bolger said finally, "but I wasn't sure when you'd be coming back."

"I don't really know either. Maybe in a couple of days."

"There's something I wanted to talk to you about."

"Ringmar is running the investigation while I'm gone."

"I don't know Ringmar, and you can think of this as a call from an old friend if you prefer it that way."

Winter reached back and turned on the light over the stove. The splash guard and fluorescent lamp were reflected in the computer screen.

"Erik?"

"I'm still here."

"Somebody called me and was a little concerned."

"Uh-huh?"

"It was about that young inspector of yours."

"Bergenhem?"

"The guy you sent to get some leads from me. Bergenhem, that's the one."

"Somebody called you?"

"An old contact. He thought your guy was being too nosy."

"Too nosy about what?"

"Too nosy about a legal, well-run business."

"The whole idea is for him to be nosy. That's his job, for Christ's sake."

"Customers have started to ask questions about what's going on, why the police keep showing up and that kind of thing."

"This is a murder investigation, not a high school prom."

"I know."

"Bergenhem wasn't in uniform, was he?"

"Not as far as I know."

"He's got a stubborn streak, and that's fine with me as long as he makes some progress. I can't worry about the sensitivities of customers at a strip joint."

"It seems that Bergenhem has gotten a little too interested."

"What do you mean by that?"

"He's been following one of the women around."

"Women?"

"One of the strippers."

"Who says that? The customers or whatever you call them? Or your old contact, whoever the hell he is?"

"I'm just repeating what I've heard."

"Why are you telling me all this, Johan?"

"Dammit, Erik, you know me. I'm the one who put him onto this trail. Of course I'm going to be nervous."

"Bergenhem knows what he's doing. If he's hanging out with one of the women, there's a reason for it."

"There usually is."

"That's not what I'm talking about."

"I think the kid has lost his bearings."

"He knows what he's doing."

"He may be wandering into dangerous territory."

"Wasn't it a legal, well-run business we were talking about here?"

"Yes, but . . ."

"Then he's in safe territory, right?"

"You know what I'm getting at. If there's any truth to your suspicions, it's plenty dangerous."

Danger is the name of the game, Winter thought. Bergenhem's job is to get as close to danger as he can and then pull back. That's exactly what he's going to do, and it will make him a top-notch inspector. "I appreciate your keeping an eye on all this," he said.

"That's an overstatement. I'm just telling you what's come my way."

"Let me know if you hear anything more."

"You do realize this is serious business?"

"Yes, I understand."

"So what's on the docket for tonight?"

Winter looked at the diagram. Would it be his night out? Or would he spend it dozing in front of the TV? He hadn't turned it on once. He checked his watch. The news was starting just about now.

"Aren't the London police wining and dining you?" Bolger asked.

"I needed to be alone tonight."

"So what are you going to do?"

"I'll go out and grab a bite to eat in a little while."

"An Indian restaurant?"

"Something nearby. Chinese, I think. There's an old place I like on one of the side streets."

Winter watched the news. The picture quality was just as impersonal as in Sweden, flat and depthless as if the color had been added as an afterthought.

The local news featured the same garrulous reporters, a windblown face at the scene of a crime or an accident or a conference. An outdoor market had been robbed; a car was upside down in the river; MPs were shouting at each other again; Princess Diana was on her way out of Kensington Palace, not far from where Winter sat with his feet on the table in a hotel suite lit up by a television screen.

The skies would be clear for the rest of the week. The weather girl's face shone as brightly as the sun on the chart behind her.

Nothing about a murder. What did you expect? Winter asked himself. A big photo of Per? A tattered notice like the one on the pillar that holds up the ceiling at Victoria Station?

His cell phone rang again. He was about to let the caller leave a message but remembered Macdonald. "Winter."

"With a simple tulip on your special day . . ."

"Thanks for the musical greeting, Mom."

"Happy birthday!"

"Nice of you to call."

"What kind of mother wouldn't call her son on his birthday?"

"I appreciate it."

"Dad sends his best."

"Tell him I'm thinking of him too."

"What's the weather like in that horrid city?"

"Sunny."

"That's a lie. You can't fool your old mother."

A new program had started. Two people were poking fun at each other on a stage. It was hard to hear what they were saying because the audience was laughing so loudly. Winter picked up the remote and turned down the volume.

"It was a beautiful day here," she said.

"Naturally."

"Have you solved the case yet?"

"Almost."

Winter heard another voice close to the phone.

"Dad wants to know if you bought any cigars."

"Yep."

"Your sister is dying to hear from you."

"I know."

"I talked to her the other day, Erik. She's having a rough time."

"I realize that."

"So how are you celebrating your big day?"

"I'm drinking tea and making some notes on my laptop here in the hotel."

"That must be dreadfully boring."

"It's the life I chose for myself."

"Are you staying at the same place?"

"Yes, the same old place."

"Then you have a suite, at least."

"Absolutely."

"The traffic is horrible on that street."

"I'm expecting a call from the London investigator, Mom."

"On your birthday?"

"That's what I'm here for—to work."

"You need to relax once in a while too, Erik."

He heard water gushing through the pipes behind the wall. Someone in the suite above him had flushed the toilet. It's like they've been eavesdropping on the phone call and they're trying to hint that I've talked long enough, he mused. "Thanks for calling, Mom."

"Have some fun tonight, dear."

"Bye." Winter hung up.

He picked up the remote again and turned up the sound. The stage show was still on. There were more people now—two couples competing to put soccer uniforms on their partners while keeping a ball inside their own jerseys. The contestants were laughing like lunatics. Nor were the audience and host to be outdone. The longer Winter watched, the louder he laughed too, as if he'd been waiting forever for this chance. Tears ran down his cheeks and his gut ached. Your face muscles are out of shape, he thought.

He went over to the refrigerator and took out a bottle of Cava that he had bought at the Oddbins liquor store on Marloes Road, just a few blocks away. The bottle popped when he opened it. He poured a little of the sparkling wine into a regular drinking glass.

It's pretty seedy but it's the life you chose for yourself, he thought, the bubbles rolling down his tongue.

He carried the glass back toward the couch, but the computer screen glared at him like a stern reminder of the world's evil. He walked by the couch and opened the window. The night was yellow and grimy from the light behind the buildings. He heard the echo of traffic on Cromwell Road, then a siren that howled to the north and stopped abruptly.

The city's own riff, he thought. The sky was a long stretch of indigo when he looked up. A night for jazz. He lit a Cocinero Liga Especial cigar and savored it—the leather, the dried tropical fruit—and then exhaled through the open window into the night air. The smoke swirled upward.

Just before it vanished, he saw the face of a murderer. The features were indistinct but their cold-bloodedness was plain.

You've got to get that idea out of your head, Winter told himself. Murderers may have learned to shut themselves off, to push away what they can't handle, but there's always a wellspring of feeling deep down. That's where we've got to look. All we do is reinforce our own preconceptions when we chase the evidence that mounts afterward, rather than diving down and exploring the murderer's first intent.

Murder is traumatic for everyone involved. It's got to be that way. Otherwise we're doomed, he thought, taking another puff on the cigar.

A face appeared before him again, clearer than before, but it dissipated with the wisps of smoke. Memories, he thought. There's a memory somewhere that can help you with this case. What is it? Something in your own past? Lost memories? What had Macdonald said? Worn-out pictures are like worn-out memories. Someone else told you something too. Memory, he thought, clutching his forehead. You have an answer, but that's not good enough. You're not even capable of asking a real question.

He walked over to the table and poured another glass of Cava. It tasted like carbonated vinegar. I won't be able to live with myself if we don't solve this, he thought, shoving the glass aside. He turned off the television and dialed Ringmar's home number.

"Hello."

"It's Erik."

"Möllerström's computer crashed yesterday."

"What happened then?"

"What happened then was that he had the chance to show us how far he's gotten and how clever he was to back everything up all over the place."

"His big day, in other words."

"But it was a warning sign. Our computers are literally bursting with extraneous information."

"You don't have to tell me that."

"We're under enormous pressure now, especially when you're not around to talk to the British reporters who keep descending on Gothenburg."

"I've managed to avoid them so far over here, but Macdonald says my luck is about to run out."

"What's he like?"

"Smart."

"Are you getting anywhere?"

"I think so. I'm going to question a few witnesses tomorrow."

"We've got some new witnesses ourselves."

"Anything interesting?"

"Nothing we've had the chance to confirm," Ringmar said, "but one of them seems worth following up on."

The cigar went out in Winter's hand and he placed it in an ashtray. The window scraped shut of its own accord.

"The underworld is rising to the occasion," Ringmar said.

"We never stop working with them, do we?"

"We got a letter today from a professional burglar who claims that he broke into an apartment and found some bloody clothes."

"That's a new one for you."

"Hmm."

"How many apartments in Gothenburg have had bloody clothes in them the past few weeks?"

"Don't ask me."

"A lot."

"This guy doesn't seem to be a nutcase."

"Is that all he had?"

"He says that it was shortly after the murder."

"Which one?"

"Geoff."

"Did he mention the address of the apartment?"

"Yes."

"Nothing about who lives there?"

"Only that it's a man."

"Anything else?"

"No."

"Why are we wasting our time talking about this, then?"

"I don't know. Maybe because there's something about the tone of the letter. Or just because it's from a burglar. He seems to have a sixth sense about what he saw."

"Okay."

"We'll put this aside for now, but I'm keeping it in the back of my mind."

"You can discreetly check out the apartment and tenant when you get around to it."

"I sent Halders out there."

"I said discreetly."

Ringmar chuckled.

"How's Bergenhem doing?"

"What?"

"Lars. Has he found anything?"

"I don't know, to tell you the truth. He seems determined to learn everything he can about the porn industry."

"Have a little chat with him."

"I doubt that he'd be into it. As far as I can tell, he thinks you've dispatched him on a special mission from God or something."

"Tell him that I want him to report to you from now on."

"Okay."

"Bye."

Winter hung up and headed for the shower. Afterward he toweled off and dressed, letting his tie hang loose. He slipped into a pair of casual shoes and walked a block to Crystal Palace. The food was delicious, as always. He brooded some more about memory.

32

HE RAN INTO THE OWNER'S SON ON THE STAIRWAY ALMOST
every time he left his room or returned to the hotel. The guy was mentally disabled, no doubt about it. Hour after hour, he climbed the winding stairs all the way to the seventh floor, turned around and walked
down again, continuing through the lobby and out to the sidewalk.

The guy gave a peculiar smile, his face breaking up and his eyes turning inward. He always walked by him as fast as he could.

If he listened from his room, he could hear the guy's steps like clock-
work.

He had never seen the owner except when he first checked in. The
lobby was always empty and nobody was ever behind the front desk.
You could ring the bell for the clerk, but he had everything he needed.

He had already scouted out the two Greek restaurants across from
the hotel, so he decided to walk south on a new street. He had never
seen such awesome houses, at least a hundred years old with ivy growing up the sides. He passed a few people washing their cars. The street
was long, and it took him a while to get to Grove House Tavern, where
he sat down at one of the three tables on the sidewalk. The sun made
its way over the rooftops on the other side of the street and shone in his
face. He bought a glass of beer in the pub and went back outside.

The other tables were empty. Three men, all white, sat inside. This
was a typical white street. You could tell by the houses.

Which was sort of odd, because the street he was staying on and
the main thoroughfare that led to downtown Brixton got blacker and

blacker the farther you went. It was like coming home, he thought. Things were different here. He sat all alone, surrounded by white people.

A black guy at a white pub.

How strange it had been to feel white among all the black people and yet blend in with the crowd. It was never like that in Sweden. Christian Jaegerberg was a white name but that's not what he looked like.

The trees along the street shrouded him in silence. He patted the CDs in his jacket pocket.

There had been a white customer at Red Records when Christian was there. The guy had heard him talking to the clerk. He was tall, maybe thirty-five or forty years old.

"Are you Swedish?" the guy asked, walking out at the same time as Christian.

"Does my accent give me away?"

"You sure surprised the clerk."

"I guess I don't look like a typical Swede."

"No doubt he's seen stranger things." The guy laughed.

Christian nodded as if he'd seen stranger things too.

They stood on Brixton Road across from the underground station.

"Did you find anything good in there?" the guy asked.

"Too much."

"*Somma I?*"

Christian looked at him. "How did you know that?"

He threw out his arms and Christian got the impression he was flexing his muscles—a bodybuilder on his day off. "You looked like you kept up with the music scene."

"That's why I'm here," Christian said.

"I figured as much."

Christian started walking toward the pedestrian crossing on the left.

"I come to London every once in a while to stock up on music," the guy said.

"Stock up?"

"I have a distributorship in Scandinavia."

"For reggae?"

"If it's black music, we carry it."

"So here you are."

"This is the place."

"What did you buy this time?" Christian wondered if he knew his stuff.

The distributor rattled off the best there was.

"Do you buy a lot of music?" Christian asked.

"Yep, but I hardly take anything back home."

"Gothenburg?"

"It's a hard dialect to disguise, isn't it?"

"But you don't have a store or anything?"

"Just what I distribute in Scandinavia, and a little bit in northern Europe. I have a few samples I could show you, or even give you just to see what you think of them, but there's not enough time."

"Too bad."

"I'm supposed to be at a meeting in half an hour."

"I understand."

"It was a pleasure meeting you. Good luck with your musical adventures."

"Thanks."

"And your Swedish accent."

Christian's face felt colder, as if the sun had gone behind the clouds, and he opened his eyes. Somebody was standing directly in front of him. He waited until his pupils readjusted to the light and saw that it was the distributor.

"I thought you looked familiar."

"Hi," Christian said.

"It's a small world." The distributor moved to one side.

Now the sun was in Christian's face again. He squinted, then cupped one hand over his eyes. The distributor's features were obscured by the shade. His teeth glistened and it looked like he was smiling.

"One of my contacts lives on this street. An honest-to-goodness Jamaican. Up by the hospital—have you seen it? The biggest one in south London."

"No, I haven't," Christian answered. "I didn't think any black people lived around here."

"It's a strange part of town—like a chessboard, you might say."

"Uh-huh."

"I'm on my way to see another guy down on Coldharbour Lane, and he's white." The distributor's teeth flashed again. "I'd ask you to come along, but he doesn't like to have more than one guest at a time."

"That's okay."

"I think I can squeeze in a quick beer. Do you want another one?"

"Sure."

The distributor went into the pub. The sun was behind a chimney on the other side of the street, lighting it up like a torch. An ambulance passed and Christian remembered the hospital up on the hill, or wherever it was.

A woman and a man came from the direction of his hotel and sat down at the next table. After a few minutes, the man got up and walked inside. The woman stared at the chimney, now surrounded by a halo of sunlight. The distributor came out carrying two pints of beer with foam running down the sides. Christian felt the cold glass in the palm of his hand. He put it down and reached for the wallet in the inside pocket of his jacket.

"It's on me," the distributor said.

"Okay, thanks."

"So tell me about your favorite CDs."

Christian gave him a quick rundown.

"Brilliant. I've got to remember this." Taking out a pen and a small notebook, he asked Christian to repeat a few of the titles. "A whiz like you could come in handy," he said.

"I don't know about that."

The woman's companion stepped back out of the pub with a glass of beer and something that could have been wine. He sat down across from her.

Christian heard her say that they had left home too late and missed the sunshine.

"At least it's warm," the man said. "I don't ever remember it being so nice this early in the year."

"I've really got to go," the distributor said.

"Okay."

He stood up. "Are you staying nearby?" he asked.

"It's not too far," Christian said.

"Stop me if I'm being pushy, but I was wondering if you could do me a favor."

"Me?"

The distributor took a stack of CDs out of his briefcase. There must have been at least eight of them. He sat back down. "I'm meeting with one of my other contacts tomorrow, and we're going to discuss these. I was planning to listen to them tonight. Maybe it's not so important, but he wants his customers to know what they're getting. I have to be able to say something about them."

It was colder now. The couple at the next table took their glasses and went inside.

"I have a little lady here in London who needs her man, if you know what I mean."

"I think so."

"You could listen to them for me."

"Sure, but . . ."

"And give me your expert opinion."

"Hmm."

"I might have time to come by and pick them up later tonight, but my lady friend will be with me, so it would be better if you could leave them at the front desk."

"But then you won't know what I thought of them."

"Damn, how stupid of me."

"You must have that chick on your mind."

"Yeah, and then it's not exactly the thing between your shoulders that you think with." The distributor laughed.

"No."

"If I put off my meeting for one day, I can stop by for a few minutes tomorrow night and go through the CDs with you."

"I probably won't be able to tell you anything you don't already know," Christian said.

"The CDs are yours, that goes without saying. You can keep all of them."

"What time will you come by?"

The distributor took out his notebook again. "I have a dinner date at eight, so I could come right after that. Is eleven too late?"

"No, that's fine."

"Are you sure?"

"No problem."

"My friend might be with me, but she can sit in the corner while we talk."

"Okay."

"Here's my cell number in case something comes up." The distributor tore a page out of his notebook and jotted something down. "Shit, I forgot that my phone doesn't work in London for some crazy reason." He put the piece of paper in his pocket. "I don't remember the number of my hotel, but I'll call and leave it at the front desk of your place when I get back."

"Sounds good."

"Now I'm really late."

Christian felt a little dizzy from the two beers. He was starting to like this guy. A little speedy, maybe, but businessmen were like that.

The distributor was on his feet. "Just one more detail."

"What?"

"You'll have to tell me where you're staying."

33

THEY HAD SEEN EACH OTHER THREE TIMES AFTER THEIR CON-versation at the club in the Vasastaden district.

Bergenhem had turned into two people, or maybe three, each with a conscience that bumped up against the others like ice floes.

When he was at home with Martina, he couldn't understand what he saw in Marianne. When he put his hand on her belly and felt the baby kick, he hated the other person who was also him.

She called herself Angel when she danced. A pair of small wings were attached to her shoulder blades. They were white and glittered like fish scales. Everything—her name and costume, if you could call it that—went perfectly with the sleaziness all around her. He couldn't think of another way to describe it—everything was sullied, like the world seen through a dirty car window.

The third person in him was the policeman. Somewhere in the dimly lit underground chambers, that person disappeared. So he got together with Marianne elsewhere. That's what he would say if anyone asked, but nobody asked except him. He had also seen a question mark in Martina's eyes, as if she knew, and realized that he knew that she knew.

He was on his way to Marianne's place. She lived on a boat at Gullbergskajen Wharf. He hadn't believed her at first, but she did.

It was an old fishing vessel that had outlived its usefulness, surrounded by others.

People in Gothenburg called it the Wharf of Dreams. He had heard the name all his life but never made it out there. An odd way to experience it for the first time, he thought.

It was best in the summer, she had said. The boats that still had any life in them put out to Älvsborg Fortress and back, the only time they sailed all year. It was something of a competition.

She had called it the Regatta of Shattered Illusions.

"You haven't told me much about your life," Bergenhem said after she had poured the coffee.

"This is unbelievable."

"What?"

"I can't figure out why I'm sitting here talking to you."

He listened for some kind of noise outdoors, like water lapping against the side of the boat, but they were encircled by silence.

"You're taking advantage of me," she said.

"That's not true."

"Then why are you here?"

"Because I *want* to be here."

"Everybody takes advantage of someone."

"Is that what your life has been like?"

"I don't want to talk about it."

"How long have you had the boat?"

"Years and years."

"Do you own it?"

"Yes."

"Do you know any of the others who live here?"

"What do you think?"

He drank his coffee and heard a motorboat hum out on the river.

"Do you hear your buddies?" she asked.

"What?"

"It's the marine police making their rounds. You never know what you might happen to find, right?"

"They might happen to find me."

"What would they say then?"

"They don't know who I am."

"Just like me. I don't know who you are."

"And I don't know who you are."

"Is that why you're here?"

"Yes."

"It's insane."

"You don't have any more information about those movies, do you?" he asked hastily, switching to another role.

"No."

"Nothing about the hidden part of the industry or whatever you call it?"

"No," she said again, but he heard a hint of something else.

"Are you afraid?"

"What do I have to be afraid of?"

"Is it dangerous to talk about?"

"The dangerous thing is for us to see each other."

"What do you know?"

She shook her head, like she was tossing his questions overboard. "Do you really think nobody knows you're seeing me? Someone might even have followed you here to check out what you're up to."

"You're right."

"Is that what you're hoping for?"

"I'm not sure."

"You want to make somebody slip up. And that's what you're using me for."

"That's not true."

"Yes it is."

"I wouldn't be sitting here if you had told me straight out that you never wanted to see me again."

"That's exactly what I said."

"Not enough times." He smiled.

She seemed to be thinking about something they had discussed earlier. She chewed on her lower lip—he'd never seen anyone do that before.

She lit a cigarette and opened one of the portholes. Her eyes were dark and fathomless in the dim artificial light when she raised her chin to exhale the smoke. Her hand shook, but that could have been from the damp chill outside.

She inhaled again and her whole body trembled. It's like she's sucking on an icicle, Bergenhem thought. Her skin is blue and her hands must be colder than snow.

"I want you to leave," she said.

She's afraid, he thought. She knows something horrible has happened and can happen again. She might have a name or an incident, or something somebody said, but that's all. And that's what scares her.

How did she find it out? What is it? Who? Is this bringing you any closer to what you're looking for? Or is it just wishful thinking? Or do you want her to be afraid of something she's heard so you can justify coming here?

"Give me some time to think about it," she said.

"What?"

"I need some time to think. Leave me alone now, for Chrissake."

Bergenhem dialed Bolger's number and left a message.

Bolger had given him the names of a couple of contacts, both of whom seemed slightly amused when he showed up, as though he were a welcome break from their humdrum lives.

He felt like a derailed train. He thought about Marianne, then Martina. It's none of her damn business what I do, he thought. This is my job.

He was hoping Bolger could give him some advice. Winter was an old friend of his and seemed to trust him. The occasional sarcastic comment Bolger made about Winter left little doubt that they went way back.

"Mr. Supercop," Bolger had called him a couple of days before.

"He's good," Bergenhem had said.

"He's always been like that. The world revolves around your boss. He had a friend named Mats who died this winter, and he was my friend too."

"And?"

"Erik grieves like he's the only one who ever lost anybody. He claims everything for himself."

Bergenhem didn't know what to say. But he sensed he'd been entrusted with a confidence and he relished the feeling.

"That's just one example," Bolger had gone on, recounting details about the city when they were growing up.

"Did you live near each other?"

"No."

"But you hung out together."

"In our midteens. Earlier, maybe."

"It's so hard to keep track of everything," Bergenhem had said. "It all goes by so fast, and when you try to think back to the way it was, you don't remember, or else you remember wrong."

Bolger had said something he didn't catch.

Bergenhem had asked him to repeat it.

"Skip it," Bolger had said.

34

"WE DON'T DO ANYTHING FOR BLACK PEOPLE ANYMORE," ADDAE
Sawyerr said. "All the employment subsidies are gone."

Sawyerr ran a consulting firm from an office above the Brixton Road
Pizza Hut, where Winter had met him. He'd invited Winter upstairs
to chat.

"But blacks aren't the only ones who live here," Winter said.

"We're in the majority." Sawyerr had come to London from Ghana
many years earlier. "But whites hang around the street corners too."

"You mentioned that downstairs."

"I can see them from this window. Come and look."

Winter went and stood beside him. Sawyerr was on his toes and
Winter had to crouch down.

"There are always a few of them outside Red Records, right across
the street," Sawyerr said. "It's one of the new places."

"I'm planning to go there next."

"They won't tell you anything in there."

"Then I'll just have to listen to some jazz."

"Nobody reveals anything in Brixton."

"People are afraid everywhere."

"Maybe so."

"Show me somebody who has the guts to tell you what they know,"
Winter said.

Sawyerr shrugged. He was talking about his world, in his way.
"There's terrific potential around here, with all the knowledge and skills
people have, but little of it ever gets used. This is Europe's biggest center

for black culture. We should be bringing others here to see and experience it."

Winter said good-bye and walked down the creaky steps. The smell of strong spices and disinfectants was everywhere. Lysol, Winter thought.

Earlier, he had wandered among the arcades in the food market, the largest in Europe for Africans and Caribbeans. The odor of animal flesh filled his nostrils; the floor was greasy and slippery with blood and guts. This is the real soul food, he thought: cow's feet, goat's and pig's intestines, hairy clumps of bull's testicles, mangoes, okra, chili peppers.

Now he handed a photo of Per Malmström to the clerk at Red Records.

"So many tourists come into this place," the clerk said.

"He might have been with someone else."

The clerk looked at the photo and shook his head. "I really couldn't tell you. We're the center of the world again. We get customers from all over."

"Lots of whites?"

"Just look around. What do you see?"

That afternoon, they drove over to talk with the Hilliers. Winter thought he was getting to know the city landscape, but maybe it was just because all the buildings looked so much alike.

"I was supposed to stay home today and catch up on unread reports," Macdonald said. "But you know how it is."

"Monotonous," Winter said.

"Monotonous isn't the word for it. When you've been on a case this long, you end up with a stack of papers a mile high. You can only take in a certain amount of information at a time. After that your instincts start to play tricks on you."

"Is that what you go on? Your instincts?"

Macdonald gave a short laugh that sounded like someone pushing an ice scraper across the roof of the car. "Isn't that why you came to London?" He glanced quickly at Winter. "Instinct might be our most important asset. That and intuition, deciphering the subtext of what people say, either right away or later on."

"Procedure takes us halfway there. After that, we need something more, something else."

"Sounds profound."

"But don't you have to be at the scene of the crime?"

"We have an on-duty system. Eight teams rotate for one week at a time. From Tuesday to Tuesday, starting at seven in the morning."

"Not ideal."

"No, but people can't always be available."

"You might be in the middle of another investigation too."

"Absolutely."

"But if you're on duty and another team takes over after four or five hours, you've spent all that time for nothing."

"Yeah, that happens occasionally."

"It's wasted."

"Not a good situation, I agree."

"Who's on duty this week?"

"Yours truly."

"And still nothing new has turned up."

The trains came and went outside the Hilliers' house. Nothing had changed. Winston sat on the couch and the room reeked of booze. Karen appeared with a tray. Winston took three glasses and filled them to the rim with whisky. Macdonald nodded in Winter's direction and they sat down.

Winston placed their glasses in front of them. "I have nothing more to say," he announced.

"We're doing all we can, and it's going to pay off eventually," Winter said.

"That's what he told me too." Winston pointed at Macdonald.

"He was right."

"Were you the one who called from Sweden?"

"No, it was another investigator."

"His English was good. Studies have shown that encounters with police personnel are critical for both victims and survivors."

Winter nodded.

"A supportive attitude on the part of the police has been shown to be a protective factor against depression, whereas negative reactions by the police at an acute stage appear to contribute to deeper despair."

Winston said this in a monotone, gazing to Winter's right as if he were reading from a teleprompter mounted on a camera.

"Do you think we've been slighting you in some way, Mr. Hillier?" Winter asked.

"Police can exacerbate the difficulties of victims by making them feel guilty or afraid," Winston droned.

Macdonald turned to Karen. "You haven't found anything else that belonged to Geoff, have you? Like a letter, for example?"

"The victim's emotional needs may conflict with the search by the police for detailed information about the crime." Winston took another drink.

"They're not mutually exclusive," Winter said.

Macdonald shook his head discreetly and glanced over at the door.

"You'll have to excuse us," Karen said.

"See what you've done," Winston said. "You've gotten my wife to apologize again."

"We really wanted to help," Karen said.

"Help? What are you talking about?" Winston asked.

Macdonald and Winter stood up.

"We'd like to come back again if that's possible," Macdonald said.

"I'd rather spread my wings and fly to Coventry," Winston said.

Macdonald swung the car out on the street. "Pub time?"

"Sure."

"Skilled waitresses trained in dealing with people who have suffered as the result of crime or its consequences can help the police," Macdonald said.

Christian plugged his Discman into the TV speakers. The owner's son would hear Beenie Man when he passed by. Christian felt sorry for him. He had given him a friendly nod, but the poor soul looked straight ahead like he was walking a tightrope.

It was getting late. The CDs the distributor had given him were good, but he already knew that, and he grew tired of them after a while. The guy wasn't going to show up, and that was just as well.

He could go out tonight, down to Brixton Academy or the Fridge, where he'd already been twice. He would take the distributor along if he ever came, but he must have been there before.

He heard the owner's son shuffle by again. He's gotten as far as the banister, Christian thought. After that he always scrapes against the door. I've seen the marks. I bet it's been going on for years.

The door rattled. So he's come after all, Christian thought. Wonder if he brought the chick along. Good thing I bought some beer.

When he opened the door, a strange man stood on the other side with a smile on his face. Christian thought he must have come to the wrong room. Then he saw that the man was wearing a Rasta wig, or a long black wig that he had twisted some Rasta curls into.

What a weird prank.

The distributor was inside now. He closed the door behind him and started to rummage around in his duffel bag.

35

IT WAS MIDNIGHT WHEN WINTER GOT OUT OF THE CAB IN FRONT of his hotel. He paid, walked up the half flight of stairs to the second floor and unlocked the door. Standing in the hallway, he heard voices from the suite above him. A TV set was keeping someone company.

His mind was empty, cleansed by the jazz at the Bull's Head down in Barnes. He had jumped into the taxi right after the Alan Skidmore Quartet finished their last encore.

Skidmore played the tenor sax, occasionally the soprano sax, his music heavily influenced by Coltrane. British music didn't get any better. Winter had sat right in the draft, which had helped clear his head.

Music is like sex, Winter thought as he walked into his suite. When it's good, it's terrific and when it's bad, it's still pretty good.

He had gone out wanting to find someone to sleep with, but the music had satisfied him. He hadn't even looked at the women all night long, the package of condoms in his wallet forgotten.

He opened the window and pulled back the drapes. He smelled of smoke and sweat against the breeze, and when he washed his face, his head still had that pure, empty feeling. He undressed and stood under the shower. The water restored his body, and he reveled in the strength and purpose it gave him.

He pulled on a pair of clean boxer shorts and sat on the couch. The taste of smoke lingered in his mouth. He got up and brushed his teeth again. Sitting back down, he listened to the last strains of the music fade away inside him. Finally there was nothing left but silence. He tried to remember further and further back. Memories, fragments of conversations, continued to swirl around him when he went to bed.

Sound asleep, he heard a tenor sax wail to him in a maniacal Coltrane meditation, trying to split his subconscious in two.

The wail turned into a jangling sound that woke him up. His cell phone rattled on the floor where he had plugged it in. The room was as dark as the night outside.

He rolled out of bed and onto the floor, picked up the phone and pressed the green button. "Winter."

"Steve here. We'll pick you up in ten minutes."

Winter stretched as far as he could and snatched his watch off the nightstand. Three o'clock.

"It happened again," Macdonald said.

"No."

"Throw something on and wait outside for the squad car."

"Where was it?"

"Camberwell, between Peckham and Brixton."

"At a hotel?"

"Yes."

"A Swede?"

"Yes."

"My God."

"Get dressed now."

"When did it happen?"

"Tonight, but get a move on, dammit."

The room at the New Dome Hotel was full of people when Winter arrived. Everything was hideously familiar.

"I had to come right away," Macdonald said.

The police were hard at work. Blood clung to every surface in the room. The forensic team's plastic bags glistened under the bright lights.

"Of course, it's not necessarily Hitchcock," Macdonald said.

"No."

"It happened late last evening." Macdonald handed Winter a piece of paper. "I have the kid's name here."

Winter read it: Christian Jaegerberg.

The victim had already been removed. Winter saw stains on the floor, footprints tracing a pattern from the door to the chair in the middle of the room.

The bed hadn't been slept in. A little stack of CDs lay on top of it. The shades shut out the night. Voices droned on in low-key professionalism. Cameras flashed.

The plastic bags were everywhere, coded on the outside, filled with hair, teeth, bloody skin, flesh and bodily fluids.

We're in hell, Winter thought. Hell on earth is right here, in this room.

He moved his head from side to side. Blood—swelling behind his forehead, roaring in his ears—had replaced the pleasant vacuum.

Macdonald told him what he had found out so far.

It was a critical moment for everybody.

"He was interrupted," Macdonald said.

"What?"

"The owner's son walked by and heard something. He pounded on the door and wouldn't let up."

"And then what?"

"He's sitting in a room by the lobby. He's mentally disabled, not to mention shocked as hell. We tried to talk to him but didn't get anywhere. I'm just about to give it another shot."

They went out into the hallway, which reeked of vomit that Winter hadn't noticed before.

"One of our men," Macdonald said. "It happens all the time."

"They're only human."

"We've got dozens of officers knocking on doors in the neighborhood."

They were sitting as though someone had screwed them into their chairs. The owner held the hand of his son, who was around thirty but could pass for twenty-five. His disability exaggerated his features. His eyeballs moved back and forth but lacked focus. He wanted to get up, but the owner held him firmly in place.

"I want to go-o-o," he rasped, as if his vocal chords were weighed down by rocks.

"Soon, James," the owner said.

"Go-o-o."

"He walks around the hotel all day long," the owner said. "That's the only thing he does."

Macdonald nodded and introduced Winter. They sat down on a couple of chairs that a uniformed policewoman had brought from the lobby.

"Tell us again what happened," Macdonald said to the owner.

"James came down and started screaming and stamping his foot. He kept pulling on me, and I went back upstairs with him after a while."

"Did you see anyone else on the staircase?"

"No."

"No doors opening?"

"Not right then."

"What happened next?"

"What?"

"What did you do after that?"

"We got upstairs and I saw it, all the blood."

"What did James do?"

"He screamed."

"Did he see anyone or anything?"

"I don't know. I've been trying to get him to talk."

"You didn't notice anyone go up to the room?"

"No, I probably don't spend as much time at the front desk as I should."

"Nobody ran down the stairs afterward?"

"No."

"Nobody at all?"

"I didn't hear anything."

"But James heard something unusual?"

"He must have, because he never bothers the guests otherwise."

"He interrupted it," Winter said.

James turned his face toward Winter, and his eyes regained their focus. "He-e-e came ou-ou-out."

"He came out?" Winter repeated.

James nodded and squeezed the owner's hand.

"Did the guy come out?" Winter persisted. "The guy who was staying there?"

No answer.

"Did a big man come out?"

James's eyeballs began to roll again, then stopped when they got to Winter. "I pou-ou-ounded."

"Go on."

"I pou-ou-ounded on the door."

"Keep going."

"He-e-e came ou-ou-out."

"Who came out, James?"

"Hi-im."

"The guy?"

James shook his head harder.

"Hi-im."

"Somebody else? Not the guy?"

"Hi-im," James said, trembling.

"He must be talking about a visitor," the owner said. He turned to James. "Was he white like him?" He took Winter's wrist and pointed at the palm of his hand.

James continued to tremble, rocking back and forth as if a song were playing in his head.

"James," the owner continued. "The man who wasn't staying in the room, was he white like these two men who are sitting here now?"

James didn't react.

"I think we need to get him to the hospital," the owner said.

"Bla-a-ack," James said suddenly, grabbing his head and running his hands down his cheeks.

"Black?" the owner asked, pinching himself and holding his arm up to James's face. "Black like you and me?"

"Bla-a-ack." James repeated the gesture with his hands.

"Black hair, did he have black hair?" Macdonald pulled on the strands that hung over the right side of his forehead. James gave a start.

Macdonald removed the rubber band from his ponytail and let his hair fall over his shoulders. "Long black hair?" he asked, tugging on his own. James twitched, continuing to sway from side to side like a mourner. His eyes resembled caves.

"Bla-a-ack," he said again and pointed to Macdonald.

"And white?" Macdonald asked, running his fingers across his face and pinching his cheeks. "White? A white man? White skin?"

"Whi-i-ite."

36

THEY SAT IN MACDONALD'S OFFICE, ALONE FOR THE FIRST TIME in twelve hours. Macdonald's eyes were nuggets of coal. The skin of his face looked like it had been taped to his cheekbones. His hair still hung loose over his shoulders.

Winter was wearing a sport jacket and black jeans, a gray button-down shirt without a tie, and dark boots. His chin and cheeks were unshaven.

So much for Scandinavian elegance, Macdonald thought. "I hope you realize that you're more than an observer now," he said.

"When does your team get together?"

Macdonald held his wrist up and looked at his watch. "In an hour."

It was dusk. The dying light filtered through the blinds and shredded Macdonald's face into blue strips.

"We're never going to be this close again," Winter said.

"Assuming he's our man."

"If not, we have a brand-new problem, right?"

"Then he's got to be our man."

A stack of papers started to vibrate. Macdonald brushed them aside and picked up the phone. Winter noticed that the papers came from a printout of Macdonald's policy file. I follow the policy to a T, Macdonald had told him. It gives me cover for everything I do. That way I can justify my decisions when the top brass call me in for my monthly grilling.

"Hello?" Macdonald picked up a pen and asked a few short questions, taking notes.

Winter studied Macdonald as he played his role in the eternal cycle of evil that both of them and every other homicide investigator around the world were part of. He could have been sitting there himself with the receiver pressed against a sore ear, Macdonald could have been in Winter's chair, or they could have been two other detectives in a crowded room in Singapore, Los Angeles or Stockholm. Or Gothenburg. It was all the same, and everyone was interchangeable. It's bigger than life, he thought. It was there before we came, and it will be there after we're gone.

Macdonald clenched his pen harder. "That was the lab—at Lambeth."

"Yes, I remember."

"He went about it the same way."

"Exactly the same?"

"As far as they can tell right now."

"Marks on the floor?"

"Yes."

"Jesus."

"All of a sudden he was in a hurry to get out of there."

The sun had set and Winter saw Macdonald's face in silhouette.

"Our poor witness pounded on the door and howled like a baby," Macdonald said. "The murderer didn't panic, but he stopped whatever he was doing."

"But it might have made him a little careless."

"What do you mean?"

"I was just wondering if he slipped up at that point."

"Actually, he did."

"How?"

"They found a loose metal sleeve from one leg of the tripod."

Winter felt like he'd been locked inside a walk-in freezer. The roots of his hair tingled and his fingers turned to rubber. "The Lord is with us after all," he said.

"So you believe in a merciful God?"

"Yes."

"Maybe he's looking down on us right now."

"That metal sleeve. It's not just something that happened to be in the room?"

"You're selling some of the world's best forensic specialists short."

"Sorry."

"There's a streak of defiance in this," Macdonald said. "It makes me wonder if it really was sloppiness."

"That's occurred to me too."

"The defiance?"

"Yes, and that it could be a message of some kind, or a greeting."

"Or a cry for help. But we'll have to leave that up to the forensic psychologist."

"Not help. It's something else, more intimate. I can't find the word for it."

"Just as long as you can say it to yourself—the Swedish word, I mean."

"I can't find it in any language."

The north wind had risen and Bergenhem felt the boat rock from side to side for the first time. The porthole was whistling like a flute. "The porthole is drafty," he said.

"It doesn't bother me," Marianne said. "I'm used to it."

"I can fix it."

"I'd probably be nervous without it."

"When you're Angel . . ."

"What?"

"When you're working."

"Yes?"

"When somebody follows you into the other room."

"What are you getting at?"

"What do you do there behind the bar, or wherever it is?"

"What do you want from me?"

"I just want to know what goes on back there."

"If I fuck them?"

"No, I was just wondering if they say any—"

"You want to know whether I'm an honest-to-goodness hooker."

"No!"

"You think I'm a hooker."

"No way."

"I'm not a hooker. I've never done it for money, not what you're talking about."

There was only one thought in Bergenhem's head—that he had become someone else. His fists were clenched, and they didn't belong to him.

"Hello? Anybody home?" Marianne edged toward him.

"Stay right where you are."

"What?"

"Don't come any closer."

"So you think I'm a hooker after all."

"That's not it."

"What are you talking about then?"

He drank some more wine. They were on their second bottle. He was off duty tonight, but Martina thought he was working. I wish you could stay home, she had said. It feels like my water is about to break any minute."

"I dance for those poor bastards," Marianne said. "All I do is dance."

Bergenhem had lost interest in his question. He closed his eyes and saw a child on a table. He and Martina were watching through a screen. Angel danced for them and smiled at something she was holding in her hand.

The hull surged, as if a gale had lashed the boat, lifted it up and hurled it back into the river. Suddenly he felt sick to his stomach. His hands throbbed, the blood storming through his fingers. They weren't his hands. His head was somebody else's.

"Like when I was little," Marianne continued. "Did I ever tell you how much fun I had?"

She had told him about the child she had once been, and that was one of the reasons he stayed. He thought about the privileged and the underprivileged. There was no justice anywhere, and it wasn't going to get any better. All the signals that flashed on the road to the future were red as could be, with the same glare as at the strip joints, a light that led the human race on its pilgrimage to perdition.

"I was the star of my parents' dinner parties," she said.

Bergenhem lunged off the bed, dashed up to the deck, leaned over the gunwale and vomited. Tears filled his eyes and all he saw was a black hole. He felt a hand on his back. Marianne said something he didn't catch.

"Don't lean any farther or you'll fall over."

He breathed more easily now and he could see again. Below him the river ran dark between the boat and the stone of the wharf. The boat bumped up against the stone. Down there—that wasn't any way out.

She wiped his forehead with a damp towel. He was drenched from the rain, his shirt clinging to his body as if he had fallen into the water. She steadied him as they walked back below deck. His feet slipped back and forth on the boards.

Winter poured hot water from the coffeepot. It was eight in the morning and birds he didn't know the names of had already warbled themselves hoarse in the courtyard below his open window.

Just a few more hours and he would be sitting in a television studio with Macdonald and a bunch of reporters. The producers of *Crimewatch* had called a second time and Macdonald had accepted without hesitation.

Winter and thirteen other investigators had met the night before in one of the big offices on Parchmore Road. A bottle of whisky was on the table. Everybody said what they had been thinking. Macdonald tried to draw out the best in each of them.

Could they distill what had been said and communicate it to the public? Winter wasn't nervous, and he hoped and prayed they would get calls after the program.

"Now's the time to go for it," Macdonald had said to Winter. "We've just got to keep our fingers crossed that someone out there in the anonymous public has seen something."

"I agree."

"Television is a paradoxical medium."

"The anonymous public."

Winter spread butter and orange marmalade on two slices of toast. Earlier in the morning, he had walked down Hogarth Road to a newspaper stand on Earl's Court Road and bought the *Guardian*, the *Independent*, the *Times* and the *Daily Telegraph*.

His cell phone rang.

"I know you're an hour behind us," Ringmar said, "but I assumed you'd be up anyway."

"It's broad daylight here."

"We just got another letter from our burglar friend."

It took a few seconds for Winter to follow the chain of thought backward: burglar, apartment, bloody clothes—far-fetched, so goddam farfetched.

"Erik?"

"I'm still here." Winter washed down his toast with a mouthful of tea.

"He was insistent, as if he wanted to make up for his procrastination and set the record straight."

"And?"

"So we took a closer look at the guy who rents the apartment. Halders and Djanali had a little extra time when—"

"For God's sake, Bertil, skip the chronology and tell me what happened."

"We called him in for questioning."

"And?"

"He didn't respond right away, but finally we heard from him."

"Bertil!"

"Okay, okay, I'm coming to it. Listen carefully now. We couldn't get hold of him in Gothenburg at first because he was in London."

"What?"

"I told you to listen carefully. He was in London."

"How the hell can you know something like that?"

A chilliness began to creep through Winter's body. His scalp was prickly. Sweeping the newspapers off the table, he took three steps over to the counter and picked up his notepad. He sat down again, pen in hand.

"That wasn't so hard to figure out," Ringmar said. "He's a flight attendant, often on the Gothenburg–London route."

"Good Lord."

"And that's not all. He has an apartment in London. He lives there and has an overnight apartment in Gothenburg, or the other way around."

"Is he British?"

"Swedish through and through. Not to mention his name—Carl Vikingsson."

"Vikingsson?"

"Yes. And the name of the aircraft he usually works on is Viking something."

"Does he have a record?"

"Nope, clean as a whistle."

"Where is he now?"

"We've got him here."

Winter's throat was dry. He drank his lukewarm tea but it might as well have been kerosene or blueberry soup.

"We haven't had a chance to question him yet," Ringmar went on.

"No alibi?"

"Like I said, we don't know at this point. It could get pretty complicated."

"Where is his London apartment?"

"The address I've got is 32 Stanley Gardens."

"Hold on." Winter put down the phone and walked over to the coffee table. He picked up a *London A–Z* street atlas and checked the index. "London has six streets named Stanley Gardens," he told Ringmar when he returned.

"Shit."

"I need the postal code—NW7 or something like that."

"Wait a minute."

Winter took another gulp of kerosene and felt the hunter's instinct rise in his gut. He heard fumbling at the other end of the line.

"We have his business card here. Let me see . . . it's Stanley Gardens W11."

Winter looked in the index. W11. The address was at 7 H 59. He flipped to page 59 and found 7 H: Notting Hill, Kensington Park Road, Stanley Crescent . . . there. It was a little cross street. "Up in Portobello."

"Sounds good."

"Hold him for six hours, and make sure to get an extension for another six."

"Okay; remember, we haven't questioned him yet."

Winter had made up his mind. They had the legal right to keep him that long—with necessary rest and food. "And screw any alibis he comes up with," he said.

"Fine with me. Cohen is raring to go with the interrogation."

No doubt Cohen had read everything he could get his hands on.

"Don't turn Cohen loose on him just yet," Winter said.

"What?"

"Keep it low-key at first. Start off yourself."

"But Cohen has to be there."

"Just as an onlooker. We can't afford to make any mistakes."

"Easy does it."

"No screwups."

"Don't underestimate me. Odds are we'll still be discussing the weather forecast when you get here tomorrow."

"Good—I have faith in you."

"What time are you getting back, by the way?"

"I don't know yet. The television program I told you about yesterday is this afternoon. We've got to check out the address you gave me right away. I'll let you know in an hour or two."

"Erik?"

"Yes?"

"One thing we know for sure. Vikingsson was in London when Christian was killed."

"Not on a plane?"

"Shit, that's possible. But he wasn't in Sweden."

They hung up. Winter dialed the eleven-digit number to the Thornton Heath police station. "This is Chief Inspector Erik Winter. May I speak to Steve Macdonald?"

"Just a minute please."

Macdonald came on the line.

"It's Erik, I just heard from Gothenburg. They've called a guy in for questioning, and he has an apartment here in London. It might be a long shot, but we should take a look."

"An apartment here?"

"Up in Notting Hill."

"Nice area."

"I don't know anything about the guy. But I think we need to see his apartment."

"From the outside?"

"What?"

"I know a couple of sympathetic judges, but neither of them is going to let us search an apartment without a little more to go on."

"I want to head over there anyway. I'm leaving now. See you at the corner of Kensington Park Road."

"Kensington Park Road and what?"

"Sorry, the apartment is on Stanley Gardens."

"Okay."

"I'll be there in an hour."

"I'm out the door."

37

WINTER FLAGGED DOWN A NORTHBOUND TAXI ON EARL'S COURT
Road. It was fifteen minutes to Notting Hill Gate on the narrow streets
past Holland Park. He had hiked around there occasionally in his
younger days.

The houses on Kensington Park Road shone like marble. At the Pem-
bridge intersection, a café owner was putting checkered tablecloths on
the outdoor tables. People were already waiting for the first cappuccino
of spring.

The buildings on Stanley Gardens were surrounded by silence and
shade. Number 32 had an entrance where anybody could go in and out.
Winter continued down the street and then turned back to Kensington
Park Road. He stood still on the corner. A couple his own age stopped
before him.

"How do we get to Portobello Road?" the man asked with a Swedish
accent.

"It runs parallel to this street. Just turn right down there."

"Thank you very much," the couple said in unison and Winter
flashed them his best British smile. I'm a member of the anonymous
public, he thought.

It was a Swedish area of sorts. Within walking distance to his east
was the Bayswater district, whose hotels around Queensway Street
were the favored accommodations of Scandinavian tourists.

A taxi pulled up and Macdonald wriggled out. "A train and then a cab
from Victoria Station," he said. "It's the fastest way."

"It's over there."

"Did you go inside?"

"No."

"I've issued an order for the building to remain under 24/7 surveillance from the moment we leave."

"Excellent."

"I had a chat with a judge, who said no, of course, so that investigation of yours needs to turn up something pretty damn quick."

They went over to the building, and Winter read the nameplates. He tugged on the heavy door to the northern stairway. It was locked. "I assume you have the entry code," he said.

Macdonald nodded. "We can always count on the janitors."

The hallway had the cool smell of polished wood. The light spiraled up the stairs to the roof. They followed the light and stopped on the third floor. Macdonald put on a pair of gloves and tapped on the door with the lion-faced knocker. "A custom left over from our colonial era."

No answer. Macdonald tapped again, brass against wood. "Nobody's subleasing the apartment," he said.

"We don't know that."

"Whatever. Nobody's home right now."

Winter heard a clatter beneath them. The elevator hissed, went down and stopped. A minute later it passed by on the way back up. The passenger couldn't have seen Winter or Macdonald, who stood in the blind corner of the staircase.

Macdonald tossed a pair of gloves to Winter. "Put these on."

"I never thought you'd have the nerve to do it."

"This is dangerous as hell."

"Open the door."

Macdonald handed Winter some blue plastic hospital booties. "These too."

He must have been a burglar in a past life, Winter thought. The blood swelled in his chest.

Nothing but silence from the stairway and the other apartments. Macdonald's picklock clicked softly and they slipped inside.

It's all about ends and means, Winter thought. We're burglars, but we're fighting for the survival of others. That's what sets us apart from the real thieves.

They found themselves in the middle of the living room. It was hot in the apartment, and the sun beating down on the closed blinds provided more than enough light.

Macdonald nodded to the right side and Winter followed him. There were no leftovers or dirty dishes in the kitchen. Towels hanging in a neat row, a rack of knives on the wall.

"All the knives are right where they belong," Winter said.

"None of them double-edged."

We've invaded someone's privacy and Steve is playing it for all it's worth, Winter thought. We have no respect anymore, not for anything. But I'm glad we're here.

They picked up and examined everything in the apartment.

"The guy's a fucking perfectionist," Macdonald said.

"He's into music."

"Reggae."

"Yeah, I noticed."

"He's got quite a bit."

"Lots of locked chests," Winter said.

"And cabinets."

"Right."

"Something's not right about this place," Macdonald said. "Do you feel it too?"

"I'm not sure."

"Here's a photo of him." Macdonald leaned over a desk. Vikingsson smiled unassumingly at the camera. He had short, straight, blond hair. "Wh-i-ite."

Winter went and stood next to him.

"How can a flight attendant afford an apartment in Notting Hill?" Macdonald asked.

"I don't know what Scandinavian Airlines pays."

"I couldn't live here on my salary."

"That's because you fly too close to the ground."

"That doesn't seem to be a problem for you, judging by your clothes."

"No."

"So you're independently wealthy?"

"You might say that."

"Damn, I knew it."

"It's a mix of old and new money."

"You're like a British officer," Macdonald said. "Their salaries pay the bill at the mess hall and that's about it."

"We'll have to do a little checking into Vikingsson's finances. Remember, he's got that place in Gothenburg too."

They opened all the closets. The clothes were impeccably stacked.

"Perfectionist," Macdonald said.

"What were you expecting? Another garbage bag of bloody clothes?"

"Once doesn't count."

"We'll come back."

"You'll be gone by then."

"I'll be with you in spirit."

"What time is your flight?"

"Seven o'clock."

"Will Vikingsson still be there when you land?"

"Just barely. Unless we get a detention order."

"Somebody has to convince the D.A."

"Everybody's nervous now. We can take advantage of that."

"Or else Vikingsson will be cleared by the time you get home."

"That would also be a step in the right direction."

"The process of elimination. That's our stock-in-trade."

They came out on Stanley Gardens and walked over to the intersection. Macdonald nodded at someone in a Vauxhall that was parked across the street.

Winter called Gothenburg.

"Ringmar here."

"It's Erik. How's it going?"

"No disagreements about the weather forecast, anyway."

"What's he like?"

"Cool."

"Too cool?"

"Not exactly. But he's obviously hiding something."

"Good to hear."

"It may or may not be important."

"My plane lands at ten o'clock."

"That's too late."

"So we're still not close to having probable cause?"

"We haven't got a thing."

"This is moving fast, but that's the way I like it. Make sure you've got something on him by the time I arrive. I'm counting on results."

Winter hung up. It was late afternoon and more people were out, on their way to the markets. He heard cheerful Scandinavian voices.

"Vikingsson isn't talking."

"That's hardly surprising," Macdonald said.

"It'll happen. We just need a little more time."

"They're waiting for us at the studio."

"I'd forgotten all about that."

"They haven't forgotten about us."

Winter played the part of Macdonald's advisor. It was a small studio. The lights were bright but Macdonald wasn't the least bit sweaty.

This might do some good, Winter thought. You never know.

They didn't mention the interrogations in Gothenburg. If it had been just three days from now, or five, Winter thought, we would have had a photo to hold up, a head of short, straight blond hair.

They held up other photos. People could call in during the program. The crew recorded all the calls. But when Macdonald listened to the tapes afterward, he didn't hear anything that merited immediate attention.

Winter thought about Vikingsson. The events in Gothenburg were a welcome distraction.

After the show, they sat in Macdonald's car outside the studio, then rode to a pub for lunch. As soon as they were through the revolving door, Winter was assaulted by the smell of beer, fried liver and cigarette smoke. They ordered their meal.

"We're going to hear from some witnesses this time," Macdonald said.

"About Christian?" Winter lit a cigarillo.

"Yes."

"Because of the color of his skin?"

"Yep. The victim was a black person from another country. People aren't so afraid. And considering that the murderer was white . . ."

"That's an assumption on our part."

"We have no reason to believe otherwise."

"Here comes the beer."

"And your quiche."

"Now I won't get a chance to meet your family," Winter said.

"That makes two of us."

"Do your kids remember what you look like?"

"Just as long as I don't get a haircut."

"Do you have a picture of them?"

Macdonald put his glass down and took his wallet out of his inside pocket. His holster strap stretched tightly across his chest like a big leather bandage. The metal revolver gleamed under his arm.

He pulled out a photo, a side view of a dark-haired woman sitting between two teenage girls. All three of them had ponytails.

"That's the way they wanted it." Macdonald smiled.

"Where's the other half of the mug shot?"

"They're a wild bunch."

"Twins?"

"Uh-huh. Here's another shot of them."

"They look like your right side."

"It's the hairstyle."

They ate in silence. Macdonald ordered coffee for both of them. He drove Winter back to the hotel. The traffic was hardly moving on Cromwell Road.

"London is a hellhole," Macdonald said. "At least to drive in."

"I always end up back here. It's one of the few truly civilized cities there is."

"You just can't resist our cigars."

"The diversity is what most appeals to me."

"Right, real diverse—murderers and rapists and pimps and junkies."

"And soccer teams and restaurants and jazz clubs and people from all over the world."

"It's true. The eternal empire, although we call it the Commonwealth these days."

"Could you imagine living anywhere else?"

"Somewhere other than London? I don't live in London. I live in Kent."

"You know what I mean."

"No."

"No what?"

"No, I can't imagine living anywhere else."

"Not to mention that you can sunbathe when it's still winter in Sweden."

Winter picked up his bags from the hotel. Macdonald coaxed the car back onto A4 and drove through the borough of Hammersmith onto M4 south of Gunnersbury Park. Winter looked out at the urban landscape. Children were playing soccer in Osterley Park, the wind ruffling their hair. Nothing ever changed. Middle-aged men strolled past, golf carts in tow. Three horses trotted by below him. He couldn't tell whether the riders were women or men. He saw the last horse leave a trail of manure without breaking its elegant stride.

Winter felt the cold air as soon as he was out of the terminal. Spring was dawdling over the North Sea.

Ringmar was waiting in the car. "We had to let him go," he said.

Winter waited.

"But he doesn't have any alibis."

"That's good."

"He can't prove where he was during any of the murders."

"Fine."

"We've contacted the airlines, and he wasn't on duty when they were committed."

"Hmm."

Out on the expressway, they drove through the town of Landvetter at eighty miles an hour. The lights of Gothenburg glimmered ten miles away.

"He was in London when it happened there and in Gothenburg when it happened here," Ringmar said.

"What does he claim he was up to?"

"This and that. Laundry, cooking, going to a movie."

Ringmar tapped his fingers on the wheel, as if to make the car go faster.

"No holes in his story?" Winter asked.

"Nope."

"Have you checked whether he was working on the days that the victims were en route?"

"Yes."

"And?"

"He was on all the flights."

"That's a little too good to be true."

Ringmar switched on his turn signal and passed another car. They zipped by the suburb of Mölnlycke, a cluster of lights on the left. "Aren't you the one who wanted quick results?" he asked.

"It wasn't long ago that we were wondering if somebody had been on one of the flights, and now we've got a man who was on all of them."

"And that's too good to be true?"

Winter rubbed his eyes. He had dozed for half an hour on the plane, had shaken his head when they'd come around with the food and coffee. "All this is based on the suspicions of a self-confessed burglar," he said.

"It wouldn't be the first time we solved a case that way."

"How discreet have you been?"

"We're not going to botch a lineup."

"We can't afford to."

"That's what I'm saying. We won't jeopardize what we've got."

Waving photographs around before you can get a proper lineup together is a mortal sin, Winter thought. It's spending your best ammunition, maybe for good. They had tried a photo lineup once, ten pictures in a row in front of the witness, but that was a huge risk.

"We've got to play by the book all the way," Winter said, thinking of his escapade with Macdonald on Stanley Gardens.

"We took Vikingsson's keys, but we didn't have the chance to search his apartment very thoroughly."

"I'll go there right away."

"If we want to know anything more about this guy, we'll have to get a detention order," Ringmar said, "so we can sit down with him and get to the bottom of things."

"What does Birgersson have to say about it?"

"He told the D.A. that he's never going to talk to him again unless he issues an order."

"That's quite a threat."

"Birgersson is willing to take the chance. Also, the D.A. can consider it a promise. But so far he's looking at whether we have probable cause."

"And he's decided that we don't."

Ringmar parked outside police headquarters.

Winter's whole body was stiff as he got out of the car. Welcome to Sweden, he told himself. "What's going on with Bergenhem, by the way?"

Ringmar locked the door with the remote. "He sniffs around like a bloodhound."

"Has he come up with anything?"

"He says he's waiting for a name."

Winter meandered through Vikingsson's two-room apartment. It was suffused with an air of transience and sudden departure. What does he need this place for, anyway? he wondered, looking around. Something's wrong in here. I can sense it.

He rummaged through the drawers. Vikingsson's apartment on Stanley Gardens was lived-in and comfortable, but these walls—this floor and this ceiling—were mute and impassive, and the rooms rejected him like a foreign object. Had the burglar really been here? What an insolent lot they are.

What are you looking for?

Where would you keep something important, even if you were just passing through?

Papers, rolls of film, addresses, receipts? Where?

Where would you put something that you don't want anybody to see even though you have no reason to believe that someone is going to come barging in?

He went into the sparsely furnished bedroom: a bed, chest of drawers, bookshelf, chair with a telephone on it.

A telephone.

People had called Vikingsson and he had called them. Winter closed his eyes and imagined the chart on Macdonald's wall. Phone calls like satellite orbits high above the Western Hemisphere, a map that tracked every last sneeze that went out over the lines.

That was one approach they could take. If Vikingsson was innocent, they would help him prove it.

He opened his eyes and moved around. Nothing on the walls. The chest looked like someone had flung it across the room. He went over and pulled out the drawers, one by one, each of them scraping as it resisted.

He couldn't budge the bottom drawer. Had the police been in here and tried before?

He pulled harder. The drawer came loose and he fell down and felt like an idiot. He looked around. The drawer was empty.

He lay back on the floor and looked up at the room. A mirror dangled from a hook on the wall above the chest, which now had a gaping hole like a missing row of teeth where the drawer had been. Even eight feet away from the mirror, he could see behind it. Something stuck out like a silhouette in the light that filtered through the space between the mirror and the wall.

Praise the Lord, Winter thought, standing up. He turned the mirror around and looked for the silhouette in the brighter light of the room.

It was gone. He gazed down at the floor. No paper, no photo, no receipt—nothing. A piece of fabric stuck out from the back of the mirror. He didn't see anything else in there.

He hung the mirror back up and lay on the floor once more, trying to position himself at the same angle. He saw the space and the silhouette again. It was the loose piece of fabric. I'm letting all this get to me, he thought.

He had saved the photos for last. A collage was tacked up on a little bulletin board over the kitchen table. Ringmar had said that Vikingsson was vain. People like that don't go very far without a mirror or a photo of themselves.

The collage was the only object in the apartment that revealed who lived there. Winter leaned over the table and looked at it. He counted the photos—eight in all, and Vikingsson the only person in each of them.

They had been arranged in a circle. He followed them clockwise, returning to the one on top: Vikingsson sat at some kind of counter that looked like a bar. He took up most of the photo. You could see behind his shoulders and five or six feet along the counter. Somebody had stood behind it and taken the picture with a wide-angle lens. Winter's gaze meandered from Vikingsson to the area in back of him and off to the side.

Something about the place was familiar. The windows behind Vikingsson . . . Winter closed his eyes and saw the windows emerge from the past. The same bar. He saw himself sitting there and saying something to the man on the other side.

Take it easy, he told himself. It's just a coincidence. The city is full of popular bars—and ones that aren't so popular.

38

WINTER COULD ALMOST SMELL THE ADRENALINE IN THE CON-
ference room. The mood had changed drastically since his departure for
London, investigators now in motion, having found their direction.

Winter spent ten minutes telling them about London. "I want to
know what each of you is thinking at this very minute," he said. "Don't
worry if it comes out all jumbled up. Ringmar will write everything
down. Okay—lights, camera, action."

The semicircle they formed around Winter was like half a clock
without the hour hand, as if they expected to solve the case before it
came around again.

"Welcome back, boss," Halders said.

Damn ass kisser, Djanali thought. He's trying to sound ironic, but
everyone knows he's just sucking up.

"Sara?" Winter said.

"The marks on the floor indicate that the murderer was not only
very strong, but beside himself with rage," Helander said.

"Rage?"

"That's our interpretation based on the way he moved around the
room."

"Hmm."

"Something he had repressed finally got the chance to come out."

"The bastard ran amok," Halders said.

"Do you have people looking at Vikingsson's past?" Winter asked,
his eyes on Ringmar.

"You bet."

"It seems to start quietly," Helander continued. "Like a system or a pattern, and then it spirals out of control."

"You can say that again," Halders interjected.

"Hold your tongue, Fredrik," Winter said, "and let us know when you have something constructive to contribute."

Halders's neck turned red, and he gave Djanali a sideways glance. She sat impassively and blinked her eyes.

"It's the same story over and over again," Helander said. "The murderer has a plan that gets out of hand, but the scary thing is that it gets out of hand exactly the same way each time."

"What do you mean?" Möllerström asked.

"The patterns look the same, as if a robot had lost its mind, or was programmed to go crazy just like the time before."

"C'est la folie," Halders muttered, a naughty child who can't keep his mouth shut.

Does he really know French? Djanali mused to herself. Maybe he's taking an evening class.

"Except for the second murder in London," Helander continued. "The photos I got from Erik show another pattern. It's like a couple of sequences are missing."

"He was interrupted," Winter said.

"It shows."

Everyone sat quietly and looked at the photos. It's the way it keeps repeating itself that's so horrible, Djanali thought. It's revolting, but without this constant repetition, we would be totally lost. The art of monotony, that's our specialty. She cleared her throat.

"Aneta?"

"We chatted with some of Vikingsson's neighbors," Djanali said. "People keep to themselves there. It's your typical apartment building. But when we asked about his habits, somebody said he worked out a lot."

"Worked out?"

"I don't know if he meant anything special by it. But Vikingsson was carrying a big duffel bag the two or three times the neighbor ran into him."

"Bertil?" Winter said.

"We just heard about the duffel bag today," Ringmar answered. "We didn't know about it yesterday or bring it up with Vikingsson."

"I was referring to what you found in his apartment."

Ringmar picked up a file folder from the table, flipped to one of the pages and read from a list. "No duffel bag," he said.

"Nothing at all—not even a travel bag or a rucksack?"

"No—one of those roller bags that flight attendants use, that's all. But we didn't have time to turn the place upside down."

"And now he's home tidying up," Halders said.

"Find out whether he has a gym membership," Winter said to Halders.

"Okay."

"Check out every health club in town if you have to."

"Aye, aye, Captain."

"Where is he now, by the way?" Möllerström asked.

"Somewhere over the North Sea," Ringmar said.

"There's something I wanted to bring up about the victims' backgrounds, or however you put it," Halders said. "We were supposed to look for whatever they might have in common, so we spent dozens of hours talking to their acquaintances and their girlfriends and boyfriends."

"Possible boyfriends," Winter corrected him.

"We're pretty certain about that."

"Go on."

"Sure enough, there's a place that Jamie, Per and Geoff all went to on a fairly regular basis," Halders said.

"Not Christian?"

"We don't know yet. It might be the kind of place that most kids their age go to."

He said the name and Ringmar looked over at Möllerström.

"Halders mentioned it this morning," Möllerström said.

"A lot of information came together last night," Halders said. "But I haven't had a chance yet to find out anything about Christian."

Erik looks totally exhausted, Djanali thought. I wonder how the rest of us would appear to a stranger who just happened to drop by.

"Does Vikingsson have a car?" Winter asked Ringmar.

"Not one that's been registered, in any case."

"That doesn't tell us much. We need to check the resident cards on the windshields of all the cars parked in his neighborhood. If we find one that nobody will own up to, it could be Vikingsson's."

"Or it could be mine," Halders said.

"What?"

"My car was stolen again, and this time I didn't catch the S.O.B. who did it."

Winter longed for a cup of coffee and a cigarillo. "We're going to call him in for questioning again," he said.

"Good," Ringmar said.

"We've got some new information to ask him about."

"He's not home," Möllerström said.

"Find him," Winter said. "He's not off the hook, no matter what he might think. If worst comes to worst, we'll try a photo lineup and hope we can get him arrested that way. And we've got to know more about his personal life. Friends, acquaintances, what he does at night. Clubs, bars, movies."

He thought about the photos on the wall in Vikingsson's kitchen.

He turned to Bergenhem. The guy looked sick. Winter couldn't remember him ever being so skinny. Had he sent him on a fool's errand? Or was he a bundle of nerves because his wife was about to have a baby? Winter was clueless when it came to that kind of thing.

"Lars?"

Bergenhem glanced at Winter as if by accident. "Yes?"

"What do you have to say?"

"I have a source, and it might lead to something."

He acts like he's got a hangover, Winter thought.

"The porn industry seems to be reeling from something, or was reeling from something up until very recently . . . something completely new."

"New?"

"A kind of anxiety. And I don't think it's just because I'm going around asking questions. It's like somebody has the answer but isn't talking."

"Has anyone told you that?"

"I might be able to come up with a name."

They all waited. Just a simple name, and everybody would finally be able to relax over that cup of coffee, close Ringmar's folder and Möllerström's database.

"Somebody who has the answer," Bergenhem repeated.

Bergenhem drove back over the bridge and caught Martina by surprise. She stood in the kitchen looking down at the floor as if she expected her water to break and splash onto the tile. It wouldn't be long now.

He kissed her and put his arms around her. She smelled like apples and cotton. He placed his hand on her belly.

"Aren't you on duty?"

"You're not going to turn me in, are you?"

She laughed. "Do you want something to eat?"

"Do we have any pork chops?"

"Pork chops?"

"I want some fried pork chops. I feel like I haven't had an appetite in weeks."

"You *haven't* had an appetite in weeks."

"Fried pork chops with onion gravy and boiled potatoes and absolutely no vegetables."

"That's not very PC."

"What's not?"

"To leave out the vegetables."

"I can go to the grocery store."

"If you want pork chops, that's your best bet. We don't have any."

He walked down to the familiar corner and turned left. Three teenagers whirled by on skateboards. They're playing hooky too, he thought.

The sky was breathtaking. Not a cloud in sight. He passed a school and heard a loud bell. It sounds just like it used to, he thought. Education reforms come and go but the bells never change. All those hours that I just sat at my desk waiting for it to ring. Waiting and waiting.

He felt like he had woken up from a confused dream, the darkness dispelled by the cold.

Was it that Winter had come back? Are you so fucking dependent on him? Who are you, anyway? Things may not be so hazy now, but you're still asking yourself the same questions. It's like you have to prove something to yourself and everyone else. I'll show them . . . I'll show them. Who are you, Lars?

The store appeared on the right. The newspaper placards in the window were the color of coltsfoot blossoms. In two or three years the baby would run in with the first fistful, and they would put it in a vase and finally press it between volumes A and B of the encyclopedia.

Who are you besides a rookie cop on his way to buy a pound of pork chops with a guilty conscience for something he hasn't actually done?

He thought of her as Angel, as Marianne, as Angel again. He didn't know anymore who was attracted and who was doing the attracting. It's like a drug, he thought. Is it over? Is what over?

You've got things under control, he told himself. Nobody can say you're not doing your job. You even wrote a report.

Östergaard sat in the kitchen and tested Maria on her French. As far as she could tell, her daughter's pronunciation was perfect.

She was thinking of renting a house in Normandy for a couple of weeks the following summer. The form was already completed. The name of the village was Roncey, and it was near the town of Coutances. She had been there once, before Maria was born. The cathedral was the highest point but had survived the bombs—the only unscathed church in northern Normandy. It stretched out a finger to God. She wanted to go in and light another candle, seventeen years later or however long it had been: a servant of God from Gothenburg and her daughter.

When they were finished with the pronunciation exercises, Maria read the paragraph out loud and translated it. Her French was better than her mother's. They could order a meal at the village restaurant. *Un vin blanc, une orange, merci*. Buy picnic food for the deserted beach. When the tide ebbed, the oyster farms glittered in the sun. They would walk along the white sand, dig for French-speaking crabs with their toes.

She looked up and Maria was gone. The television went on in the living room, a raucous guest.

Un vin blanc. She opened the refrigerator and took out an open bottle. The sides of the glass misted over when she poured it. She took a sip. It was too cold. She put the glass down and left the bottle on the counter.

It was Thursday night. The outdoor thermometer showed twenty-six degrees. Last week the crocuses had been out and now they were iced over. The question was how the summer lilac was faring.

She heard the sirens again on Korsvägen Street. It's like a training camp down there, she thought.

Maria would be at handball camp all weekend, and Östergaard was looking forward to having some time for herself—a rare treat for a minister. She would go to a movie, read a book, make some fish soup, put on three layers of clothing, take the long hike around Lake Delsjön and come home with a warm glow on her face that would last all evening long.

"Did you mend my track suit?" Maria shouted from the living room.

"Yes," she shouted back.

"How about my white jersey, did you wash it?"

"Yes, and if you want anything else, you'll have to come in here."

"What?"

"If you want anything else, you'll have to come in here."

She heard Maria giggle, once more engrossed in the movie.

The week had exhausted her. She hadn't been able to set her own priorities or break away from all those sessions with the officers.

A traffic accident on Tuesday, conversations afterward that could have sent a younger woman home in despair.

Was it really a job for a woman? That was just like asking whether it was a job for a man. It wasn't a question of muscles or how big you were. It was a question of humanity. Sometimes she wondered if it was a job for anyone.

She got up and went into the living room. "I'm going to take a bath," she said to Maria. "If anyone calls, tell them I'll call back later."

Maria nodded with her eyes on the TV. Östergaard glanced at the screen. Four people were talking at the same time. Everybody looked upset. A family.

She took the glass of wine into the bathroom and plugged the tub, adjusting the temperature of the water until it was the way she liked it. Throwing her clothes into the laundry basket, she drank some wine, then set the glass on the edge of the bathtub. She turned around and looked in the mirror on the door of the medicine cabinet.

She inspected herself. You're not thirty-five yet and this is your body, she thought, cupping her breasts. They were taut in her hands. She ran her fingers over her stomach—she still had a waistline but had gotten a little heavier. Heavier than when? she wondered and turned sideways. Her butt looked a little flabby, but that was only the angle.

The roar of the water died down as the bathtub filled up. She turned the faucet off and lowered one foot in. It was delightfully hot.

She lay there for a long time. The skin on the front of her fingers and the bottom of her feet turned into rolling sand dunes. The French beach flashed through her mind again. She finished the wine and closed her eyes, her forehead perspiring.

The most painful experience had been visiting Christian's mother. A mailbox that looked like a birdhouse stood outside their door. Her husband had flown to London immediately after getting the news.

They had adopted Christian. Did that make any difference? For a second it had felt that way. She asked Winter in the car afterward, but he was unwilling or unable to answer. He drove silently with his eyes fixed on the road. The only sound was the swish of the windshield wipers, battling something wet that was neither rain nor snow. The buildings of the Old City were colorless in the northern haze.

"This was the beginning of the end," Winter had said suddenly.

"What do you mean?"

"Now is when it all comes together," he said, putting some jazz in the tape deck. "Get ready."

Winter took the ferry to Asperö Island as the sun was setting. He got off at Albert's Pier and walked up the hill. Taking the path to the right, he continued to the top. Bolger sat outside his cottage. "Goddam beautiful, isn't it?" he shouted, waving as Winter approached.

The archipelago lay below them, beyond the pine forest. They could see the docked ferry through the glow over Styrsö and Donsö islands. Winter caught sight of another ferry—Stena Line—winding its way between the rocks on Dana Fjord.

"And it's all mine," Bolger said. "My kingdom come."

"Has it really been a whole year?"

"Weren't you here last summer?"

"No, I don't think so."

"I wanted you to see how lovely it was."

"Very."

"When I first invited you, I mean. It's most beautiful in late March."

"In what way?"

"No green haze to block the view. Only water and cliffs and sky."

"No sailboats either?"

"Above all, no sailboats."

"I heard that you were worried about Bergenhem's safety again," Winter said.

"Just relax and enjoy the view."

"Has he stumbled across something big, Johan?"

"Nothing bigger than all this." Bolger stretched out his arms.

The sea wind filled Winter's nostrils, and the bushes in front of the cottage bowed under a sudden squall.

"Do you come out here a lot?" Winter asked.

"More and more."

"And you spend the night?"

"Sometimes, if I don't feel like starting the motorboat."

The boat, open at the top and made of the same timber as the cottage, was floating in the shadow of the pier.

"He's going out with a stripper," Bolger said. "She's among the most popular ones."

"I'm sure he's got his reasons, and you told me all that before. When I was in London."

"Okay—he's your man," Bolger said.

"Who is she?"

"A stripper, that's all."

"Is that why you wanted me to come out here?"

"Weren't you the one who said you needed a little fresh air to clear your head?"

"Who is she?" Winter insisted.

"This chick has been a junkie, and they're capable of imagining anything."

"Do you know her well?"

"No."

"But you're worried."

"This kind of thing is never safe, Erik."

"What do you think I should do?"

"Find out what he's up to."

"I know what he's up to."

"I forgot. You know everything."

"What?"

"Where is . . ."

"What did you say?"

"Mats is . . ."

"What are you mumbling about, Johan? What about Mats?"

Bolger looked up at Winter. "Never mind."

"What do you mean?"

"Nothing, I told you." Bolger got up. "Come on in and we'll have something to drink."

Winter watched the evening descend over the water and glimpsed the lights of two boats out on the fjord. They approached each other and merged for a second like a powerful lamp.

They drank coffee and schnapps. The only light came from the fireplace.

"What time does the ferry go back?" Bolger asked.

"Eight o'clock."

"You can sleep over if you like."

"I appreciate the offer, but I don't have the time."

"Something has been going round and round in my head," Bolger said.

Winter drank his coffee and felt the sting of the locally brewed schnapps. He took a bite out of a sugar cube.

"Now that I've thought about it a little," Bolger continued, "I wouldn't be surprised if one or two of the victims had been at my bar."

"And you waited all this time to tell me?"

"I never actually saw them, but most kids their age show up once or twice a month. It's become something of a meeting place on Thursday nights."

"I see."

"It could be worth checking out."

"Good idea."

"I might even have served one of them. It never occurred to me before."

"Hmm."

"Let me see their photos again."

Bolger lit an outdoor brick fireplace that he had recently built on the rocks. He had insisted that Winter join him. The evening was a vault above them. The logs caught fire and Winter saw them shift from orange to crimson. Bolger's features faded in and out. The flames rose with the smoke. For a moment Winter thought he saw something move in the fire, shadowy figures or writhing bodies.

39

WINTER READ THE TWO LETTERS THAT THE BURGLAR HAD WRIT-
ten. The way he described the bloody clothes and the phone call he
had heard from under the bed took on a new and ominous significance
in light of a couple of the most recent developments. Bloodstains had
turned up in Vikingsson's Gothenburg apartment, and Macdonald had
found more in the Stanley Gardens flat.

Blood drips no matter how careful you are, Winter thought.

The stains in Gothenburg were composed of both human and animal blood. It could have been the same mix as on the clothes the burglar
had seen, but who knew? The blood in London hadn't even been ana-
lyzed yet.

What a strange conversation the burglar had overheard. Vikingsson
had used the word "celluloid"—what was that all about?

They had traced all the calls Vikingsson had made from his cell
phone. He never phoned London. He didn't call anyone in Gothenburg
very often either. He had dialed a downtown pay phone the day the
burglar was there.

This was all assuming there was some truth to the burglar's claims
and he wasn't just another lunatic. He seemed sane enough, but you
never could tell.

Vikingsson had come back, and they had convinced the D.A. to issue a detention order, which gave the investigators a chance to proceed
more deliberately.

They tried to postpone the hearings for an arrest warrant as long as
possible. The judge could rule at any time, but Winter hoped he would

wait the four-day limit. We'll never get him arrested on the evidence we have right now, Winter thought, putting the copy of the letter back on his desk.

Four days max.

They would place Vikingsson in a lineup. Beckman, the streetcar driver, would stand on the other side of the glass wall. They would find out how good a memory for faces he actually had.

Winter had read a lot about the cognitive neuroscience of memory. A lineup could either make or break the prosecution's case.

Police screwups always resulted from clumsiness or ignorance. The human psyche was specially equipped to distinguish between different faces, no matter how similar, and the brain employed a separate system for storing and processing facial information.

He dialed Ringmar's extension. "Could you come in for a minute, Bertil?"

Ringmar arrived, a flush of excitement in his face.

"You're looking frisky," Winter said.

"This might be the light at the end of the tunnel."

"What tunnel?"

"The one at the beginning of the light."

"I've read through Beckman's interrogation, and I think he'd be willing to tell us more now," Winter said.

"Could be, but he's not much of a witness. He didn't actually see a crime being committed."

"We'll question him again, and take a more cognitive approach."

"You took the words right out of my mouth," Ringmar said sarcastically. There were certain expressions that always perturbed him. Winter didn't understand why.

They would ask Beckman new, more open-ended questions. Leave more pauses for him to fill in. The purpose of the cognitive method was to impose various memory-improving techniques on the witness. They would get Beckman to describe each detail, to relate everything he had seen in a different order and from different points of view.

"We can't afford to slip up," Winter said.

"You're starting to repeat yourself."

"I want seven decoys in the lineup."

"You got it."

Just enough people to fill the first couple of rows of a streetcar, Winter thought.

They would do the same with Svensson, Jamie's boss. He might be able to recognize the face of the new customer who had popped up at his bar from time to time.

"It's important to find exactly the right ones," Winter said.

"You mean the decoys?"

"Yes."

"That goes without saying."

They couldn't very well put Vikingsson next to seven homeless people. Finding the right combination was always a nightmare.

"Cohen is going to question Vikingsson again," Ringmar said.

"I know. I'm about to head for his office now."

"We've found out a little more about Vikingsson's background, or personal life."

"He hasn't got a family, from what I've heard."

"Neither a wife nor children, if that's what you mean by family."

"Yes."

"He's not gay."

"I thought so at first," Winter said.

"Really?"

Winter remembered the unauthorized search he and Macdonald had conducted in London. No need to mention it, not yet at least. He had seen certain signs, little details that were familiar to him. He thought of Mats. "It doesn't mean much one way or the other," he said.

"Except that all the victims were young males."

"And that there might be a sexual motive that has escaped us thus far." Winter suspected that such a motive did exist, at least indirectly. The murderer had taken advantage of the victims' confusion, their search for a sexual identity. It was the simplest thing in the world to do. They might call themselves the ironic generation, or maybe it was adults who referred to them that way. Perhaps they had it together on the outside, but they were looking for something deeper. Beneath it all was a kind of faith. That was both their salvation and their vulnerability. "Kids are so defenseless," he said.

"Only kids?"

"They're the easiest people to lead astray."

"You're not so old yourself."

"People take advantage of me, but not that way."

"You mean it's all society's fault."

"Certainly."

"Has it always been like that, do you think?"

"Society ends up with the adults it deserves. It's just a little more obvious nowadays."

"So there's nothing left to hope for?"

"I don't know, Bertil."

"What are you doing next New Year's Eve?"

"If you're asking whether I'll have a reservation at a restaurant, the answer is no."

"You'll sit in your living room and play Coltrane for a beautiful woman."

"That's a pretty safe bet."

"Which reminds me. We've already talked to a couple of Vikingsson's female acquaintances in Gothenburg. He's got his share."

"I saw that in the report. Does he sleep around?"

"You're thinking about another time."

"What time was that?"

"Just before a homosexual flight attendant brought HIV from Africa to New York."

"Have you asked him about that urban legend?"

Winter felt Vikingsson's eyes on him as he walked into the interrogation room. He was taller, his hair longer, than the photos had suggested, and he looked like someone who could account for his actions. He's got a good memory, Winter thought.

Cohen shuffled his papers. Winter nodded briefly and sat down. Vikingsson fidgeted in his chair, searching for the right defensive posture.

"This is Chief Inspector Erik Winter," Cohen said. "He'll be sitting in on our conversation."

Winter nodded again. Vikingsson raised his index finger as if to say he had decided to play along.

Cohen began this interrogation the same way he had so many before. He focused on what Vikingsson was doing at the time of the murders.

At several points, Vikingsson apologized sarcastically for not having walked around with a diary strapped to his chest.

COHEN: The friend you claim to have been with on Saturday is unable to confirm that you spent the whole evening together.

VIKINGSSON: Nobody's got a perfect memory.

COHEN: Are you saying she forgot what happened?

VIKINGSSON: Yes.

COHEN: Okay, we'll get back to that. Tell us what you did on the twenty-fourth.

VIKINGSSON: I had just returned from London and picked up a few things at my apartment.

COHEN: What kinds of things?

VIKINGSSON: Toiletries.

COHEN: You have two apartments, is that correct?

VIKINGSSON: You already know . . .

COHEN: I didn't catch your answer.

VIKINGSSON: That's not something you have to ask me.

COHEN: How long have you had two apartments?

VIKINGSSON: I wouldn't call it an apartment.

COHEN: What wouldn't you call an apartment?

VIKINGSSON: The place in Gothenburg. It's more of a . . .

COHEN: I didn't hear what you said.

VIKINGSSON: It's a crash pad.

COHEN: How long have you had it?

VIKINGSSON: A while. You can check up on that easier than I can.

COHEN: I'm going to ask you again how long you've had the apartment.

VIKINGSSON: Six months, maybe.

COHEN: Why did you rent it in the first place?

VIKINGSSON: The pad in Gothenburg?

COHEN: Yes.

VIKINGSSON: I wanted somewhere to get together with friends when I wasn't working.

COHEN: But you don't get together with friends in Gothenburg.

VIKINGSSON: What?

COHEN: You can't prove that you were with anyone at the times we asked about.

VIKINGSSON: That's your misfortune.

No, it's your misfortune, Winter thought. He scrutinized Vikingsson. There wasn't a drop of sweat on his forehead, nor was he squirming in his chair anymore. No nervousness to his gestures. Winter wondered how crazy he actually was.

COHEN: You said you rented the apartment so you could get together with friends.

VIKINGSSON: That's right.

COHEN: Where do you see your friends?

VIKINGSSON: What kind of question is that?

COHEN: Give us an example of where you meet your friends.

VIKINGSSON: At somebody else's place, not at mine because it's not very big.

COHEN: Have you ever had any guests there?

VIKINGSSON: Only a woman or two who weren't in the mood for their husbands.

COHEN: Your neighbors say that people often come to see you.

VIKINGSSON: Not when I'm there, anyway.

COHEN: Do you work out much?

VIKINGSSON: What?

COHEN: Do you spend a lot of time at the gym?

VIKINGSSON: No.

COHEN: Are you sure?

VIKINGSSON: I get all the exercise I need on the job.

COHEN: On the job?

VIKINGSSON: Yes, I spend the whole flight going up and down the aisle.

COHEN: So you don't work out at all?

VIKINGSSON: Once or twice, but that was a long time ago. Anyone who claims that he's seen me at a gym is lying.

COHEN: Nobody has claimed that.

VIKINGSSON: Good.

COHEN: On the other hand, you've been spotted with a big duffel bag more than once.

VIKINGSSON: What?

COHEN: You heard what I said.

VIKINGSSON: That's for the stuff I carry between Gothenburg and London.

COHEN: We didn't see it in your Gothenburg apartment.

VIKINGSSON: It's in London.

COHEN: We couldn't find it there either.

VIKINGSSON: Did you go into my London apartment?

COHEN: Assistant Chief Investigator Ringmar informed you that we searched it.

VIKINGSSON: Like hell he did.

COHEN: You've been informed of everything you need to know.

VIKINGSSON: This is nuts.

COHEN: Just tell us where your duffel bag is.

VIKINGSSON: What?

COHEN: Where is your duffel bag?

VIKINGSSON: If I had to guess, I'd say that one of your men got his grubby fingers on it.

COHEN: Do you ever keep it anywhere else?

VIKINGSSON: It's in London, for God's sake. The other flight attendants can verify that I had it the last time I was there. Yesterday, I mean.

COHEN: It's not in your apartment.

VIKINGSSON: Then the cops have it.

COHEN: We talked to the other flight attendants, and none of them saw you carrying a duffel bag.

VIKINGSSON: Then they must have had more important things on their mind.

COHEN: Do you have two duffel bags?

VIKINGSSON: What?

COHEN: Just answer my question.

VIKINGSSON: Are you guys starting to see double?

COHEN: Cut it out.

VIKINGSSON: The answer is no.

COHEN: Do you own a car?

VIKINGSSON: No.

COHEN: Is there a car in Gothenburg that you drive occasionally?

VIKINGSSON: Do I ever borrow somebody else's car? Sure, once in a while.

COHEN: Any car in particular?

VIKINGSSON: I don't understand what you're talking about.

You understand exactly what he's talking about, you bastard, Winter thought. Hold on a minute and you'll understand even better.

COHEN: Is there any particular car in Gothenburg that you borrow on a regular basis?

VIKINGSSON: No.

COHEN: You never drive a 1988 white Opel Kadett Caravan, license plate number ANG 999?

VIKINGSSON: What?

COHEN: Just answer the question.

VIKINGSSON: What was the question again?

COHEN: Do you ever drive an Opel Kadett Caravan, license plate number ANG 999, recently reregistered?

VIKINGSSON: No.

COHEN: We found it a couple of blocks from your apartment in a paid parking spot on Distansgatan Street.

VIKINGSSON: And?

COHEN: The parking spot belongs to an acquaintance of yours named Peter Möller. According to him, you sublease it from him.

VIKINGSSON: That's a lie.

COHEN: It's a lie that you sublease it?

VIKINGSSON: It's a lie.

COHEN: So you've never seen the car?

VIKINGSSON: Nope.

COHEN: It's registered in the name of Viking Carlsson.

VIKINGSSON: You don't say?

COHEN: Is that a coincidence?

VIKINGSSON: Is what a coincidence?

COHEN: The name of the owner.

VIKINGSSON: What was his name again?

COHEN: Viking Carlsson.

VIKINGSSON: I don't have a clue.

COHEN: You don't own the car?

VIKINGSSON: For the umpteenth time, no. You just said who the owner was.

COHEN: We found fingerprints in the car that match yours.

VIKINGSSON: That's a lie.

COHEN: We also found bloodstains in the trunk and other places in the car.

VIKINGSSON: I don't know anything about that.

COHEN: You have no idea where the bloodstains might have come from?

VIKINGSSON: Not the slightest.

COHEN: Why are your fingerprints in the car?

VIKINGSSON: The only explanation I can think of is that I rode in it. I've taken a few illegal taxis in my day.

COHEN: So you're saying you might have ridden in it?

VIKINGSSON: How else would my fingerprints have gotten there? All I can come up with is that it was an illegal taxi.

COHEN: Why is your acquaintance lying about the parking spot?

VIKINGSSON: What?

COHEN: Why do you think your acquaintance claims that you rent the parking spot from him?

VIKINGSSON: Wait. Now I remember . . .

COHEN: I didn't hear what you said.

VIKINGSSON: My God, I had forgotten all about it. I rent it from him and sublet it to someone else.

COHEN: You're sub-subletting a parking spot?

VIKINGSSON: Certainly.

COHEN: Can you give us the name of this other person?

VIKINGSSON: Sure, but the problem is I haven't heard from him for months. He hasn't been paying.

COHEN: But you've continued to pay on your sublease?

VIKINGSSON: Yes, I don't want to lose the spot.

COHEN: And you haven't heard from the person who rents it from you?

VIKINGSSON: Not in the last few months.

COHEN: Meanwhile, there's a car standing in a parking spot that you don't know anything about, a car that's got your fingerprints on the wheel and door handles.

VIKINGSSON: Wonders never cease.

COHEN: Our tests show that the bloodstains in the car match some of the blood we found in your Gothenburg apartment.

VIKINGSSON: How many blood types are there altogether? Three?

COHEN: We also have witness statements that there were bloody clothes in your apartment.

VIKINGSSON: Who says that?

COHEN: According to witness reports, a garbage bag in your apartment had bloody clothes in it.

VIKINGSSON: That's a lie.

COHEN: Where did the blood come from?

VIKINGSSON: What blood?

COHEN: The bloodstains.

VIKINGSSON: Okay, I might as well come clean before we go any further.

Winter exchanged glances with Cohen.

COHEN: What were you going to tell us?

VIKINGSSON: I'm no murderer.

COHEN: You'll be better off once you confess.

VIKINGSSON: What?

COHEN: All this questioning will be over and you'll feel an enormous sense of relief.

VIKINGSSON: I didn't do it, dammit.

COHEN: What didn't you do, Carl?

VIKINGSSON: I didn't . . .

COHEN: What did you say?

VIKINGSSON: I'm not . . .

COHEN: I can't hear you.

VIKINGSSON: There's a simple explanation for all of this. I do a little hunting on the side with a friend of mine.

COHEN: A little hunting on the side?

VIKINGSSON: Yes.

COHEN: What kind of hunting?

VIKINGSSON: Moose, deer, rabbits, game birds.

COHEN: Poaching, in other words?

VIKINGSSON: Yes.

COHEN: I asked whether you're a poacher and you answered in the affirmative. Is that correct?

VIKINGSSON: Yes.

COHEN: When do you hunt?

VIKINGSSON: Whenever I'm in Sweden. That's why I don't have any alibis.

COHEN: And where do you go to hunt?

VIKINGSSON: The woods north of here, in the Dalsland and Värmland provinces. It's not for . . .

COHEN: I didn't catch what you said.

VIKINGSSON: It's not for the money, even though it . . .

COHEN: Could you please repeat that?

VIKINGSSON: Even though it pays well.

COHEN: Why do you poach?

VIKINGSSON: For the thrill of it.

COHEN: You hunt for the thrill?

VIKINGSSON: Do you have any idea what it's like to be at the beck and call of a bunch of whining passengers all day long?

COHEN: No, I don't.

VIKINGSSON: You should give it a try sometime.

COHEN: So you hunt whenever you're in Sweden?

VIKINGSSON: Yes.

COHEN: And you use the car we were talking about before?

VIKINGSSON: Yes.

COHEN: A 1988 white Opel Kadett Caravan, license plate number ANG 999?

VIKINGSSON: Yes.

COHEN: Where do the bloodstains come from?

VIKINGSSON: From the game, of course.

COHEN: From the game?

VIKINGSSON: When we cut up the carcasses.

COHEN: There's human blood in the car and your apartment.

VIKINGSSON: Somebody must have cut himself.

COHEN: Who could have cut himself?

VIKINGSSON: My buddy cut himself once.

COHEN: What's his name?

VIKINGSSON: Do I have to say?

COHEN: Yes.

VIKINGSSON: Peter Möller.

COHEN: The same Peter Möller you rent the parking spot from?

VIKINGSSON: Yes.

COHEN: Did you cut somebody up, Carl?

VIKINGSSON: What?

COHEN: Did you kill those kids?

VIKINGSSON: No, goddammit. You've got to believe me.

Vikingsson was ushered back to his cell.

Cohen turned off the tape recorder and gathered up his papers. The room felt vacant, as if Vikingsson's voice had been a piece of furniture, now removed.

"What do you think?" Cohen asked.

"I'm speechless," Winter said. "I've never met anyone like him."

"A raving lunatic."

40

VIKINGSSON WAS ARRESTED THREE DAYS LATER. WHEN THE D.A.
walked out of the judge's chambers, he looked as though he were searching for a bowl to wash his hands in. They had requested that he be held for a month and had been given fourteen days.

Vikingsson shook his head—he, a petty criminal who didn't qualify for the major leagues.

They lined him up next to seven other six-foot two-inch blond or ash-blond men, who could just as easily have been Winter, Bolger or Bergenhem—or Macdonald with a wig on.

Or the victims, Winter thought. They could have stood there with a thumb in their pants pocket, already hungry even though it was still a couple of hours until lunch. Feeling immortal.

None of the witnesses could point out Vikingsson. Maybe they had chosen the decoys too carefully.

Winter had talked with Macdonald, who had arranged a photo lineup in Clapham. Anderton couldn't identify Vikingsson as the man he had seen with Per in the park. He had the wrong kind of hair.

There was another difference too, but Anderton couldn't say exactly what it was. Something about a jacket.

The whole idea of finding someone who would recognize Vikingsson had been hopeless from the start. They were clinging to what little they had, Winter thought, and time was passing.

McCoy Tyner was playing the introduction to the John Coltrane Quartet's "I Wish I Knew." It was past midnight. Winter sat and waited for dawn to stretch out its hand through the darkness. Coltrane's music was for the seekers and the restless at heart.

He got up and made a full circle around the room. The computer shone from the desk behind him, its reflection in the window a square of liquid radiance.

He had created a new scenario and closed the document just as the gruesome story came to a head. Coltrane was playing "It's Easy to Remember (but So Hard to Forget)." I'm not so sure about the first part, Winter thought as the short piece drifted through the room. He had been six years old when it was recorded.

The CD over, he put on Charlie Haden and Pat Metheny. It was music to bring back memories, even the ones that flew around the room in circles.

He went back to his scenario. Scrolling to one of the key paragraphs, he cut and pasted it three pages later. That made it part of the climax. He worked some more on the end of the story.

His thoughts had descended to a place where he didn't want to be. They swirled around an image of Bolger's bar. Vikingsson sat on one of the stools. What was he doing there? Winter had tried his best to rule out a connection between the two men but had come up short.

He forced himself to think about Bolger. He knew him, but only up to a certain point. He had dragged Bolger into this case as a consultant. Wasn't that the way it had been? He had turned to an old friend for help.

He needed to question his assumptions, use his analytical abilities. Assuming he had any left.

Why had Bolger talked about Red Records as though he had been there many years earlier when it had opened just recently? Winter had checked into it. Bolger claimed that he hadn't been in London for a long time. He made a point of repeating it on several occasions.

Winter went over to the stereo and put on *New York Eye and Ear Control*. The free-form jazz filled the room.

It seemed like a hundred years since Bolger had played the album for him.

The clerk at Ray's Jazz Shop had played it when he was there. Another

Scandinavian had been through shortly before. It's as if the clerk was following instructions, Winter thought.

The other Scandinavian had also bought the album.

When calling Winter on his cell phone in his London suite, Bolger had asked whether he had been to any music stores.

Winter raised the volume until it shook the room, then returned to the desk with the latest phone bill in his hand. Something had bothered him when it arrived the day before.

He looked at it with fresh eyes. The monthly charge was at the top, followed by a separate list. Domestic calls. Special services. That must be call forwarding, he thought.

Overseas calls—they referred to it as roaming. And calls from other countries to his phone. He paid for those.

He put his finger on the call to his suite. He had done some calculations the day before but couldn't make the charges add up. He and Bolger had talked for quite a while. The bill wasn't high enough.

Bolger hadn't called from Sweden. It was a local call. He must have been in London.

Bergenhem steadied himself with his feet planted on the deck. The only light was from Marianne's porthole.

When she opened the door, he put his arms around her and held her to him.

They found something to drink. It was warm in the galley.

"This is the last time," he said.

"No more days off?"

"You know what I mean."

"So your snooping is over."

"It's my job."

"I thought there was something more between us."

"There was something more, but not any longer."

"Then I think you should leave."

"Can't I just sit here with you for a while?"

"Poor guy, you don't know whether you're coming or going."

"That's not true."

"Do you want me to give you some information or don't you?"

"What?"

He felt the boat rock, a sensation so familiar that his body immediately knew which muscles to activate.

"You have a job to do, right?"

"A bigger one than I ever knew," Bergenhem said.

"You're hopeless."

"I mean it."

"You took advantage of me."

"No."

"The hell you didn't."

"In that case, I took advantage of myself too."

"Do you want a name?" She flung the words at him in desperation. "Isn't that what you're looking for?"

Bergenhem's mouth felt dry.

"There's somebody you don't know anything about, even though you think you do. I have no idea what he has to do with all of this, but he scares the shit out of me. And I don't think he's alone."

"What?"

"Forget it."

The boat swayed again and the jackdaws screeched above the old tobacco building, the din growing louder and louder.

"I don't know very much about it," she resumed. "But I saw him with one of the victims."

"What did you just say?"

"Maybe with two of them."

The screeching stopped.

"When?"

She shrugged. "He's a night owl like me."

"A night owl?"

"That's not so strange. He's in the industry too."

"The porn industry?"

"Yes, and he's totally crazy, a psychopath or whatever you call it."

"What's his name?"

She told him, and Bergenhem made her repeat it to be sure he had heard correctly.

He felt delirious. A voice told him the right thing to do, but he ignored it. He was alone and he wanted to act alone. "Why didn't you tell me before?" he asked.

"I thought my memory was playing tricks on me. All I could

remember was a face. I've been so confused about everything—about you too. And I'm not ready to die yet."

"There's not going to be any more dying here."

Bergenhem stood outside the door. It was lunacy to play the lonesome hero like this. He saw a finger on the bell but it wasn't his. He pressed again.

Bolger raised his eyebrows when he opened the door. He was wearing a terrycloth robe. "Hi, Lars."

"Hi."

"It's a bit late, isn't it?"

"I'd like to come in for a minute."

"Can't we talk tomorrow?"

"Preferably now."

Bolger moved out of the way and Bergenhem stepped inside.

"You can leave your jacket there." Bolger nodded at a splintery chair under a mirror. "Do you want some coffee or tea?"

"No, thanks."

"This way," Bolger said, leading him through the short hallway. "Have a seat." He pointed to an armchair and sat down across from it on the other side of a glass table.

Bergenhem looked around the room but couldn't take it in. You can get up and leave, he told himself, and say that Martina is about to go into labor.

"You had something to tell me," Bolger said.

"Sorry, what did you say?"

"You've got something on your mind, right?"

Bergenhem searched for the right words. He had just found them when Bolger went on. "You've been talking to that stripper, I assume. She says I'm a shady character. I'm surprised you didn't come by earlier and ask me about her accusations."

"I came now."

"Am I right?"

"I have a couple of questions."

"You ring my bell in the middle of the night just to ask a couple of questions?" Bolger said. "You think you're onto something, I can tell it from your face. You couldn't wait until morning."

"We talked to a witness."

"We? You mean the stripper passed on some juicy gossip."

"I need a little help from you."

"It's too late to switch tactics."

"What?"

"You didn't come here to ask for my help. You came to point the finger at me."

"No."

"I've done all I could for you, you snotty-nosed brat. I've been covering for you while you chase that crazy stripper. Don't you think I know what you're up to? You're not a detective. You're a baby. She says something about me and the first thing you do is come running here. Erik's going to get an earful about your nighttime adventures."

"I haven't talked to her about you."

Bolger sat still in the glare of a lamp, blocking the light every time he moved his head.

He looks like he has a halo, Bergenhem thought. "You're the one who did it," he said.

"What the hell are you talking about?"

"I wasn't completely sure before, but I am now."

"Then where's the SWAT team?"

"You motherfucker."

Bolger laughed. His robe parted and the hair of his chest gleamed in the semidarkness. "You're too much, pal."

"You murdered those kids. I don't know why you did it, but I'm going to find out."

"Did you shoot up with that junkie chick of yours or are you just drunk?"

"Will you come with me?"

"What?"

"I want you to come with me. You're under suspi—"

Bolger was on his feet. "If you leave now, we can pretend this little incident never happened."

"I'm not going anywhere."

"Then I'll call Erik."

"I'll call him."

"Go ahead. You've got your cell with you, don't you?"

"No," Bergenhem said, standing up. He spotted a phone on a

crescent-shaped desk next to the window. He made his way between the armchair and the table. Bolger stepped in front of him as he was about to pass. They were the same height. Bergenhem looked Bolger in the eye.

"I'll call," Bolger said.

"Get out of my way," Bergenhem said, raising a hand, but Bolger lunged at him, and Bergenhem staggered backward. Recovering his balance, he started toward Bolger again.

"Come on," Bolger said, jabbing at Bergenhem's shoulder.

Bergenhem lost his footing. His legs buckled and the back of his head struck the edge of the table with a blow that sounded like iron against iron. The glass didn't break. He looked as if he were hovering in the air with his head pinned to the table, his eyeballs rolling as he slid to the floor. A twitch snaked its way from his head to his legs and back again.

Bolger heard sounds coming from Bergenhem's mouth and throat. Leaning over, he heard them again, a groan that seemed detached from the injured man beneath him.

Bergenhem appeared to be unconscious, but then he opened his eyes. Bolger couldn't tell whether they saw anything. Then they closed again. The horrible sounds resumed.

Bolger hadn't asked for trouble, hadn't invited Bergenhem to come. He raised Bergenhem's head and placed his forearm on the throat that was making the hideous noise. Shifting his weight, he pressed down, felt Bergenhem's body lurch sideways and pressed even harder.

After a while, the moans died out. But Bergenhem's eyes were open and continued to move in their eerie way.

Bolger stood and pulled on Bergenhem's legs. They were still twitching. Bolger picked him up.

He had never had the slightest interest in Bergenhem or what he was up to. Bergenhem meant nothing to him.

Bolger carried him out to the stairway as if they were the only people left in the world.

41

WINTER WAS SCALING A CLIFF. A STEREO SPEAKER JUTTED OUT
at the top. "What's New" was playing. Coltrane peered down over
the cliff, took the mouthpiece from his lips, lit a Gitanes cigarette and
shouted to Winter *What's New, What's New, What's New,* and the cell
phone attached to his tenor sax jangled against its straight neck. A tenor
sax is supposed to be bent, Winter thought. It's soprano saxes that are
straight. He was just about to say so aloud, but now Macdonald was
holding the phone instead and screaming, *Answer you snob, answer before
the kid hangs up.* Winter tried to take the phone but it was stuck to the
instrument. The phone rang and rang.

He woke up and the phone on his nightstand was ringing. It stopped
and the cell phone on the desk took over. He barreled out of bed and
grabbed it but nobody was there. The landline started all over again.
Darting back, he stubbed his big toe on the leg of the bed. The pain
surged through his body after a numb second. "Hello?" he said. His eyes
were watering from the pain. He reached for his toe but it rebuffed his
hand. He was sure he had broken it.

"Is this Erik? Erik Winter?"

She sounded more or less like he felt, a cold gust of agony through
the receiver. Out of his other ear, he heard Coltrane's music stuck on
repeat in the living room. It wasn't the first time he had fallen asleep
before turning everything off and getting ready for bed.

The pain in his toe, now his whole foot, had gone from red hot to a
dull, malevolent throb. He concentrated on the voice at the other end of
the line. "Yes, this is Winter."

"I'm sorry if I woke you. This is Martina Bergenhem."

They had met several times. Winter liked her. She possessed a calm maturity he hoped would rub off on her husband. "Hi, Martina."

Winter leaned over the nightstand and turned on the lamp. He blinked a couple of times to get used to the light. He held up his watch. It was cold in his palm. The hands pointed to four o'clock.

"I can't get hold of Lars."

"What did you say?"

"He hasn't come home tonight and I have to go . . ."

Winter heard her start to cry—or cry some more.

"I have to go to the hospital."

"Hasn't he called?" It was one of those meaningless questions. But maybe they had to be asked anyway.

"No, I thought he was out on some . . ."

"I don't know," Winter said. "But it's certainly possible."

"You don't know?"

"No, Martina, but I'll find out as fast as I humanly can."

"I'm worried about him."

My God, Winter thought. "Are you all alone?"

"Yes. I called my mom but she lives in Stockholm."

She might as well have said the Caribbean, he thought.

"I just called a taxi," she said.

"Is there a neighbor or somebody else nearby who can help you?"

"I didn't want to bother . . ."

"I'll send someone to pick you up."

"But the taxi . . ."

"Can you hold on a minute, Martina?"

"What?"

"Don't hang up, I just want to make a quick call on the other line." He put the phone down, took a step to the side and shouted from the pain. Hopping over to the desk, he picked up the cell phone and made his call. When he was done, he returned and sat back down on the bed, his injured foot dangling over the edge. "Martina?"

"Yes?"

"Somebody will be there within ten minutes to pick you up and take you to Sahlgrenska Hospital. You can lie down in the car if necessary. I asked a friend to go along and assist you. Her name is Angela and she's a doctor. She'll be in the car when it gets to your house."

"I . . ."

"Get ready, and they'll be there before you know it. Meanwhile I'll make sure that Lars goes directly to the hospital. I'll look for him as soon as we hang up."

Winter sat still. He carefully flexed his ankle and felt the toe. It was tender but there wasn't any swelling. Maybe it wasn't broken after all. It hardly mattered one way or the other—you didn't put a splint on a toe.

He'd wear a pair of clogs if necessary.

He limped to the bathroom, intimations of disaster coursing through his body.

He was examining his toe under the lightbulb when the phone rang again. He hobbled back. A woman introduced herself as Marianne Johnsén. Winter listened.

Bergenhem was found at eight o'clock in the morning. Unable to resist any longer, the proud owner of a new sailboat had driven down to the Tångudden Road Marina to feast his eyes on it before the season started.

Bergenhem was sitting straight up, wedged between two rocks at Hästevik Bay. The gulls were more raucous than usual at this time of day. The boat owner had seen the legs sticking out and forgotten his plans. The patrol officer responding to the alarm had recognized Bergenhem.

Winter had dragged his sore toe behind him over the meadow and down into the crevices. He stood next to the spot where Bergenhem had been, as if offering his protection. The meaning of life could have become a moot question for you, Lars—for me too, he thought.

The morning drifted blue and white over Älvsborgsfjorden Bay, the light lucid as if it had been scrubbed clean. Stena Line ferried people to Denmark as though nothing had happened. The Stora Billingen fields would be bursting with life in less than a month. As though nothing had happened, Winter repeated to himself. The bus makes its scheduled stops, passengers get on and off. Tonight people will sit down at the dinner table as always and gather in the living room with their eyes glued to the television.

"It's my fault," he said. "Tell me that it's my fault."

"It's like you're pleading with me," Ringmar said.

"Just say it."

"He's your man."

"More, say more."

"You're his boss."

"I want to hear it all."

"Pull yourself together."

Winter looked south over the meadow. They had cordoned it off from the road. The ruts were fresh, but lots of people had driven down to the water in the past few days. Fishermen, boat owners, lovers. "There's nothing more for us to do here," he said, down on one knee next to the rocks.

"His neck was bleeding," Ringmar said.

"Suffocation. Ask the doctors and they'll tell you someone tried to choke him."

The forensic team was at work all around them.

"You're right, we can't do anything more here," Ringmar said.

Winter stared at the rocks. He wasn't sure how old Bergenhem was. Twenty-six? Martina was a few years older, he knew that. "His wife just had a baby girl," he said, looking up at Ringmar.

"You mentioned that in the car."

"Everything went fine. Angela was there the whole time, and her mother is coming this afternoon. From Stockholm. Bergenhem's mother-in-law, I mean." Winter stood up. "Why haven't you asked me?"

"What?"

"Why haven't you asked me when I'm going to tell Martina?"

"Jesus, Erik, it's only . . ."

"I've got to tell her today. We can't keep it from the press."

"No."

"Today."

"Let Östergaard go with you."

"I'll do it myself. She can take care of me afterward."

Ringmar drove them back to the city through the old center of Kungsten. Långedragsvägen Way had been patched together and repaired century after century. They went under the viaduct and continued across the Sandarna district. Winter gave a start when the car hit a bump.

"How's your foot doing?" Ringmar asked.

"It's my toe."

"At least you can still walk."

"That's what counts."

"Right."

"And Marianne has disappeared?"

"We're looking all over for her," Ringmar said.

"No trace of her anywhere."

"It's only been a few hours."

"Do you think she's dead?"

"No, just afraid. Bergenhem was completely unprofessional. He didn't keep us up to date on what was happening, and it almost cost him his life."

Winter looked out at the cemetery. "Act unprofessionally and get killed. That's a good way to sum up our line of work."

They took the Mariaplan roundabout. Gothenburg is made up of twenty-five small towns, Winter thought, and they're all just as dangerous.

"Do you think he's going to make it?" Ringmar asked.

"He's over the worst of it now. A hell of a headache, but he's hanging in there. He's young and strong."

"But no hero."

"Not this time, anyway."

"She knows," Ringmar said.

"Who, Marianne?"

"She knows."

"She's not the only one. So do I."

"What do you mean?"

"It's almost over."

Winter called the bar and got the answering machine. He hailed a taxi.

He rang Bolger's bell and waited. He rang again, then walked back down the two flights of stairs, crossing over to an alley on the other side of the street. The store windows were dark. Night arrived without warning in April, almost like a burglar.

I've been blind and deaf, he thought. Maybe I'm to blame, maybe not. There have been hints, innuendos, but who could have . . .

He swatted away those thoughts. He had already been through them more than once.

Bolger drove up, parked his BMW and got out. He raised the remote and Winter heard the lock click shut in the stillness of the night. Bolger disappeared through the front door of the building.

Maybe you're the one who's crazy, Winter thought. Your story is the figment of a madman's imagination. No rules apply any longer, and never have. Each thought crumbles and falls to pieces that fly off in all directions and come back—often broken, rarely whole. Nothing can be polished or even forced into a symmetrical pattern. Nothing is unblemished, not even on the surface.

A gust of wind blew in from the street and swirled behind him.

He'll come back out any minute, Winter thought. You can shoot him on the spot and that will be it for your career.

Bolger walked out five minutes later. He extended his arm and the lock clicked. After settling into the driver's seat, he took off.

How strange that not a single person has passed by while you've been standing here, Winter thought. It's like a movie in which a thousand people gather outside a cordoned-off area and follow what's going on. The eye of the camera watches from a privileged position above it all.

He stepped out of the alley, limped across the street, climbed the stairs and rang the bell again. He took out his ring of skeleton keys and tried one of them. The steel felt soft through his glove.

The lock gave way and he opened the door. He slowly made his way from room to room.

The first place he looked was the chest of drawers, but there was nothing in it except socks and underwear. Bolger was a stickler for neatness.

He checked the closets: shoes, clothes, belts and ties.

A thick envelope, open like a defiant challenge, lay in the third desk drawer from the top. Inside were three passports, each under a different name, none of them Bolger's. But the photographs were of him. None of the pages were stamped—the brave new Europe had no use for that sort of thing. He's got more of these somewhere, Winter thought.

One of the passports was in the name of someone who had flown to London the day after Christian.

The investigators had focused all their attention on the passenger lists for the three days around the victim's arrival.

It was a monumental discovery, but Winter simply filed it away in his mind like a bread crumb that had been laid out for him. I've been blind, but now I see, he thought. I'm holding this passport. My hands are trembling.

Maybe it's just another inexplicable coincidence.

He found lots of papers—accounting records, invoices, bills, business contracts—but they didn't interest him. Some porn magazines, nothing alarming, were stacked neatly in the bedroom dresser.

No receipts, no copies of tickets or vouchers.

He went back to the desk and picked up a pile of paper from the hutch. There were at least twenty sheets, each of them scribbled all over in a pointed, angular longhand. It looked like a screenplay written in a state of rage. He couldn't make out the words, then suddenly caught sight of his name in clear, straight letters. He flipped to the next sheet. There was his name again. It was all he could read. The incomprehensible words sprawled out in all directions.

A chill more wretched than any he had ever felt before ran down his back.

A cloth was draped over a foot-high rectangular object on the desk.

He removed the cloth and stared at a photograph of himself, taken shortly before high school graduation. The glass frame looked new.

42

"WHERE IS HE, THEN?" RINGMAR ASKED. "WE'VE BEEN IN HIS apartment and gone to his bar. Nobody knows."

"I know," Winter said.

The wind swirled above the fjord like a crazed wanderer. Winter pulled his cap down over his ears. His thoughts were frozen in place.

"You're all alone," he told himself as the boat docked.

The sea heather bowed over the cliffs as in prayer.

Bolger stood by his outdoor brick fireplace and jabbed at the coal with his poker. Winter had seen him walk over to the structure as he approached.

"First you never come and now you show up every day," Bolger said when Winter stood next to him. He continued to stoke the fire without looking up, then tapped the brick with the poker.

"We found Bergenhem."

"Where was he? With his stripper?"

"In a crevice by the Tångudden Road Marina."

"That kid will do anything to avoid you."

"I want you to come with me now, Johan."

"What did you say?"

"It's over."

"Do you know who the murderer is? Don't tell me it's Bergenhem."

"I have a boat down at the pier."

"I might have a thing or two to say about what Bergenhem was up to." Bolger threw the poker to the ground. It bounced back against the brick with a clang. "But you don't want to listen. You've never wanted to listen to me, Mr. Smarty Pants."

"Let's go, Johan."

"You've always thought you knew it all, Erik. Ever since I can remember. If you're so damn smart, why haven't you solved this case yet? You haven't gotten a step further than when you came to the bar and asked for my help a million years ago. My help!" He swayed slightly. The wind cried, delivering a cryptic message from the opposite shore.

"There were all kinds of things that could have helped you, Erik, but you couldn't see them. You're not so smart after all."

They walked down the hill, Bolger as if in his sleep.

"While you're taking this stroll with me, it could happen again. Has that occurred to you?"

They had been questioning Bolger for three hours when another inspector came in and said that Winter had a call. It was Marianne, obviously in a phone booth. He could hear the roar of traffic in the background.

"You don't know how happy I am to hear from you," Winter said.

"It's dreadful. I just read about it. He was a fine man."

"He's going to pull through."

"What? Is he alive?"

"Yes."

Winter heard something that sounded like a car splashing water over the curb. He looked out the window. Rain clouds had blown over Gothenburg. "You don't have to be afraid," he said.

"Why not?"

"We have him here."

"Him?"

"Yes."

"Bolger?"

"That's right."

"You knew. It was like you knew even before I called and told you the first time."

"He said it himself."

"Just now?"

"A long time ago."

"I don't understand."

"I'll explain. But I have to see you."

"I don't know if I can."

"It's absolutely necessary. There's a good chance that he'll be released otherwise."

"But you told me . . ."

"I'll explain everything."

Four hours later they obtained a detention order for Bolger on suspicion of murder. He flatly denied everything, insisting that he needed to sleep. Maybe I'll remember more when I'm rested, he repeated over and over.

Marianne had agreed to meet Winter and told him she had seen Bolger with two of the victims.

How did she know? She recognized them in the photos that were circulated afterward. Where had she seen them together? Someplace that few people went to. Why hadn't she said anything? She couldn't explain it. Nobody else was really in a position to see them, she had offered, and Winter didn't press her on it right then.

There was something in her manner, a kind of hesitation, when she talked about Bolger. About the way he was. Winter kept that in the back of his mind while he moved on to other things.

"But Lars didn't say he was going straight to Bolger's apartment the last time you saw him?"

"He didn't have to say it."

Winter knew what time everything had happened. Bolger could have been Bergenhem's assailant.

Where had Bergenhem been injured? Not among the rocks, certainly. Someone had driven across the fields and carried him down there.

They had turned Bolger's apartment upside down.

"Can he get out?" Marianne had asked.

"No," Winter said.

"Will he be arrested?"

"Tomorrow."

"Who's going to believe anything I say?"

"We've got other evidence too."

"Enough to convict him?"

"Yes."

But he didn't know the true answer to that question. They had strong circumstantial evidence, that was all. Winter had thought Bolger would confess but there was no guarantee, and now he was worried that Bolger would maintain his innocence forever.

"We're going to need you," he'd said to Marianne.

"I can't go back to the boat."

"Is there some other reason?"

"What would that be?"

"Fear."

"Would that be so strange?"

"Are you afraid of someone else?"

"*Is* there someone else?"

"I can't honestly tell you."

"Are there more murderers?"

"We don't know."

"Jesus."

Winter could tell she had more on her mind.

"I feel like somebody's after me," Marianne said. "He has an accomplice or whatever you call it. But I'm not sure."

"Do you know who it is?"

"No."

Macdonald called, his voice equal parts agitation and relief. "Is it going to stick?" he asked.

"Sooner or later," Winter said. "We might have a murder weapon too."

"That will make your Viking happy."

"He'll have to be a witness if we don't find anything else. Assuming that Bolger flew on Vikingsson's plane under one of his pseudonyms."

"Didn't you say Vikingsson was crazy?"

"What are we going to do with him? He claims he's never set eyes on Bolger. He's been to Bolger's bar, but it's just one of many. Why would he remember that particular bartender? We got hold of Möller, his hunting companion."

"And?"

"He says he doesn't know a thing about it."

"The poaching story?"

"All he has to say is that Vikingsson is nuts and he doesn't know what the guy is talking about. How are things going there?"

"Under control."

"Are the papers ready?"

"Almost."

"How many people have you told?"

"We're operating on a need-to-know basis."

"That's good."

"Maybe we're being overly cautious."

"You're doing the right thing."

"God have mercy on us."

"Have you received the photos?"

"You Swedes all look alike. How the hell can we set up a photo lineup with a bunch of fucking clones?"

The line crackled with static, as if the North Sea were eavesdropping on the conversation.

"We share the same sky and the same north wind," Macdonald said. "But you guys look different from us. It's hard to explain."

"Aberdeen is at the same latitude as Gothenburg."

"On the map?"

"Where else?"

"Talk to you soon. May God be with us."

Cohen had asked Winter to conduct the interrogation but he'd declined. He sat in the background like a shadow from another time. He could get up and leave if he was in the way.

Bolger's somnambulistic behavior had reversed itself. He was full of life, derisive, aggressive, and Winter recognized the tough teenager he had once known. Bolger was a perpetual-motion machine back then, constantly talking about everything he was going to do, the person he would someday become. He would succeed where nobody else could. He was going to prove he was smarter than all the rest.

Winter had sat for hours and thought about what Bolger had said so long ago, what he had done, what he himself had done, what had become of Bolger during all those years that had pursued them with growing fury and finally caught up with them here in this interrogation room.

COHEN: You haven't satisfactorily accounted for your comings and goings on Friday, March thirteenth.

BOLGER: Like I said, it was an unlucky day and I didn't want to see anyone. I never left home.

COHEN: Is there someone who can confirm that?

BOLGER: That's your job to find out.

COHEN: You'd be better off if you cooperated.

BOLGER: Cooperated? Who with? I'm innocent.

COHEN: You've said that several times now.

BOLGER: A lot of good it does. The big boss over there in the corner doesn't believe a word I say. With friends like him, who needs enemies?

COHEN: We found three passports in your apartment. They're in the following names.

Bolger listened while Cohen recited the names.

COHEN: What do you know about those passports?

BOLGER: Nothing.

COHEN: Are you sure?

BOLGER: Somebody planted them.

COHEN: Who would put three passports in your apartment?

BOLGER: Chief Inspector Erik Winter, who else?

COHEN: You're claiming that the assistant head of the homicide division of the county criminal investigation unit put passports in your apartment. Is that right?

BOLGER: He broke in, didn't he? That's against the law. Planting evidence, or whatever the hell you call it, is the logical next step.

COHEN: We have no knowledge of someone breaking into your apartment.

BOLGER: But I do.

COHEN: What were the passports used for?

BOLGER: Are you deaf or something? I have no idea.

They went on and on in the same vein. Winter studied Bolger from the side. His jowls were much heavier than when he was a kid. Something had drawn them to each other back then, and it had continued through the years. They had both remained bachelors, chosen not to have families—or families had chosen not to have them. Winter remembered Macdonald's ponytail-clad kin. He had felt a pang of regret when he thought about the photo afterward. What did he have but the remnants of a family? If even that. When had he called his sister last?

Was Bolger plagued by the same regrets? Winter listened distractedly to the interrogation, the questions, the short answers, a couple that were a little longer. The voices came together in the middle of the room and he could no longer tell who was saying what.

Cohen ended the session, and Bolger followed the guards out without looking at Winter.

"I'd like to get a psychological profile of this guy," Cohen said.

"I'll arrange for one."

43

MACDONALD CALLED AGAIN. HOUR AFTER HOUR, WINTER SAT
deep in thought with his palms pressed against his forehead. Days had
come and gone, bringing light and darkness and the whisper of a new
kind of wind when he crossed Heden Park.

His phone jolted him out of his reverie.

"Publicizing those photos of Bolger may have yielded us some results," Macdonald said. "For whatever it's worth."

"You said yesterday you'd never manage to sift through everything."

"That was yesterday."

"So what happened?"

"A couple called. They live near Christian's hotel and say that they
saw him sitting with a man outside a pub on Camberwell Grove."

"Where's that?"

"It's that upscale street with Georgian architecture. I pointed it out to
you when you were here. Our inspectors had knocked on all the doors
in the neighborhood, but this couple was away at the time and we never
had a chance to go back."

"Okay."

"They saw a black guy around twenty years old drinking beer with a
tall blond man who could have been in his midthirties."

"And they're sure about that?"

"They're sure it's your high school buddy."

"Don't call him that."

"What?"

"Please don't use that expression."

"Sorry. Anyway, the woman is positive. She watched them out of the corner of her eye when her boyfriend was inside the pub."

"But all they've seen is a photo."

"She also said she figured the kid was a foreigner because it's so unusual to see a black person at that pub."

"Local blacks are afraid to go there."

"Right."

"And she thinks it was Bolger?"

"Yes, but I'm going to reserve judgment until we can arrange a real lineup."

"And suddenly they'll all look the same to her."

Silence at the other end of the line. The static was like fragments of Macdonald's thoughts, crystallized in the emptiness of space.

"How's the interrogation going?" Macdonald asked.

"He's not talking. When he opens up a little, he claims he can't remember. He's had a lot to say about amnesia the past few days."

"It's not so unusual for a murder suspect to say he can't remember."

"I have my doubts. Deep down I know for sure, but I still have my doubts. Maybe it's time for someone to take over the investigation who's more capable. Or at least less emotionally involved." He heard his own breathing in the receiver. "I've talked with Skogome, the forensic psychologist. He's working on a profile of Bolger."

"I have a lot of respect for those guys."

"So do I."

"As you know, people can feign amnesia to avoid confessing."

"Yes."

"Or it can be for real. That would make things a bit tougher for us, wouldn't it? We'd find ourselves in unknown territory."

Winter didn't respond.

"Am I right, Erik?"

"He's never going to confess under interrogation. I know what he's like, and he's simply not going to do that."

"Are you sure?"

"I also know what his motive was."

"What?"

"I'll tell you as soon as I've thought through it, finished writing."

"Writing?"

"My story."

Macdonald waited, but Winter had nothing more to say. Macdonald was breathing heavily, and it sounded to Winter like he'd caught cold in the middle of the British spring.

"How are things with Frankie?" Winter asked.

"He'll never let himself get drawn into something that endangers his own safety."

"But what's he looking for? Remember all that stuff he had to say about torture scenes?"

"I couldn't tell you. He left a message for me this morning. I called back but he was out."

"Maybe he's found something."

"Frankie? You never know."

"Do you trust him?"

"Depends on what you mean by trust."

"You know what I mean."

"Frankie may be black, but his soul is white as snow."

"Would he appreciate that comparison?"

"Of course not. Would you? I'll call you right away if he comes up with anything you need to know."

"Great."

"Going back to Bolger's memory problems—according to the statistics I've seen, 30 percent of the most violent criminals claim they can't remember what happened."

"The numbers are about the same here in Sweden."

"We do lots of simulations, and it seems they have a naïve hope of holding on to their innocence."

"Exactly."

Winter knew that memory lapses needed to be taken seriously. If you wanted to get as close to the truth as possible, they had to be acknowledged and diagnosed. It was called dissociative amnesia. "But many offenders with amnesia have had mental problems at some point in their lives," he said to Macdonald.

He had just spoken to an expert about it. Amnesia might be limited to the point at which the actual crime was committed. Or it could involve a personality change and loss of identity for several days. Or a split personality.

Winter had a moment of terror during their conversation. He had given the expert the photograph and handwritten material from Bolger's apartment, and they'd discussed possible connections.

The expert explained that one cause of genuine amnesia was trauma or profound, emotionally charged conflict earlier in life.

Committing a crime was accompanied by strong feelings and extreme stress.

Criminals don't generally exhibit any anxiety about their amnesia.

Bolger didn't exhibit any anxiety. He alternated between indifference and scorn, his eyes darkening as he insisted he was doing his best to remember. He carried himself as if he were asleep.

But there were clear indications of feigned amnesia. Winter had read what the researchers said about it—how you had to be on your guard if the amnesia started right after the crime, or if it varied from one interrogation session to the next.

That's the way it was with Bolger. No two sessions were the same. But he was now certain that he wouldn't be able to remember what happened even if he had more time or more clues to help him out.

It's like permafrost that covers the whole world, Winter thought. Only a huge explosion in the brain can save us and rescue the victims from the scourge of their assailants' willful ignorance.

"You still there?" Macdonald asked.

"I'm still here."

"No turning back, then."

"It's our only chance."

"Do you know how much it's going to cost?"

"Money is no object for me."

"I forgot about that."

Winter was scouring his brain for one particular event, and if he could remember what it was, the answer would be there. Everything would be over.

How many hours had he devoted to thinking about the past? The early years, when he and Bolger had spent so much time together . . .

What had it been like?

There was the rivalry. He hadn't thought about it much at the time, but it was always there. And he had always turned out to be right. Or he had won the game, which perhaps was the same thing.

He surrounded himself with silence that night. The intermittent cries of the city were his only link to the years he had spent there, beyond the balcony.

Bolger had been briefly committed for mental problems. It had all been hush-hush. His father was like barbed wire coiled round and round the family secrets.

Bolger had always walked one step behind him and slightly to the side, and Winter had rarely turned around. How must that have felt?

Was that an oversimplification? Maybe that's what he was looking for—the simple, unadorned truth.

They give you funny looks at police headquarters, he thought. Unless it's the phantoms in your brain making you imagine things.

His conjuring might be a reconstruction of events, another caper of the phantoms, but he could follow the signs of the last few months backward like a thin but unbreakable thread. A series of messages, clues.

There had been words, fragments of music, as if Bolger had planned the whole scenario far in advance: if you're so brilliant, pal, here's something to get your mental juices going. Winter was starting to see the pattern.

His friend had challenged him. Was that the word for it? There was an unspoken plea in everything Bolger did, explicit but coming from another place—one step behind him and slightly to the side.

Bolger had known Winter would go to London, could read his intentions. Nothing that he had said was a matter of chance. It was all in the story, the one Winter had thought he was writing.

Maybe you've spent your days and nights dreaming, he thought. This could all be an illusion. Everything is unfounded, a misunderstanding. There's no concrete reason to hope that our efforts have succeeded, that we've found the real murderer.

Do you want to be right or wrong?

Winter tried to persuade himself that it wasn't about him, that it was something bigger. You could be anyone—a pawn in his fury to commit deeds so terrible that no hand can undo them.

Another memory emerged. His memories were like a photo album and a diary lying open side by side. Something had happened to Bolger, but he couldn't recall what it was.

There were two days left before they would have to release Bolger, unless something else happened in the interim.

He splashed water on his face and fell into a dreamless sleep.

44

THEY TOOK BOLGER DOWN TO THE SECOND FLOOR. WINTER FELT like his throat had been stitched shut.

Bolger bumped against the wall of the corridor. He looked at Winter, his pupils nonexistent. Then he spoke to him like a hiking companion on their way down to the shore. He said they could be friends again once all this was over.

Outside the lineup room, Bolger said something nobody understood and bumped against the wall again. The hair on the back of Winter's neck was cold from sweat. His revolver chafed under his arm. Bolger started to rock back and forth on his heels, the sway extending to his whole body. The guards tightened their grip.

The door opened. Winter caught sight of a ponytail and leather jacket, but Macdonald ignored him and followed Bolger's every move. The guards led Bolger sideways through the doorway.

Macdonald walked slowly toward Bolger and stopped when he was six inches away. Winter noticed they were exactly the same height.

The April sun through the window blended with a floor lamp in the middle of the room, the light softer than in the corridor. Seven decoys stood along one of the walls opposite a horizontal one-way mirror.

A growl rose from Bolger's throat. He shook, and the muscles of his forearms tensed. Everything was frozen in the eternal now.

Winter walked out of the lineup room and into the area on the other side of the mirror.

The bed was in the far corner, the wheels locked in place. It looked like one of the old-fashioned cots hospitals once used, but it was designed to take aboard present-day aircraft.

The face peeked out like a black mask against the pillowcase and gauze. Winter had never seen him in real life, only in photos.

Christian's eyes shone as he stared into the lineup room. He seemed to be straining to raise his bandaged arm, which followed the contours of his body on the bed.

He moved his head back and forth, echoing Bolger's gestures a few minutes earlier. He gazed at Bolger as a ghost inspects his murderer and finally nodded.

Winter walked up to Christian and listened to his soft voice. All doubt vanished.

Winter returned to the lineup room. The decoys were still there, but he was blind to them. Bolger looked at Winter, then nodded at the mirror. He's nodding at both of us, Winter thought. He knows who's behind the mirror. He isn't rocking back and forth anymore.

What did you expect? Winter thought. That he would start trembling and frothing at the mouth when he realized what was happening?

Winter closed his eyes and imagined Bolger lunging forward and dragging the guards behind him with a horrific display of strength.

When he opened his eyes again, Bolger stood there quietly as if in meditation. Nobody was touching him. He was staring at Winter now. There was a clarity to his gaze that Winter hadn't seen since they'd first brought him in.

"It's not over, and it never will be," Bolger said, and his eyes clouded over again.

They were sitting in Winter's office. All his sweating had cooled him down. Macdonald's face was pale and drawn, his cheekbones stark.

"I thought we had lost him for good," Winter said.

"Hmm."

"He's still on this side of madness, but it was a close call." He lit a cigarillo. His hands trembled slightly, still reverberating from the day's events. "He said it's never going to end." The smoke curled toward the ceiling.

"I know what he means."

"You do?"

"At least part of it."

Winter took another puff but tasted nothing.

"Remember how disappointed you were when you had to let Vikingsson go?" Macdonald asked. "Or even before that, when he gave you all that bullshit about poaching?"

"Yes."

"He's still on the loose."

The blood drained from Winter's face.

"Think about the photo collage you found in his apartment."

"Please cut to the chase, Steve."

"Neither of us has dismissed him from our thoughts, or from the investigation, or whatever you want to call it at this point."

"Of course not."

"I was disappointed too. So we talked with Vikingsson ourselves when he was in London. It was just like you said once. There was more to him than he was letting on to; I could also sense it. So I did what you said, or what you wanted."

"What are you getting at?"

"Listen carefully now. You sat in my office once and told me that you believed in a merciful God. And here's your reward. It happened late last night. I wanted to wait to tell you in person."

"Tell me what?"

"We kept Vikingsson under surveillance. Something about him kept bothering me, so I put two men on him for a few days just to see what would happen. Frankie had also said—"

"Steve!"

"Hold on, I have to say this first. Frankie ran across someone who had something to sell. Nothing you'd ever see at a porn theater in Soho. Be that as it may, it all ends up in that part of the city eventually."

"Vikingsson was in Soho?"

"Some blond guy was making the rounds with a special offer. He was extraordinarily discreet, but not discreet enough to escape the attention of Frankie and his sources."

"Who are his sources?"

"Neither you nor I want to know that."

"So what happened?"

"Nothing has made it to the market yet, according to Frankie."

"Then how can we get any further?"

"We have gotten further."

"What?"

"Vikingsson let down his guard last time he came back to London," Macdonald said. "He had been released after all, and he apparently figured that the path was clear. We stalked him to Heathrow, but he wasn't there to report for work, at least not above sea level."

As Macdonald leaned forward in the chair, his jacket tightened across his shoulders. He was paler than ever and his voice was thin and strained. "He went to his locker and removed a little sack, and we strolled up and helped him empty it out. Lo and behold, it was the tripod."

"The what?"

"The tripod we've been looking for. I'm sure of it, and do you know why? Because one of the legs was missing a sleeve. The technicians at the Yard aren't finished yet, but there's no doubt in my mind."

"You're putting me on."

"Do you really believe I'd do that, after what we've been through together?"

"No."

"No, what?"

"No, you're not putting me on."

"Thanks."

"The tripod," Winter said. His mouth tasted of blood and vinegar.

"The wizards at the Yard assure me it's got fingerprints all over it, and it doesn't matter how old they are."

Winter started to sweat again.

"And that's not the end of it. An envelope was taped to the top of the locker and they found the key to a safe-deposit box inside."

"A safe-deposit box?" Winter's cigarillo had gone out ages ago but he held on to it.

"Vikingsson's safe-deposit box in London."

"Have you been there?"

"You'd better believe it. And, sure enough, we found another key."

"Another key." Winter's voice was barely strong enough to get the words out.

"It's to a locker at one of London's railroad or underground stations."

"How many of those are there?"

"Lockers? Tens of thousands, and hundreds of stations. But we'll find it."

"What does Vikingsson have to say for himself?" Winter asked.

"Not a thing. He seems to think he'll be in the air again tomorrow."

"Where is he now?"

"At headquarters in Eltham."

"And he's not talking?"

"Not yet."

"Do you think the tripod is all we need?"

"We're getting there," Macdonald said.

"So there were two murderers."

"That explains quite a bit."

"What?"

"How they got away so fast without leaving any of their equipment behind."

"It could also be coincidence."

"No way."

"We don't have any other evidence that Vikingsson and Bolger know each other. Apparently we haven't been looking in the right places."

"We're going to find it now. That's the way it always is."

"If we want to get Vikingsson convicted, we need more than circumstantial evidence."

"We'll put the squeeze on him."

"That's not good enough. And I'm not as optimistic as you are."

"The squeeze," Macdonald repeated.

Half an hour later, Winter strolled through the park outside police headquarters. The fragment of an idea had rattled around his brain since the conversation with Macdonald.

He remembered the times he had talked to Marianne. There had always been someone else lurking in the back of her mind, and she'd seemed confused whenever he brought up Bolger. Or when he talked about Bolger alone. As if Winter had sown the confusion and caused her to doubt her own eyes and ears. Or to forget that other, most important detail, whatever it might be.

The feeling he had after talking to her was like a pebble in his shoe. He had to question her again, or at least sit down and talk to her.

But that's not what bothered him most now.

Bolger was trying to show him something.

Scratching his scalp as if it were responsible for a traffic jam in his brain, Winter thought again about all the hints Bolger had dropped over the previous months.

They had been looking out over the archipelago, and Bolger had made a remark about beauty and having a clear view . . .

Winter stood still. He looked down at the ground without seeing it. The scraps of thoughts in his mind were beginning to converge.

He saw Bolger in front of his cottage. They had just stepped out. Bolger talked about building the new fireplace for himself, then lit it and walked slowly around his proud creation.

When Winter had gone out to the island the last time, Bolger threw his poker at the glowing stones.

The fireplace.

Bolger's cliff-top monument of brick.

Winter ducked under the police cordon. The cottage was amorphous in the reflected sunlight. He said a couple of words to the officer who was keeping an eye on the place and sent him down to the boat. Then he laid his coat on the ground, slipped on his work gloves and picked up the sledgehammer he'd brought for the task.

He moved from left to right, smashing the brick to pieces, feeling the heat gather in the small of his back as the blood flowed to his arms. The fireplace slowly gave way under the relentless blows. He took a break to wipe the sweat from his neck and threw his sport jacket onto the grass, relishing the cold wind against his back. When he resumed his assault, his sore toe throbbed from the effort.

After an hour of hacking with the sledgehammer and then prying with a crowbar, he glimpsed the edge of a flat oilcloth bag in a little space between the bricks. But he couldn't dislodge it. His forehead was pounding, and not just from physical exertion. You should have taken a tranquilizer or two before coming out here, he told himself.

Carefully he pried at the mortar around the bag and tried to wrench it loose with his gloved hands, but to no avail. Then he swung the sledge-hammer in six inches below it and the mass finally gave way.

Exhausted, he leaned on the sledgehammer. His breathing was heavy, but the wind soothed his back and neck again, and he watched the heather sway on the surrounding cliffs.

The bag was light and fragile when he picked it up. He walked over to the cottage and unlocked the door.

Opening the sack in the kitchen was like peeling away layers of bark. A videotape was inside. A sheet of typing paper had been folded in half and taped to the front. To ERIK, it said in tall letters, meticulously traced with a blue felt-tip pen.

He closed his eyes, but the words were still there when he opened them again.

He tore off the sheet of paper and crumpled it up in the palm of his hand, then threw it to the ground.

There was more. Credit card receipts from stores and restaurants. Bus passes, underground tickets.

Everything was from London. Winter poked at the pile as if it were alive. A taxi receipt lay on top. Someone had scrawled STANLEY GARDENS across it with the same felt-tip pen.

He saw a letter to Geoff from Sweden.

One of Bolger's last bread crumbs, Winter thought, but I haven't watched the videotape yet. This is where it all comes together.

He had seen the television set last time he was here, a small LCD monitor with a built-in video player. After checking the main switch on the power strip, he turned it on.

Our Father who art in heaven, hallowed be thy name, he thought, pushing the tape in.

The speakers roared. He turned the volume down and watched the static dance on the screen. He recognized the music immediately, and it made him sick to his stomach. *New York Eye and Ear Control.*

The video started off with a panorama of Bolger's bar; the camera must have been perched on the mirror behind the counter. Winter saw himself. The screen filled with static and quickly cut to the next scene: Per Malmström on a bar stool. Cut. Winter again, a glass of beer in his hand. Cut. Per. Cut. Winter. Cut. Jamie Robertson. Cut. Winter. Vikingsson sat ten feet behind him and smiled. The camera zoomed to his face. Cut. Geoff. Cut. Winter, smiling at an invisible figure in front of him. Cut. Vikingsson, at the bar. Cut. Winter. Cut. Vikingsson. Cut. Per again. Cut. Back and forth, faster and faster.

The music stopped and the screen went blank.

A room appeared. A naked boy sat in a chair. A man came into view, bare chested with a piece of cloth covering his thighs. Winter stared at

the boy's eyes and heard his muffled cries as a rag was stuffed into his mouth.

The man took off his mask and peered into the camera. It was Bolger.

Winter heard a male voice.

Bolger's lips weren't moving and the boy was in no condition to speak.

Winter's jaws began to ache. He tried to open his mouth but couldn't. He grabbed his chin and pulled down. His mouth opened and the pain subsided.

He stopped the tape, rewound it a few seconds and hit play. There was the voice again. It sounded like an announcement. Winter replayed it, catching something about a camera.

Somebody else was in the room. It could be the same voice they had on the interrogation tapes. Vikingsson's voice. Bolger wanted him to know that Vikingsson had been there. The police had experts who could compare and match voices. It was only a matter of time and effort. The eternal routine.

Winter let the tape run this time, for another three minutes, then stopped it and walked quickly out of the cottage to inhale all the oxygen he could find there at the top of the cliff.

45

EVERYBODY GATHERED AT WINTER'S PLACE. THE MOOD WAS hushed, dominated by an overpowering need to be together. Some of them were drinking, but Winter refrained, having numbed himself sufficiently after hours under the shower.

"Get as drunk as you want," he had said when they arrived, ushering them into the dining room, where the bottles were lined up on the table.

Winter hugged Bergenhem, careful not to touch the bandage around his head, and then Martina, who had an easier time hugging him back.

They all oohed and aahed over the baby.

"What's her name?" Djanali asked.

"Ada," Martina answered.

"Permit me," Winter said, coming back with a box of Cuaba Tradicionales he'd bought at Davidoff.

"I was supposed to bring those," Bergenhem said.

"Right," Winter said. "But that headache of yours isn't quite gone yet, and in the meantime I'm going to hand out these fine old cigars as tradition dictates."

Halders poured two glasses of whisky and handed Macdonald one.

Winter was off talking to Möllerström and Bergenhem, both of whom were sipping wine. They stood by the windows and looked out at the sunset. Djanali and Martina joined them.

"There was a chance that Christian would survive," Macdonald was explaining to Halders. "We decided right away to keep it secret. His parents knew, of course, plus anybody else who needed to, and then we just sat back and waited."

"Jesus Christ," Halders said. "I almost fainted when Erik came back and told us about it."

Winter walked over from the window. He had finally broken down and poured himself a glass of wine.

"Are you actually drinking?" Macdonald asked.

"Sometimes you've got no choice."

The hours passed. Ada slept in Winter's bedroom. Macdonald told Möllerström all about HOLMES—the Holmes Office Large Major Enquiry System—and caught up on the latest developments in Sweden. Östergaard, Djanali and Martina were back at the window, glasses in hand.

Halders brooded by the clutter of bottles. He had given Macdonald the lowdown on all the recent car thefts in Gothenburg.

"In such a lovely little town?"

"We have the highest figures in the European Union," Halders boasted.

Winter and Ringmar sat in the kitchen. Ringmar's voice was getting ragged around the edges. A beer and half a highball were on the table in front of him.

"You're saying there was animal blood in his apartments?" Ringmar asked.

"He's confessed," Winter said.

"Fucking Viking." Ringmar picked up the beer bottle and knocked over the whisky glass. A rivulet ran toward the edge of the table. "Shit," he said, looking around for a dishcloth.

"Don't worry about it."

"What a bastard."

"He thought he'd found the ultimate kick."

"But still . . ."

They fell silent and listened to the music from the living room.

"He never managed to sell the tape?" Ringmar asked.

"I think he ran out of time. Assuming that was ever his intention."

"Why wouldn't it be?"

"It might not have been the most important incentive."

"If you ask me, we're talking about big money here," Ringmar said. "Business is business. It's hard to believe it wasn't a consideration."

"Perhaps for Vikingsson. Macdonald says he'll find out if anybody bought the tape. He has some sources with sources of their own."

"And Bolger had his motives too." Ringmar avoided Winter's eyes. "They used each other. Two madmen, coming from opposite directions."

"I called my mother," Winter said.

"You did what?"

"I asked her about the past twenty years. Suddenly she was razor-sharp."

"Razor-sharp?"

"I wanted to find out about a few things I didn't know back then, or was too young to notice, and it turns out she remembers quite a lot."

"About you and Bolger?"

"The stuff that went on in those days. What he was like and everything that's happened since."

"What stuff?"

"How screwed up he was."

"Did he really hate you that much?" It occurred to Ringmar that he wouldn't have asked the question sober.

"I can't answer that."

Ringmar drank his beer.

"But he wanted to meet me on my terms," Winter said after half a minute. "It consumed him day and night. He wanted to challenge me on my own turf. That's the conclusion I've come to anyway."

Ringmar didn't want to talk about it any longer.

"The music has stopped," Winter said.

"What did you say?"

"I'll go in and put on some more."

"What's this?" Halders asked.

"Charlie Haden and his Quartet West," Winter answered.

"Good stuff."

"Yes."

"Even though it's jazz. They call this jazz, right?"

"Immortal music of the forties and fifties."

"What?"

"You're right, it's jazz."

Möllerström was telling Östergaard and Djanali about his last relationship. Helander held his hand to steady him.

Winter sat down on the floor next to Östergaard.

"I was just kidding," Möllerström said. "She picked up a pebble and threw it in the water."

"Was the moon out?" Djanali asked.

"What?"

"Was it a moonlit night?"

"I can't remember. Anyway, I said, Did you know it took ten thousand years for that pebble to make its way up to the beach? Or something like that."

"Oy," Helander said.

"Was that such a terrible thing to say?"

"It's no big deal, Janne," Djanali assured him.

"It sure as hell was a big deal. She was angry, or hurt. Things were never the same between us after that."

"May I borrow that album, boss?" Halders asked, coming over to them.

Winter and Östergaard took the elevator down and crossed the street to Vasaplatsen Park. The fountain was like an iron anvil in the night. When he turned around and looked up, he saw the lights shining in his apartment. He thought he glimpsed a ponytail swinging in the shadows of the balcony.

They looked for the comet and spotted it right away.

May was approaching. It never got completely dark anymore.

He picked up a pebble and threw it across the grass.

"It took ten thousand years for that pebble to make its way from the obelisk up to this bench," she said.

"Let's go look at it."

"Wait a minute."

"Why?"

"How are you doing, Erik?"

"I'm making it. Tomorrow's another day and all that."

"I meant how you're feeling."

"Better than I expected. Honestly."

"What have you been thinking about these last few days?"

"The meaning of life, but Halders taught it to me an hour ago."

"Just in time."

"No kidding."

A car passed.

"For a while there, I thought everything might be my fault. Who knows, maybe I'm indirectly responsible, but nobody could have stopped Bolger. If we hadn't finally stumbled across a way to do it, he would have kept on going for God knows how long."

"Yes."

"He wanted it to continue, but he also longed for it to end."

She let him talk.

"I think my numbness has finally worn off," he said.

They went down and walked around the obelisk.

"Does an obelisk have six sides?" he asked.

"It could be four."

"This one has six."

"But it looks like one." She strained to make out the inscription.

> *Wild birds plow their way through the far reaches of space.*
> *How many never reach their final destination.*
> *But what difference does that make?*
> *They die free.*

They walked back to the bench. She sat down and he put his head in her lap. The coolness of the earth soothed him. He heard a fluttering above them.

"Do you want to pray?" she asked.

"I'm already saying my prayers. The free association kind."

The wings fluttered again.

"Explain it all to me," he said.

"Later."

"I want to know everything."

"It's getting warmer day by day," she said.

20-stupid! 97,

Frozen Tracks
A Chief Inspector Erik Winter Novel

The autumn gloom comes quickly on the Swedish city of Gothenburg, and for Detective Chief Inspector Erik Winter the days seem even shorter, the nights bleaker, when he is faced with two seemingly unrelated sets of perplexing crimes. The investigation of a series of mysterious assaults and a string of child abductions takes Winter to "the flats," the barren prairies of rural Sweden, whose wastelands conceal crimes as sinister as the land itself. Winter must deduce the labyrinthine connections between the cases before it is too late and his own family comes into danger.

ISBN 978-0-14-311358-4

Never End
A Chief Inspector Erik Winter Novel

It's summer in Sweden. As the coastal city of Gothenburg suffers through a heat wave, Chief Inspector Erik Winter broods over a series of unsolved rape-murders. The crimes bear an eerie resemblance to a five-year-old case that the mercurial detective has refused to let go cold. Has the same rapist reemerged to taunt him, or is a copycat at work? And can Winter find a common thread among the victims before there are more of them?

ISBN 978-0-14-311243-3

Sun and Shadow
A Chief Inspector Erik Winter Novel

Erik Winter is the youngest chief inspector in Sweden. He wears sharp suits, cooks gourmet meals, has a penchant for jazz, and is about to become a father. He's also moody and intuitive, his mind inhabiting the crimes he's trying to solve. In this atmospheric, heart-stopping tale, Winter's troubles abound—and a bloody double murder on his doorstep is just the beginning.

ISBN 978-0-14-303718-7